LL

LINETTA

Check into the Pennyfoot Hotel . . .
for delightful tales of dete~~ct~~

Room w~~ith~~

The view from the Pennyfoo~~t~~ for Lady Eleanor Danbury, ~~…~~ saw. Now Cecily must find ~~…~~ society matron falling to her ~~…~~

Do Not Disturb
Mr. Bickley answered the door knocker and ended up dead. Cecily must capture the culprit—before murder darkens another doorstep . . .

Service for Two
Dr. McDuff's funeral became a fiasco when the mourners found a stranger's body in the casket. Now Cecily must close the case—for at the Pennyfoot, murder is a most unwelcome guest . . .

Eat, Drink, and Be Buried
April showers bring May flowers—when one of the guests is found strangled with a maypole ribbon. Soon the May Day celebration turns into a hotel investigation—and Cecily fears it's a merry month . . . for murder.

Check-Out Time
Life at the Pennyfoot hangs in the balance one sweltering summer when a distinguished guest plunges to his death from his top-floor balcony. Was it the heat . . . or cold-blooded murder?

Grounds for Murder
The Pennyfoot was abuzz when a young gypsy was hacked to death in the woods near Badgers End. And now it's up to Cecily to find out who at the Pennyfoot has a deadly axe to grind . . .

Pay the Piper
The Pennyfoot bagpipe contest ended on a sour note when one of the pipers was murdered. Cecily must catch the killer—before another piper pays for his visit with his life . . .

MORE MYSTERIES FROM THE
BERKLEY PUBLISHING GROUP . . .

SISTER FREVISSE MYSTERIES: Medieval mystery in the tradition of
Ellis Peters . . .

by Margaret Frazer

THE NOVICE'S TALE	THE BISHOP'S TALE
THE OUTLAW'S TALE	THE BOY'S TALE
THE SERVANT'S TALE	THE MURDERER'S TALE

PENNYFOOT HOTEL MYSTERIES: In Edwardian England, death
takes a seaside holiday . . .

by Kate Kingsbury

ROOM WITH A CLUE	EAT, DRINK, AND BE BURIED
SERVICE FOR TWO	GROUNDS FOR MURDER
CHECK-OUT TIME	PAY THE PIPER
DO NOT DISTURB	

GLYNIS TRYON MYSTERIES: The highly acclaimed series set in the
early days of the women's rights movement . . . "Historically accurate
and telling." —Sara Paretsky

by Miriam Grace Monfredo

SENECA FALLS INHERITANCE	NORTH STAR CONSPIRACY
BLACKWATER SPIRITS	THROUGH A GOLD EAGLE

MARK TWAIN MYSTERIES: "Adventurous . . . Replete with genuine tall tales
from the great man himself." —*Mostly Murder*

by Peter J. Heck

DEATH ON THE MISSISSIPPI

A CONNECTICUT YANKEE IN CRIMINAL COURT (*coming in December*)

CHIVALRY IS DEAD

KATE KINGSBURY

BERKLEY PRIME CRIME, NEW YORK

CHIVALRY IS DEAD

A Berkley Prime Crime Book / published by arrangement with the author

PRINTING HISTORY
Berkley Prime Crime edition / October 1996

The Putnam Berkley World Wide Web site address is
http://www.berkley.com

ISBN: 0-425-15515-3

Berkley Prime Crime Books are published
by The Berkley Publishing Group,
200 Madison Avenue, New York, NY 10016.
The name BERKLEY PRIME CRIME and the BERKLEY PRIME CRIME
design are trademarks belonging to Berkley Publishing Corporation.

PRINTED IN THE UNITED STATES OF AMERICA

10 9 8 7 6 5 4 3 2 1

CHIVALRY IS DEAD

CHAPTER

1

The month of April simply had to be the most beautiful time of the year, Phoebe Carter-Holmes decided as she pranced along the Esplanade that bright, breezy morning in the warm spring of 1909.

When she had left the vicarage that morning, the daffodils were in full bloom, their nodding heads bathing the gardens of the churchyard in a blaze of warm sunshine and chasing away the dull, gray chills of winter.

Soon the tulips would join them in a mass of glorious pinks and reds and brilliant yellow. If there was one thing Phoebe adored most about the vicarage grounds, it was her beloved flowers.

A gust of wind from the ocean threatened to dislodge her hat, and she clutched the wide brim with a firm hand. She should have tied the hat down with one of her chiffon scarfs, she thought, casting an anxious eye up the street just in case one of those noisy mechanical monsters should come charging out of nowhere. One never knew if it was safe to cross the street nowadays.

Stepping smartly across the road, she eyed with appreciation the gleaming white walls of the Pennyfoot Hotel. The building always looked so pretty with the sun shining on it. Though how long it would stay that way with all the dirt and soot belching out the backs of those dreadful motorcars, she couldn't imagine.

Above her head a seagull swooped down to alight on the balcony of a fourth-floor suite. Ignoring its hopeful stare, Phoebe lifted her skirts and mounted the stone steps of the hotel. Her mind was on the coming festivities.

St. George's Day was one of her favorite celebrations. In honor of the patron saint of England, the Pennyfoot's owner, Cecily Sinclair, held a grand ball each year on the fourth Saturday in April.

The following day the annual medieval jousting tournament took place on the grounds of the hotel, much to John the gardener's disgust, since he had the unfortunate task of restoring the pristine lawns.

The popular contest was the highlight of the weekend, executed somewhat clumsily but with much gusto by several of the young men in the surrounding villages. Dressed in medieval garb, complete with shields and cushioned lances rented from the Wellercombe Theatrical Society, the men attempted to whack each other off their horses until only one brave champion was left seated.

Dinner at the head table, followed by dancing was the usual prize for the winner and three guests at one of the Pennyfoot's prestigious events. The gallant victor was also paraded through the village after the joust with all the pomp and circumstance due such a brave feat.

Michel, the hotel chef, was renowned enough to induce the brawny farmers and fishermen to risk sustaining bumps and bruises for the treat, not to mention the prospect of brief notoriety and adulation of the crowd.

Phoebe's main interest, as always, was the entertainment for the St. George's Day ball. Cecily held her responsible for all the presentations at the hotel's events, and Phoebe enjoyed the task immensely.

She would enjoy it a lot more, she reflected as she swept past the footman at the door, were it not for that detestable Madeline Pengrath, the third member of the entertainments committee. How Cecily put up with the woman's snide remarks and disgraceful manners was beyond Phoebe's understanding.

Why, everyone knew that Madeline had gypsy blood. She was definitely beneath their class, in Phoebe's opinion. There were even some who regarded the enigmatic woman as a witch. She certainly had the strangest powers, or thought she did, more likely.

Phoebe nodded in answer to the hotel manager's greeting as she passed him in the dim shadows of the foyer. Mr. Baxter made such an impressive figure in his black morning coat and striped trousers, Phoebe thought warmly. Now there was a real gentleman. There were not too many of that particular breed left unfortunately.

Take dear Sedgely, for instance. Her late husband had been such a gentleman. It was too bad that his family had not followed his example. In fact, after dear Sedgely's fatal accident, the entire family had behaved like heathens, throwing her and poor little Algie out.

As always, Phoebe's spirits drooped a little at the thought of her misfortune at the hands of her dead husband's relatives. They had considered her beneath them, simply because she had not been to the manor born. It had been a long, hard struggle to achieve her present station in life as the respected mother of the local vicar.

Phoebe reached the door of the library and gave it a gentle tap. Cecily's calm voice answered her, soothing

Phoebe's depleted spirits. She was quite looking forward to making her announcement this morning.

Having been stung once too often by Madeline's comments on her choice of performers, Phoebe was determined to provide a dignified presentation for a change. This time, she thought with satisfaction as she opened the door to the warmly paneled library, Madeline would not have the opportunity to cast aspersions on her enterprises.

Cecily looked up as her visitor entered. Phoebe looked most fashionable in her pearl gray suit with its chinchilla collar, she thought with fond approval. The pale mauve blouse covered Phoebe's long throat with a lace cravat, and the lightly coiled parasol in her gloved hand matched the delicate shade exactly.

Although Cecily knew quite well that Phoebe's clothes had seen the light of many a day, the elegant woman always managed to look stylish. In Phoebe's mind, appearance was everything.

"I'm not late, I trust?" Phoebe inquired anxiously as she settled herself on a velvet padded chair at Cecily's right. She fussed with her parasol for a moment, then sat back with a little sigh. "It is such a beautiful morning, I'm afraid I loitered along the Esplanade. After the dreadful winter we've had it's so pleasant to feel the warmth of the sun again."

"You're not late," Cecily assured her, smiling at her friend. "Madeline hasn't arrived yet."

Phoebe sniffed. "Well, yes. But then, Madeline is always tardy, isn't she?"

As if in answer to her words, a sharp rap sounded on the door, after which it immediately opened. The slender woman who entered the library had the delicate features of a finely crafted doll. Long black hair flowed over her shoulders almost to her waist, and her soft blue skirt billowed out behind her as she seemingly floated across the room.

One hand lifted in a languid gesture as Madeline came to

a halt at the table. "Oh, good, Cecily, you've got a fire. I was hoping you would."

"It's no wonder you are feeling the cold," Phoebe said a trifle tartly. "You are dressed for summer in that flimsy frock. Most people would have the good sense to wear a shawl about their shoulders."

Madeline swiveled a dark eye onto Phoebe. "Ah, but as you know," she murmured, "I am not most people."

"There's no doubt about that," Phoebe muttered.

Cecily cleared her throat, recognizing the danger signals. Phoebe and Madeline could become quite heated if left to pursue a battle of words. "I can have one of the housemaids build up the fire if you're cold, Madeline," she said, hoping she wouldn't be called upon to settle their differences as usual.

"I'm not at all cold." Madeline dug in the deep pocket of her skirt and pulled out a small white cotton sack. "I mentioned the fire because I wanted to show you this." She wagged the sack at Cecily as she spoke.

Cecily peered at the bag swinging in the other woman's hand. "What is it?"

"Not one of your dreadful spells, I hope," Phoebe muttered. "I should hate for us all to be turned into toads or something equally repulsive."

"Toads are only repulsive to people who don't understand them." Turning her back on the table, Madeline skimmed across to the fireplace. "This, my friends, is potpourri. I made it myself." She opened the drawstring of the bag and poured something into her hand. With a quick movement she sprinkled what looked like dust onto the smoldering coals.

Bright sparks danced above the flames for a moment or two, then settled down. Brushing her hand on her skirt, Madeline returned the sack to her pocket and sauntered back to the table. "You'll have to wait a moment or two," she said, dropping onto a chair. "Then you'll be able to smell it."

Phoebe wrinkled her nose. "I can smell it already."

Madeline merely sent her a venomous look.

Cecily sighed. She was about to speak when the whiff of scent invaded her nostrils. Breathing in the pleasant fragrance, she said in surprise, "That's a wonderful smell, Madeline. It seems to fill the whole library, and yet it's subtle enough not to overpower the room."

"It's my own special mix of wildflowers and herbs," Madeline said, looking pleased with the compliment. "I threw some on my fire by accident, and I was quite taken with the effect. It does smell rather wonderful, don't you think?"

"I do indeed." Cecily looked warily at Phoebe, who sat in stony silence. "What do you think, Phoebe?"

Phoebe shrugged. "Well, it wouldn't do for the vicarage, of course. Poor Algie would be sneezing all day long. But I suppose it's all right if one doesn't mind the smell of dandelions and other odious weeds."

"There are no dandelions in my potpourri—" Madeline began, when Cecily hastily interrupted.

"Perhaps we should get on with the business at hand." She sent Madeline a look of appeal. "Do you have the flower arrangements settled?"

"I do." Madeline abandoned the contest and draped herself against the back of her chair. "I'm planning some quite beautiful bouquets in red, white, and blue, in honor of St. George. Lilies, I think, and asters. I also thought I'd run streamers from the balcony of the ballroom to the stage. I think they would look quite effective."

Cecily nodded. "That's a lovely idea."

"Oh, it wasn't my idea." Madeline hit a delicate yawn behind her hand. "I saw the streamers at Lord Withersgill's funeral last month and decided to use them at the first opportunity."

Phoebe made a little moaning sound. "I still can't believe he's gone. Such a gentleman. Such a pity."

"I wasn't aware you knew him," Madeline said with a sly look at Cecily.

"Well, not personally, of course." Phoebe inspected one of her elbow-length gloves and made a pretense of smoothing it out. "But everyone in Badgers End knows what a fine gentleman was Lord Withersgill. To be struck down in his prime is tragic, to say the least."

"Lord Withersgill," Madeline said solemnly, "was eighty years old if he was a day. He outlived his son, in fact."

Phoebe looked startled. "Really? I had no idea . . ."

"I understand the new Lord Withersgill is his grandson," Cecily said quickly.

Madeline's face broke into one of her lovely smiles. "So I hear. I certainly hope we see more of him than we did his grandfather. That old idiot was a total recluse. I don't know anyone who ever saw him. I was beginning to think that he was a figment of someone's imagination, dreamed up to keep us all in awe of the estate, which was actually being run by a band of gypsies."

Phoebe gasped in horror. "How can you say such a dreadful thing!"

Madeline's lilting laugh echoed around the dusty book-shelves. "Don't worry, Phoebe, I'm as relieved as you are to know that the Parson's Hill estate is in good hands." She gave Cecily a wicked little smile. "I must say, I'm intrigued about the new heir. I wonder if he is as young and handsome as people say he is. I didn't see him at the funeral."

"I think he was abroad at the time," Cecily murmured. "I only hope he doesn't take offense at our celebrations so soon after his grandfather's death."

"I wouldn't waste your time wondering about that young man, Madeline," Phoebe said silkily. "If he isn't married already, I'm sure he has a string of eligible and anxious young debutantes just dying to make his acquaintance."

"Perhaps we should get on?" Cecily suggested, wishing desperately that she could have a cigar. Her craving for them seemed to be intensifying lately. Baxter would have a fit if he knew. He made no secret of his disapproval of her unladylike habit.

"Don't worry, Phoebe." Madeline reached in her pocket for the sack of potpourri. "If I can get close enough to the new Lord Withersgill, I'll sprinkle some of my magic dust on him. He'll be mine before the hour has passed."

Phoebe tossed her head, making the oversized roses on her hat tremble. "I wouldn't jest about such things if I were you, Madeline. Witches have been known to be burned at the stake, you know."

"I'm sorry, Phoebe," Cecily said loudly, "but I must insist we get down to business. I have an appointment shortly . . ."

To her immense relief, Phoebe looked contrite. "I'm sorry, Cecily. As a matter of fact, I do have something rather exciting to tell you. I have hired an act for the ball on Saturday night, and I know you will be pleased."

"What is it this time?" Madeline asked dryly. "A ballet-dancing elephant playing the cymbals or your entire troupe performing the Dance of the Seven Veils?"

Phoebe ignored the barb. "I have acquired a classical act," she said, lifting her chin in a gesture of disdain. "More in keeping with the celebrations. A ladies' string quartet."

Madeline rolled her eyes to the ceiling.

"They sound marvelous, Phoebe," Cecily said hurriedly. "Most tasteful and refined, I'm sure."

"Oh, they are." Phoebe leaned forward, clasping her hands in her excitement. "Two of them are sisters, who are joined by two friends. They are absolutely wonderful, considering their age."

Cecily's delight faltered. "How old are they?"

"Oh, I don't know." Phoebe dismissed the question with an impatient wave of her hand. "Much older than any of us, of course."

Considering that Phoebe was at least ten years older than herself, Cecily began to feel apprehensive.

"The best point being," Phoebe went on, "is that they can be had for a perfectly paltry sum. Considering their exper-tise on their instruments, the price is quite a bargain."

"Oh, my," Madeline murmured. "Cheap and chipper."

Phoebe visibly bristled. "I'll have you know, Madeline, that I have heard them play. They are every bit as good as anything you might hear on the bandstand in the summer."

Madeline opened her mouth to answer just as a slight tap on the door distracted Cecily's attention.

"Come in," she called out, thankful for the interruption. She watched expectantly as the door opened to reveal the new visitor. Catching sight of the child standing in the doorway, Cecily smiled.

Cynthia Chalmsford was the eight-year-old daughter of Lord and Lady Chalmsford, current guests at the hotel. The wistful face of the rather plain little girl was a familiar sight around the hotel.

Given the slightest opportunity, Cynthia would escape from the watchful eye of her stern-looking parents and make her way below stairs, where she plagued the staff with endless questions.

In the three days the family had been at the hotel, Cynthia had wormed her way into the hearts of the entire staff, despite the delays and disruptions she had caused. According to Cecily's long-suffering housekeeper, Mrs. Chubb, Cynthia followed the housemaids around, making suggestions, asking questions and generally getting in the way.

The maids felt sorry for the lonely child and wasted a great deal of time entertaining the young visitor instead of getting on with their work, much to Mrs. Chubb's frustration.

Cynthia was, after all, the daughter of an aristocrat, and as such, deserved a certain amount of respect. One could hardly tell her to run along and leave the staff alone. Even so, the duties had to be carried out promptly in order for the hotel to run smoothly. It left Mrs. Chubb in a quandary as to how to handle the situation.

"What are you doing?" Cynthia asked, peering hopefully through a long blond ringlet that had escaped from the bunch piled on her head.

"Be quiet, child," Phoebe said, fixing a haughty eye on

the girl. "This is a private meeting. Have your parents taught you no manners? Children should be seen and not heard."

Cynthia's face crumpled, as if she were about to cry. "My daddy said if I want to learn I have to ask questions."

Phoebe's face turned pink.

Cecily felt a moment of sympathy. Far be it for Phoebe to dispute a member of the aristocracy. Yet it was plain to see that she had the greatest of difficulty holding her tongue.

"We are rather busy now, Cynthia," Cecily said smoothly. "Perhaps you should go back to your mother. She is most likely to be worried about you."

"She's asleep," Cynthia said, her gaze flitting about the room with avid curiosity.

"Why don't you run along and see if you can find Gertie, then," Cecily suggested. "Perhaps she'll let you take a peek at her twin babies."

Cynthia pouted her bottom lip. "I don't like babies. They're noisy and smelly. I like my dollies better."

"Then go play with your dollies," Phoebe said with a ghastly semblance of a smile.

"I'm tired of playing with them. I want to read some books."

"I'm afraid I don't have any children's books," Cecily said, with a twinge of regret. She had often thought about adding to the library of musty old tomes, but there were always other necessities to take precedence.

Cynthia wandered into the room, her gaze probing the crowded shelves. "What kind of books do you have? Do you have books I can draw in? I love to draw in books, but my daddy won't let me." She pulled a crayon from her pocket. "I could draw a picture for you in one of your books. Can I?"

"May I, if you please," Phoebe reminded the child with a frown.

In a smooth motion Madeline rose from her chair. Taking the little girl's hand she said gently, "Come, I'll give you something you can draw in. I'll also show you my magic dust if you come with me back to your rooms."

Cynthia gazed up at her in awe. "Magic dust? How does it work? Can I have some? Will it make me grown-up? I want to be a grown-up. They have more fun than children."

Madeline's musical laugh rang out. "I can promise you, Miss Cynthia Chalmsford, that you will become a grown-up much faster than you really want to. Just wait and see."

Looking at Cecily, she added, "I'll come back before the weekend to go over the floral arrangements."

Cecily nodded. "Thank you, Madeline."

Madeline flicked a glance at Phoebe. "Good bye, Phoebe. I'll look forward to hearing your ladies perform on Saturday. If they don't expire before then."

Before Phoebe could think of a suitable retort, Madeline had led the child out of the library, closing the door behind them.

"Well," Phoebe said on a rush of breath, "there are times when Madeline infuriates me almost beyond control. Yet I must say, she handled that irritating child quite well."

"Madeline means well," Cecily said, refusing to be drawn into a discussion of her friend behind her back. Changing the subject, she added brightly, "Phoebe, I have a suggestion to make. I thought perhaps it might be rather fun to have Doris sing a number at the ball on Saturday."

Phoebe's shocked expression was quite comical. "Doris?"

Cecily smiled. "You know Doris, Phoebe. She and her twin sister work here at the hotel."

"Of course I know Doris. She's a *housemaid*." Phoebe uttered the last word as if she were talking about a particularly loathsome insect.

"She also has a quite remarkable voice," Cecily said firmly. "I think it would be very nice if we gave everyone a chance to hear it." At the very least, she added inwardly, if all else failed with Phoebe's presentation, as often it was wont to do, then at least part of the evening's entertainment would be enjoyable.

"Very well." Obviously affronted and doing her best to hide the fact, Phoebe straightened her hat with a sharp tug. "One can only hope that the child can manage something suitable for the occasion."

"Perhaps you can suggest a particular piece for her," Cecily said, hoping to appease her friend. "Meanwhile, if there's anything you need—"

"I do have a favor to ask, as it happens." Shifting in her seat, Phoebe cleared her throat. "I was wondering if the ladies might be allowed to rehearse in the ballroom during the quiet period in the afternoons. The village hall is quite drafty, you know, and can be most damaging to elderly bones."

"Of course," Cecily agreed, wondering again just how ancient were the elderly bones. "They may have the ballroom from three until four, providing they leave promptly in order to allow my staff to set up for the afternoon tea."

Phoebe nodded with enthusiasm. "I'll make that quite clear." She hesitated for a moment, then murmured, "There is also the matter of transportation, I'm afraid. Some of those instruments are quite heavy, and it's too far for the ladies to carry them. Could you perhaps see your way clear . . . ?"

"I'll send a trap for them," Cecily assured her.

Phoebe rose, fanning her face with her gloved hand. "Oh, thank goodness. I have a list of their addresses right here. You are most gracious, as always, Cecily. I'm sure the ladies will be very grateful. Unfortunately they do not have the finances to hire transportation and have to rely solely on the generosity of others. If it were not for their musical engagements, I don't know how they would manage to live."

It would seem, Cecily thought with resignation, that she would have to feed the ladies as well while they were in the hotel.

She was about to answer Phoebe when the door opened once more. Madeline's face appeared in the gap, wearing a somber expression.

"I'm sorry, Cecily," she said. "I thought your discussion with Phoebe would be over by now."

Taking the hint, Phoebe made a somewhat haughty exit, leaving Cecily staring uneasily at Madeline's face.

"Is something wrong?" she asked, when Madeline continued to stand there without saying anything.

Madeline started, as if disturbed from some deep contemplation. "Pardon? Oh, not really. At least, I don't think so. It's just . . ."

Cecily knew her friend well enough to know when something was troubling her. She had never questioned Madeline's insights, even though at times they sounded quite bizarre. More often than not Madeline sensed things that were completely incomprehensible to the average person, and more often than not her dire predictions had a nasty habit of materializing in the most unexpected ways.

"I think you had better tell me," Cecily said quietly.

Madeline looked unhappy. "I sense an aura of misfortune. Someone is in grave danger. More than one. I'm afraid for the child."

And now, so was Cecily.

CHAPTER

2

"The only danger that child is in at the moment is the prospect of hearing the bite of my tongue," Baxter muttered when Cecily recounted her conversation with Madeline to him in his office a few minutes later. "You should know better than to take Miss Pengrath's gruesome forebodings seriously. These worthless notions of hers are gravely disturbing her mind."

Faintly piqued by his sharp tone, Cecily peered at him. He sat slumped at his desk, now that she took more notice. His gray eyes, usually so cool and bright, now seemed dull, and the droop to his mouth worried her.

"You are being remarkably uncharitable, Baxter," she said lightly in an attempt to hide her concern. "Has Madeline upset you, or do you perhaps have a sour stomach? If so, Mrs.

14

Chubb has some most effective powders that will make you feel better in no time."

"My stomach is quite well, thank you, madam." He gave her a morose look that did nothing to reassure her. "I am merely concerned when you accept Miss Pengrath's deceptive delusions with such naiveté."

Cecily felt a stirring of resentment. "Not always are they delusions, Baxter. There have been several occasions when Madeline's predictions have been accurate. One cannot ignore the fact that she does have unusual powers. Even you had to admit a sense of relief when she rid us of that awful ghost a few months ago."

"I'm not convinced that there was any such ghost." Baxter shuffled through a sheaf of papers on his desk without really looking at them. "After all, the hotel was teeming with Scottish pipers—it could have been any one of them."

"And any one of them could walk right through a closed door, no doubt."

As if sensing her irritation, he looked up at her. "If I may say so, madam, we are all entitled to believe whatever we wish to believe."

"You believed it at the time." She knew she was being childish, but his attitude pained her. He was not himself; that much was clear. His reluctance to discuss it with her hurt her more than she cared to admit.

"I preferred not to disagree with you, that is all," Baxter said, looking away again.

"I see." The silence in the tiny office was so thick that she felt suffocated. Struggling to ease the ache inside her, she decided to change what appeared to be a controversial subject. "I was talking to that nice American gentleman this morning, though his name escapes me at the moment. He is staying in suite five. He seems such a nice man and most charming, though rather quiet-spoken. He kept me entertained for so long with his fascinating stories about the

American way of life, I almost forgot about the committee meeting."

Instead of answering her, Baxter rested his forehead in his hand.

Thoroughly alarmed, Cecily leaned forward across his desk. "Baxter, something is wrong with you. A headache? A chill? Please tell me what is wrong. Shall I send for Dr. Prestwick?"

"No, blast it! I have no wish to see that pompous ass."

Cecily sat up straight, her back rigid. "Well!"

Dropping his hand, Baxter looked at her with despair in his eyes. "Please forgive me, madam. I humbly apologize. You are right, I am not myself. It will pass, no doubt. Please do not concern yourself on my behalf."

"I would not be your friend if I did not concern myself," Cecily said stiffly.

He gave her a weary smile. "Please, I beg you, do not worry yourself. It is nothing. Just a momentary fit of despondency, I assure you. As I said, it will pass."

She gave a slight nod, saying, "Very well. But I sincerely hope that if you should not improve, you will at least seek some professional help. Perhaps from a doctor in Wellercombe if you prefer."

"Very well, madam."

"After all, the smooth running of this hotel depends on my staff members being in good health."

She could see she had offended him and felt immediately ashamed. She had not meant to take revenge. Before he could answer, she rose to her feet. "I have promised Phoebe that we will send a trap for her musicians, so that they might rehearse here at the hotel this afternoon. Since Samuel will have his hands full storing the equipment for the tournament in the stables, perhaps we should send one of the footmen."

He barely met her glance, his gaze skimming away to rest on the door. "Very well, madam. I shall take care of it."

"Thank you. Here is the list of addresses. If he leaves at

half past two, he should have plenty of time." She let the slip of paper float down onto his desk.

She reached the door, then paused. She could not, in all conscience, leave him like this. Turning to look at him, she said quietly, "I will worry about you, Baxter."

His face softened. "Thank you, madam. I promise you, I am quite well. But I do appreciate your concern."

She had to be satisfied with that though she didn't like it one bit.

Phoebe paused in the doorway of the hotel kitchen, wincing as a loud crash erupted from the stove in the far corner. Across the room, Michel, the hotel's unpredictable chef, barely glanced at the saucepan lying at his feet.

"*Sacre bleu*," he yelled, slamming a large lid on a simmering pot, "why ees it I 'ave z' bourguignonne prepared, and the oven, he is not hot yet, *non?*"

"He is not bleeding hot yet," said the buxom young woman who stood facing him, "because Daisy hasn't kept the flipping fire going, that's why."

"And what ees wrong with you putting the coals on, eh? You break an arm, perhaps?"

"I'll break *your* bloody arm in a minute," Gertie retorted.

Phoebe jumped as another voice added to the commotion.

"Gertie!" Mrs. Chubb rushed from the pantry, slapping spilt flour from her abundant bosom with the flat of her palm. "That's no way to speak to the chef, my girl. In any case, he's right. That oven should have been good and hot by now."

"Well, it ain't my bleeding fault. Yell at Daisy if you want to yell at someone. She's the one what's supposed to take care of the fires."

Phoebe ventured a foot inside the door of the kitchen and cleared her throat, hoping to attract the attention of the housekeeper. Mrs. Chubb appeared to be preoccupied with the housemaid, however.

"Gertie Brown, how many times do I have to tell you, if you see something needs doing, then do it."

"What if it ain't my job? I got bloody things to do, too, you know. I don't just sit around looking blinking pretty."

Another saucepan hit the floor, startling Phoebe half out of her wits.

"Never mind who has the job," Michel yelled. "If someone does not put ze coals on ze fire this eenstant, we 'ave no bourguignonne for lunch. Unless the customers eat it raw, *oui?*"

"Will you be quiet, Michel," Mrs. Chubb bellowed. "How can I hear myself think when you are making all that racket?"

Deciding her word with the housekeeper could wait, Phoebe backed out of the door. As she turned to head for the stairs, she was relieved to see Doris hurrying toward her.

"Ah, Doris," Phoebe said, using her most disdainful tone. "Mrs. Sinclair has suggested—"

"I'm not Doris," the housemaid answered with a surly expression that made Phoebe itch to box her ears. "I'm Daisy. My sister is in the ballroom."

"Excuse me." Annoyed with her mistake, Phoebe charged at the stairs leading to the foyer. It was no wonder she had mistaken the girl. It was almost impossible to tell the sisters apart. Whatever had possessed Cecily to hire twin housemaids, she couldn't imagine. Things were chaotic enough at times at the Pennyfoot without deliberately adding to the confusion.

Phoebe was so engrossed in her thoughts that she narrowly avoided a collision with the young girl rushing down the stairs to meet her.

"Doris!" Phoebe cried as the housemaid passed her. "I'd like a word with you."

Doris halted, turning to look warily at Phoebe. "Yes, Mrs. Carter-Holmes?"

Phoebe straightened her back and rested her hand elegantly on the handle of her parasol while she regained her breath.

"Mrs. Sinclair has suggested that you might be interested in singing a short piece at the ball on Saturday night."

Doris's face went quite white. "Me? Oh, my."

"You are not going to swoon, I trust," Phoebe said tartly.

The housemaid's hand fluttered at her throat. "No, Miss . . . Mrs. Carter-Holmes. I'm just surprised, that's all. Flabbergasted, you might say."

"Yes, well, that's as may be. Now, about the choice of song—"

"Oo, I have the perfect one, Mrs. Carter-Holmes. I learned it just the other day. I heard the milkman singing it, and he taught me—"

"Absolutely not!" Phoebe shuddered. "If you wish to take part in one of my presentations, you must have the right material. I shall pick out a suitable aria, just a brief one, of course, and you may rehearse with the string quartet in the ballroom this afternoon sharp at three. Is that clear?"

Doris looked as if she'd bitten into a lemon. "String quartet?"

"A women's string quartet," Phoebe said proudly. "You are a most fortunate girl to have the privilege of being accompanied by such talented musicians."

Doris didn't look as if she felt privileged. Indeed, she scuttled off without so much as a word of thanks for the great honor Phoebe was about to bestow upon her.

Ungrateful wretch, Phoebe thought as she tripped up the stairs. Young people nowadays had absolutely no manners whatsoever. Whatever was the world coming to?

Belowstairs, Doris found a moment to share her frustration with Gertie. Following the older housemaid into the pantry, she pretended to be sorting out the bags of spice.

"Madam wants me to sing at the ball on Saturday night," she said, trying to sound casual about it.

"Go on!" Gertie swiveled her head to look at her. "Well, you do have a nice voice. I've always said you'd be on the stage one day."

Doris nodded. "Not exactly the stage, though, is it. I mean, it's only for madam's paying guests. Not like they're paying to see me, like."

Gertie shrugged. "You have to start some-bleeding-where, don't you? You never know, someone might hear you and before you know it . . ." She flung out an arm in a dramatic gesture. "Here she is, ladies and gentlemen, the star of the London Variety Palace—"

"It's not that kind of singing."

Gertie stared at her. "Watcha mean, it's not that bloody kind of singing? That's the only kind of singing you do."

Doris lifted her chin. "I do all sorts of singing. Mrs. Carter-Holmes says as how I have to sing one of her stupid arias, and what's worse, I've got to have some twitty string quartet playing for me."

"Oh, blimey." Gertie rubbed her chin for a moment.

Doris watched her, feeling a little twinge of excitement when she saw a slow smile creep across Gertie's face. "What?" she demanded. "What are you thinking about?"

"I know what you can do," Gertie said, grinning. "You could get someone else to play for you and bloody rehearse in secret. Then, on the night, you can spring the bleeding surprise on old toffy-nosed Carter-Holmes."

"I don't know anyone who will play for me."

"I do," Gertie said, her dark eyes dancing with mischief. "She plays the church organ and the piano for dancing in the village hall. She plays everything by ear 'cause she can't read music. She'd love to have the bleeding chance to play at the Pennyfoot. Her name is Lydia Willoughby."

"Lydia Willoughby," Doris repeated with reverence. "I'll ask her."

Gertie's grin vanished. "'Ere, hold on. I was only joking. You'll get into all kinds of trouble if you bloody mess about with Phoebe Carter-Holmes."

"It will be worth it," Doris said firmly. She was already working out in her head how to find the time for double rehearsals.

Gertie looked worried. "Per'aps you'd better hear her play the blinking piano before you ask her."

Doris shook her head, her mind firmly made up. "Don't worry. I'll teach her the song." She started as Mrs. Chubb's strident voice demanded to know what the heck the housemaids were doing in the pantry.

"Thanks, Gertie," Doris said quickly and skipped out into the kitchen.

Mrs. Chubb stood with her arms folded, her eyes glittering in her furious face. "I have to be behind you girls every minute of the day. Get those potatoes peeled, Doris, and, Gertie, I need serviettes folded and placed in the rings, and I need them right now."

"Yes, Mrs. Chubb," the girls chorused together.

Doris fled happily to the sink. The housekeeper's sharp tongue couldn't hurt her now. On Saturday night she was going to sing in public. She could hardly wait.

So engrossed in her thoughts was she that she took no notice of the young man who entered the kitchen a short while later.

Roland Young had been hired to do any necessary redecorating in the hotel rooms during the annual spring cleaning assault. Doris had met the young man only once and had taken an instant dislike to him.

She vaguely heard him behind her, saying something to Gertie, who immediately answered him in her usual forthright manner.

"Watch your bleeding tongue, Mr. blinking Young, or I'll flipping cut it off with the carving knife."

"Yeah? And who is going to help you, then, may I ask?"

"I don't need no bleeding bugger to help me. I can do it all by meself."

Roland's loud laugh pierced Doris's nerves. "Go on with yer," he said softly. "I'd like to see you try. Always wanted to get me hands on a body like yours."

"That's enough of that, young man," Mrs. Chubb snapped.

"Get out of my kitchen this instant with that filthy tongue, or I'll have Mr. Baxter throw you out."

Again Roland's high-pitched cackle rang in Doris's ears. "I was only teasing her. Bunch of bloody frumps, that's all you lot are. Can't take a bloody joke, that's your trouble. I'm going down the pub, where the girls don't mind having a bit of fun."

"Good riddance," Gertie said nastily. "Take your bleeding big head with you."

"Ah, girl, mark my words, you'll be sorry you said that one day." Roland's footsteps rang out on the kitchen floor as he strode for the door to the yard and slammed it behind him.

Doris lifted the pail of potatoes out of the sink and carried them to the stove. "I don't like that man," she said, to no one in particular.

"What man?" Daisy's voice spoke behind her.

Doris hadn't heard her twin come in. "Roland Young," she said, nodding her head at the outside door. "He is really peculiar, what with his wild eyes and weird jokes."

"I'd keep your distance from the likes of him," Gertie muttered, heading for the door with the serviettes. "That man is trouble. I can tell you." She disappeared into the hallway, leaving the twins staring after her.

"You know what I saw yesterday?" Daisy said, casting a wary eye out for Mrs. Chubb, who had bustled into the pantry. "I was cleaning out the fireplace in one of the suites when I heard this noise coming from next door. When I looked in there, I saw that Roland Young doing a really strange dance. It was really, really daffy, and he was singing his head off, all out of tune. It sounded awful."

Doris gazed in fascination at her twin. "Did he see you?"

Daisy shook her head. "He weren't the only one in the room. Cynthia Chalmsford was in there with him. She kept asking him why he sang so bad and why didn't he take lessons and why was he dancing so funny."

Doris shivered. "Go on! What did he say to her, then?"

"Nothing. He just pretended she wasn't there and went on dancing and singing while she shouted louder and louder at him."

"What are you two girls gossiping about now?" Mrs. Chubb demanded from the pantry door. "I turn my head for a minute, and there you are, wasting time again. Michel will be back any minute, and nothing's been done."

"We was talking about that daffy Roland Young," Doris said, emptying the potatoes into the huge iron pot on the stove.

Daisy said nothing as usual, while she shoveled coals into the stove.

"The problem with that young man is that he's been around too many strange people," Mrs. Chubb muttered. "Samuel told me that Roland Young worked backstage at the Wellercombe Hippodrome all last summer. After mixing with those theatrical folk, it's no wonder he acts peculiar. Everyone knows what kind of people work in the theater."

Doris didn't answer. She was too busy digesting the housekeeper's remarks. Roland Young had worked for the Hippodrome. He must have met lots of stage people there. Maybe he could introduce her to someone who could help her make her dream come true. Maybe, at long last, she had met someone who could give her that all-important step toward becoming a Variety star.

Right then and there, Doris knew she would just have to be nice to Roland Young. Even if he was crazy in the head.

CHAPTER

❖ 3 ❖

"Ah, there you are, old bean! Exciting news, what? What?"

Having almost crossed the lobby, Cecily halted in her tracks at the sound of the bellow behind her. Recognizing the blaring voice of Colonel Fortescue, she heaved a sigh of resignation.

The colonel was a regular guest at the Pennyfoot and, while harmless, nevertheless made a general nuisance of himself with his wild stories. His bizarre antics had raised many an eyebrow among the guests in the hotel.

Cecily refused to share in the general opinion that the colonel was mentally deranged. She had nevertheless, to admit that the elderly gentleman's mind was often impaired by the generous amount of gin he poured down his throat on a regular basis.

She had hoped to spend a quiet moment or two admiring the view from the roof garden before lunch. Now she would be fortunate to have time for lunch at all, she thought, as she turned to greet him.

"Good morning, Colonel. What news is that, may I ask?"

"Well, the tournament, of course, old girl." The colonel twirled one carefully waxed end of his luxurious mustache. "Just heard about it. Might have a bash at that one myself, eh?"

Alarmed by this dangerous suggestion, Cecily hid her dismay behind a smile. "I think perhaps you might want to reconsider that idea. Some of our local farmers can be quite rambunctious. I wouldn't want you to harm yourself."

"Please don't fret yourself, madam. I'm an expert horseman, you know. Cut a dashing figure on a horse in my younger days, what? What?"

Cecily seriously doubted if the colonel had achieved anything faster than a brisk trot, whereas the competitors in the joust were rather more apt to goad their steeds into a headlong gallop. Even while sober, an unusual event at best, the colonel would have difficulty keeping his seat.

"I can imagine you did," she said, hoping she sounded sincere. "I must beg you to bear in mind, however, that the shields and helmets these men wear carry considerable weight. Not to mention the lance, which is quite unwieldly, so I believe. Many a competitor has been unseated while attempting to balance with it on his rearing mount."

"If you're talking about those spears I saw arriving this morning," the colonel said as he flipped his hand in a gesture of contempt. "They don't frighten me, madam. When I was out in Africa, I faced a thousand of the blighters. You got stuck with one of those, old fruit, and they put a hole in you big enough to crawl through."

Cecily shuddered. "How utterly fascinating. I can assure you, Colonel, that on the day of the tournament, the lances will be fitted with protective covers. We really don't anticipate any holes in our competitors. Now, I must be getting along—"

The colonel nodded and tucked his thumbs inside the armholes of his waistcoat. "Only got hit once, you know."

Cecily sent a hunted look past the colonel's shoulder at the empty hallway beyond. "I'm happy to hear that, Colonel. Now, if you'll excuse me—"

"Dashed thing parted my hair." The colonel tilted his head down so that Cecily could see the top of his head. "I'll wager you were wondering why I parted my hair off center, what?"

"I must say I've never noticed." Cecily peered at the thatch of white hair. She couldn't see a parting at all.

"Aha! You would have noticed, though, if you'd seen me that day." Fortescue snapped his chin up. "Went clean through my helmet. Chin strap held it on, of course. There I was, charging all over the place with a spear stuck right through my perishing pith helmet."

"That must have been most uncomfortable for you." Cecily edged sideways in an attempt to sidle past him. "I really do have to be getting on—"

"Not so much for me, old bean. Dashed painful for the chappie riding at my side, though. I turned my head to point out an ambush. Caught him right in the mouth with the head of the spear.

"Oh, dear," Cecily said faintly.

"It was his own blasted fault, of course. Bent his head closer to hear what I was saying. Poor blighter could only talk out of the side of his mouth after that."

"What a shame."

"Had one hell of a lisp."

Cecily nodded gravely. "I imagine he did."

"Had to change his blasted name in the end. Got tired of everyone calling him Thethil."

Cecily swallowed hard. "Colonel, perhaps you'd care to have a cocktail before lunch? On the house, of course. I'd join you, but I'm already late for an appointment."

"Oh, dashed decent of you, madam. Don't mind if I do."
The portly gentleman spun on his heel, then belatedly
remembered his manners. "Are you quite sure you won't
join me?"

Cecily smiled. "Another time, perhaps."

"Very well. Must get in practice for the tournament this
afternoon, though. Have to show those young upstarts what's
what, what?"

Not if she had any say in it, Cecily thought grimly. She
would have to invent some excuse to keep the poor man out
of the competition. The last thing she needed was another
tragedy at the Pennyfoot Hotel. There had been far too many
of them already.

"We'll talk about it later," she said, deciding to ask Baxter
for his help in the matter. "Enjoy your cocktail, Colonel."

"I will, indeed, madam. Much obliged. Much obliged."
The colonel straightened an imaginary helmet, took hold of
invisible reins, and galloped unsteadily off down the hallway shouting, "Tally ho! Charge the blighters!"

Shaking her head, Cecily followed more slowly, trying to
eradicate the image of the colonel astride his horse with a
lance protruding from his head.

Doris could hear the caterwauling of the string quartet's
instruments long before she reached the huge double doors
of the ballroom. Heavy as they were, the doors couldn't
block out the dreadful noise. It sounded like an army of cats
spoiling for a fight.

Blimey, she thought as she paused in front of the ornate
archway. She had to sing with that lot. It would take every
ounce of air in her lungs to make herself heard above that
racket.

Just as she pushed the doors open, the cacophony of
screeching strings ceased. At the far end of the ballroom
four women sat on the small stage. They seemed dwarfed by
the massive pillars that supported the wrought-iron balcony.
Smiling cherubs looked down upon the dance floor from

their perches above the intricately carved portals while
enormous wreaths and vines, painted generously with gold
leaf, swirled across the ceiling.

Walking across the sprung parquet floor, Doris tried to
imagine what it would be like to be all dressed up in a
glamorous gown on the arm of a toff, gliding elegantly
across the floor in a graceful waltz.

One day, she promised herself as she approached the
stage, one day, when she was a famous singing star, she'd
come back to the Pennyfoot as a guest. Wouldn't half enjoy
that, she would. She'd treat all the maids a blooming sight
better than what she got treated by some of the guests, that
much she knew.

Smiling at the thought, she reached the stage. Her smile
soon vanished, though, when one of the elderly ladies
turned a pinched face in her direction and said in a la-di-da
voice, "Yes, what is it, gell? Can't you see we are busy
here?"

Doris dropped a resentful curtsey. Weren't no better than
she was, they weren't. They had to work for a living, just
like she did. Just because they talked through their noses,
they thought they was toffs. Well, one day she'd show them.
Even if she never learned to talk proper.

"Come, speak up, gell. What do you want?"

Doris looked up at the wrinkled face of the skinny
woman. The musician had little beady eyes like a sparrow,
which stared at Doris through a pair of spectacles. Her gray
hair was drawn back so tight that the bones stuck out of her
face. She had a violin clutched in the bony fingers of one
hand and the bow in the other. She wagged the bow at Doris
as she repeated, "What do you want? We don't have time to
stand here all day."

"If you please, ma'am, I've come to rehearse my song."

The woman's eyelids half closed. "What is your name?"

"It's Doris, ma'am. Doris 'Oggins. Mrs. Carter-Holmes
said as 'ow I was supposed to come and rehearse with you
this afternoon."

"This must be the girl who is going to sing the aria, Esme," said a plump woman holding a fatter violin. Doris thought it might be a cello.

The bird woman pursed her lips. "Thank you, Mary. Yes, well, I have no idea why we have to include a singer in our act, but I suppose if Mrs. Sinclair insists, there's nothing we can do about it. Though if Mrs. Carter-Holmes had been given the choice, I'm quite sure we would not have had this disruption in our schedule."

Doris dug her hands deep into the pockets of her apron. "I'm sorry, ma'am, but I'm only doing what I was told."

"Oh, very well." The woman tossed her head as if disgusted with the entire arrangement. "You had better get up here, I suppose."

In spite of her ungracious reception, Doris felt a little thrill of excitement as she ran up the steps onto the stage. On Saturday night she would be on this stage, singing to some of the richest toffs in the country. Anything could happen. She could be discovered and end up doing a whole summer at the Variety theater in Wellercombe.

Thinking about that reminded her of Roland Young. She would have to try to find him that afternoon and find out if he could help her. Then she forgot about Roland Young as she walked out onto the stage and looked down on the empty ballroom.

It was the very first time she'd ever set foot on a stage. The thought of standing there singing to a crowd of toffs almost overwhelmed her.

"Well, stop daydreaming, gell. Get over here and tell me your name again."

Doris came back to earth with a thump. "It's Doris, ma'am. Doris 'Oggins."

The bird woman looked down her thin nose. "Is that with an aitch or not?"

"It's with a h'aitch, ma'am. 'Oggins."

The bird woman rolled her eyes in despair. "Well, let's

hope you can pronounce your aitches in the aria. Did you bring your music with you?"

Doris shook her head, but before she could answer, the cello player said quickly, "Mrs. Carter-Holmes gave it to me, Esme. I have it right here."

"My name is Mrs. Esme Parsons," the bird woman said, taking the sheets of music from her companion. "I play the violin, of course. This is Mrs. Mary Wainscott with the cello. The lady holding the bass is Miss Beryl Barrett and the lady with the viola is her sister, Miss Hilda Barrett." She sniffed, giving Doris yet another of her mean looks. "You, of course, will address us by our surnames, if you have to address us at all."

Doris meekly nodded. "Yes, ma'am."

"Now, I suppose we had better dispense with your part of the proceedings as quickly as possible. Then we can get on with the important part of the program." Esme Parsons swung around. "Hilda! For heaven's sake, stop fiddling with that bow. It's beginning to grate on my nerves."

The tiny, mouselike woman she had spoken to jumped, thrusting her viola under her chin with such force that it jerked her face upward. Doris winced when she heard the woman's teeth snap together. Other than a faint yelp, Hilda Barrett stoically ignored the pain.

Esme Parsons studied the music, while Doris stole a glance at the bass player, who stood silently clutching the massive stringed instrument with a look of boredom on her face.

Eyeing the woman, it occurred to Doris that Beryl Barrett looked a lot like the bass she played. Tall and gaunt, with a face only a mother could love. No wonder the musician plastered powder and rouge all over herself. She needed something to help hide that big nose.

"All right, everybody, we'll run through this once, and then Miss Hoggins can try it out." Esme Parsons peered at Doris over her spectacles. "You are familiar with this aria, I hope?"

"I've never heard of it before, ma'am," Doris said, doing her best to smile. "But I'm a fast learner. I can hear something once, and I know it. Why, only the other day—"

Esme Parsons interrupted with a loud grown. "I suppose it's too much to hope that you know how to read music."

Doris stared at her. "How do you read music?"

The musician threw her hands in the air, scattering the music sheets all over the floor. "What on earth was Phoebe Carter-Holmes thinking of? This is ridiculous. You can't possibly learn an entire aria in one afternoon. It just can't be done, I tell you."

Doris felt her confidence melting away. Afraid now that she would lose the opportunity to sing after all, she snatched the music up from the floor. "I can learn it. I swear I can. Just play it for me, I'll read the—"

She broke off in surprise, staring at the unfamiliar words. "This doesn't make sense," she announced to the ominously silent group of women.

"It makes perfect sense," Esme Parsons said between gritted teeth, "if you know how to speak Italian."

"Blimey," Doris whispered, staring at the music in awe.

"Let the girl try, Esme," Mary Wainscott said, shifting her cello onto her knees. "It won't matter if she doesn't manage it all. Just let her sing whatever she learns of it. After all, none of us are familiar with the piece either."

Doris looked hopefully at the irritated face of the violinist.

"Oh, very well. I don't suppose we can do much else at this point. We'll just have to struggle through as best we can." Esme Parsons glared at Doris. "Listen carefully, now, gell. We'll only have time for one run-through or we'll never get the rest of our rehearsal finished."

"Yes, ma'am." Obediently Doris listened as the musicians fumbled into the opening chords. The tune sounded vaguely familiar, though she was sure she'd never heard it played before.

The only music she'd heard played at all was when a

friend of her aunt's used to come over to the house and play
a few tunes on the rickety old piano in the parlor. That was
how she'd learned to pick up tunes so fast. She'd only ever
had one shot at it.

The music sounded better than it had when she'd first
walked in. At least now the musicians were all playing
together. The melody was haunting, and she liked it, even if
it wasn't what she wanted to sing. She even clapped when
the song came to an end.

"That was nice," she said as the notes died away. "Sounds
a lot better than that racket you were playing just now."

Esme Parsons glared through her spectacles. "We weren't
playing anything, you idiot girl. We were tuning our
instruments."

Aware that she'd put her foot in it again, Doris wisely
decided to keep quiet. Now it was her turn, and she took her
place at the center of the stage, holding the music in hands
that trembled so much she could hardly see the words.

"Do your best with the pronunciation," Esme Parsons
said. "Just read it the way it looks." She paused as
apparently a thought struck her. "You can read, can't you?"

Doris nodded. "A friend of my aunt's taught both me and
my sister."

"Thank heaven for that." Esme wiped a hand across her
brow. "Let's just hope the audience won't be concentrating
on the words."

Doris wasn't paying attention. She was too busy trying to
calm her nerves enough to read the music.

The scratchy notes of the violin began the introduction
again, and Doris took a deep breath. She was a little late on
the melody but soon caught up. The music continued behind
her while she struggled to pronounce the unfamiliar words
and stay on key with the melody. The fact that the musicians
went out of tune every now and again didn't help at all.

Doris began to wonder if she was making a big mistake
by exposing herself to an audience with so little time to

prepare. By the time she'd reached the end of the aria, she felt like crying. That was the worst she'd ever sounded.

She would have fled the stage if it hadn't been for the small child who appeared from nowhere. The girl stood right in front of the stage, staring at Doris with a look of awe on her face.

"That was beautiful," Cynthia Chalmsford said, clasping her hands together. "You sound just like a real opera singer."

"Thank you, Miss Cynthia," Doris said, grinning down at the solemn face looking up at her.

"You sound much better than that dreadful music," Cynthia said clearly. She looked across at Esme Parsons, who glared back at her. "I can play the piano, you know. I've had lessons. May I play with you?"

"No, you may not," Esme Parsons said, looking as if she were about to explode. "I've had more than enough interruptions as it is." Staring meaningfully at Doris, she added, "Run along now, Miss Hoggins, and take this pesky child with you."

"But I don't want to go with her," Cynthia said, making for the steps that led up to the stage. "I want to stay and listen to the music." She marched up the onto the stage, ignoring the violinist's muffled sound of protest.

Doris thought she should warn Esme Parsons about Cynthia's station. "Her parents are Lord and Lady Chalmsford," she told the irate woman. "They are guests her at the hotel."

"Really. Then they should have better control over their offspring." Esme's fierce gaze followed the child, who had wandered over to where Hilda sat with her viola.

"May I try that?" Cynthia asked, holding her hands out for the instrument.

Hilda shook her hand, drawing her viola back out of harm's way.

"Get off this stage at once," Esme's shrill voice demanded.

"I want to play something. May I play this one?" Cynthia

looked up at the stoic face of the bass player and rested one small hand on the sweeping shoulder of the instrument.

"Get lost," Beryl Barrett whispered hoarsely.

"Off! Off!" Esme yelled, advancing on Cynthia with a face red with vengeance.

Cynthia took one look at her, burst into tears, and fled down the steps and across the floor.

"You shouldn't have done that," Doris said recklessly. "She wasn't doing no harm."

"Hold your tongue, young lady," Esme Parsons snapped. "One ill-mannered brat around here is quite enough. I don't care if her father is the King of England. I won't have my rehearsal disrupted any longer."

Taking that as a hint, Doris headed for the steps. But she couldn't resist throwing one last remark over her shoulder. "You'd better watch out that Lord Chalmsford doesn't come after you. Cynthia's his only child, and he won't stand for no one talking to her like that."

She glanced back as she reached the floor, somewhat aghast at her own audacity. Esme Parsons didn't appear to notice, however. The musician and Beryl Barrett were staring at each other, and it seemed to Doris as if there were a threat in the exchange.

CHAPTER
❈ 4 ❈

Doris had almost reached the doors of the ballroom when she saw a man step out from behind one of the pillars. He must have been there all the time, she thought, since she hadn't noticed anyone entering the room.

Still a little unsettled by the strange look that had passed between the musicians, she scuttled out into the hallway before the visitor could catch up with her.

He must have put a spurt on, however, as he called out to her before she'd reached the end of the hallway.

Reluctantly Doris turned to face him. "What can I do for you, sir?" she asked politely.

"I just wanted to tell you how much I enjoyed your singing," the gentleman said, coming toward her with a shy smile.

He seemed to have a funny accent, and as he reached her, Doris looked closer at him. He was quite a bit older than her, at least over thirty, she reckoned. He wore glasses and had a pleasant face. He was nicely dressed, though his clothes didn't look like the ones the toffs wore. He certainly seemed harmless enough, she thought. The quiet type.

"Thank you, sir," she said, not quite sure what else to say.

"I'd like to talk to you when you have a moment to spare," the man said, glancing at the grandfather clock in the corner of the lobby.

Doris eyed him warily. "About what?"

"About your talent." He said something else, but Doris wasn't paying attention. Out of the corner of her eye she'd seen Roland Young racing up the stairs.

She wasn't supposed to be back in the kitchen for another twenty minutes or so. Plenty of time for her to talk to the workman and find out if he could help her get her start on the stage.

Aware that the gentleman had stopped speaking, she looked back at him. "If you'll excuse me, sir, I have to go now."

Looking a little surprised, the man nodded. "Perhaps later, then."

Doris wondered what she was supposed to do later. She couldn't waste time worrying about it now, she thought, watching Roland Young disappearing around the bend in the stairs. With no more than a glance at the gentleman, who still stood watching her, she headed for the stairs.

Behind her, she heard the man ask, "Oh, by the way, what is your name?"

She scarcely paused in her headlong rush up the stairs as she called out, "Doris 'Oggins, sir."

"I'm Jerome Kern," the man called up after her.

It was a strange name, she thought. Or maybe it was just the way he said it. She soon forgot about it, however, as she reached the first landing.

There, outside the doors of an empty suite, she could see a couple of buckets with paint brushes sticking out of them. She'd found Roland Young. Now all she had to do was get him to help her.

She could hear him whistling as she approached the room, though what tune it was she couldn't say. Certainly nothing that she recognized.

Reaching the door, she pushed it open. Roland was sitting cross-legged on the floor in front of the fireplace, rocking from side to side in time to whatever song it was he was whistling. He had a paintbrush in his hand, but didn't seem to be doing anything with it other than waving it back and forth in front of his face.

"Hello," Doris said a little nervously.

Roland stopped swaying and whistling. The hand holding the brush stayed poised in midair. Without turning his head, he muttered, "What do you want?"

Doris advanced into the suite. Sheets covered the furniture and most of the floor. The carpet had been rolled up and rested against one wall. The room looked bare and somewhat menacing, she thought uneasily.

"I wanted to talk to you," she said, hoping he wouldn't speak to her the way he had to Gertie earlier. She didn't have Mrs. Chubb to stand up to him now. It occurred to her that she might have made a mistake being alone with him.

"Well, I don't want to talk to you, so hop it."

"I just wanted to ask you something."

"What about?"

Doris took a deep breath. There was a squiggly feeling in her stomach that was making her wish she'd never followed him up the stairs. "I wanted to ask you about last summer, when you was working at the Hippodrome."

"None of your bloody business." Roland turned his head then and looked at her. "So get lost, will you? Scarper. Or do I have to chase you out of here?"

He had a strange glint in his eyes that Doris did not like

at all. Deciding to wait for a better time to talk to him, preferably with other people around, she turned and headed for the door.

As she went through it she heard Roland start whistling the strange tune again. It gave her goosebumps that lasted all the way down to the warmth of the kitchen.

"Am I interrupting you?" Cecily asked from the doorway of her manager's office.

Baxter looked up. With careful deliberation he stuck his pen in the inkstand, carefully blotted the sheet he'd been working on, and then got slowly to his feet. "No, madam, nothing that cannot wait."

Cecily gave him a close scrutiny as she entered the small room. "You are looking tired, Baxter. You should get out more and enjoy the sunshine now that the air is warmer. You will have more color in your cheeks."

"Yes, madam." His face, as always, remained unreadable.

She sat herself down, knowing it was pointless to ask him to sit also. Except for very rare occasions, Baxter insisted on remaining on his feet whenever she was in his presence.

"I would dearly love one of your cigars, Baxter," she murmured, giving him a wan smile.

He tucked his fingers into his waistcoat pocket and drew out the slim package. "For someone who is so concerned for my welfare, you have precious little regard for your own," he said with just a trace of reproval in his voice. "You know very well that cigars make you cough."

Nevertheless, he handed her the package, and gratefully she took it. Extracting one of the thin cigars, she waited for him to light it for her. Then, after blowing out a stream of gray smoke, she said wearily, "Nowadays there doesn't seem much to enhance my welfare except for the occasional cigar. Smoking does relax me, you know."

He was silent, and she raised her chin to find him looking at her with an intent expression in his gray eyes. "Something is troubling you, madam?"

She managed a wider smile this time. "Nothing more traumatic than missing my son and worrying about the welfare of my manager."

He ignored the latter part of her sentence. "Have you heard from Master Michael?"

"Not a word." Cecily sighed and took another long draw on the cigar. "Of course, it's only been a matter of weeks since he and Simani left, but I can't help worrying about them. I do hope they reached their destination safely."

"I'm quite sure you would have had word had they not, madam."

"Yes, I suppose you're right." She paused, studying the end of her cigar, which already had grown a thin circle of ash. "I do miss him dreadfully, you know." She tapped the end of the cigar into Baxter's ashtray. "Simani, too, of course," she added hastily.

"You are also disappointed, no doubt, at the prospect of missing the birth of your first grandson."

Pleasantly surprised by his perception, she nodded. "Yes, I suppose I am. I can't help wondering if he will be born in a mud hut in the middle of the jungle." She looked up at him. "That's how they were married, you know. By a witch doctor, no less."

"Yes, I remember you telling me." He paused for a long moment, then added gently, "Try not to concern yourself, Cecily. I am quite sure that any son of yours knows better than to expose his child to any untoward hazards."

His use of her Christian name never failed to warm her. She met his gaze and for a long moment drew comfort from the compassion in his dear face. Then, with a brisk movement, she stubbed out the cigar.

"Well, I mustn't keep you. I'm sure you have plenty to keep you occupied this afternoon. I think I will take a rest in my suite before I get dressed for dinner."

"I think that's an excellent idea, madam."

She rose to her feet and gave him another long scrutiny.

"Did you give any more thought to paying a visit to a doctor?"

He shook his head. "I promise you, madam, should I feel the need for a doctor, I will most certainly seek one out."

"You are feeling better, then?"

"Much better, thank you."

She wished she could believe that. The droop of his mouth and the lackluster look in his eyes belied his assurances, however, although she was not about to risk incurring the irritation he had displayed that morning by questioning him again.

"I will see you later, then," she said, turning away from him so that he would not see her frown of concern.

"Very well, madam."

She closed his door behind her, aware of the dull ache beneath her breast that had troubled her so much lately. It seemed as if her treasured relationship with her manager had lost some of its vitality. That worried her even more than her concerns about Michael.

Sadly she made her way up the stairs to her room. Life, it seemed, was as unpredictable as the weather. One never knew what was waiting around the corner.

Baxter reflected on much the same thing as he entered the lobby a little later. Normally at this time of day the hotel was quiet, with most of the guests taking a short siesta before beginning the ardous task of dressing for dinner.

This evening, however, the lobby appeared to be swarming with people, all carrying some kind of musical instrument. Actually there were only five people, but they were making so much noise that he could hardly be blamed for thinking there were more.

The four ladies, whom Baxter assumed to be the string quartet, all talked at once as they argued with a red-faced, sputtering Colonel Fortescue. The colonel's unfortunate stutter, noticeable at the best of times, made it almost impossible to understand what he was saying.

The more dominant of the ladies waved a violin case in the air as she screeched at the confused gentleman, while his eyelids flapped furiously up and down as if they were about to take wing and fly away.

"Come, come, ladies," Baxter called out as he strode toward them. "Whatever is all this commotion about?"

The colonel turned bleary eyes on him, but before the agitated gentleman could get anything coherent out, all four ladies started jabbering and gesturing until Baxter held up an imperious hand.

"Ladies, please! I cannot help you if I cannot understand you."

Silence settled on the group, and Baxter lowered his hand. "That is better. Now perhaps one person will explain to me what has happened to arouse such riotous indignation." He looked purposefully at the loudest of the group, the determined-looking lady with the violin case.

"Who are you?" she demanded, after sending the colonel a frosty stare. "I hope you can make more sense than this nincompoop here."

The colonel spluttered some more, than managed a complete sentence. "I say, madam, that's a bit much, what?"

Baxter patted the colonel on the shoulder. "May I suggest, Colonel, that you retire to the bar? I'm sure that a gin and tonic will help settle your nerves."

Fortescue's eyelids flashed up and down. "Gin and tonic? On the house?"

"On the house, Colonel. It will be my pleasure."

"Jolly sporting of you, old boy. Much obliged." Turning to the violinist, he gave her a stiff bow. "I will bid you good day, madam. I won't say it has been a pleasure. By Jove, I have had more pleasant experiences fighting wild boars in Africa." In spite of his sputtering, he'd managed to make himself understood.

The violinist's face turned white. "Well," she said, exhaling a great deal of breath with the word. "I must say I am astonished to find a hotel of this stature allowing ignorant hooligans such as this to wander about willy-nilly. I will have a word with Mrs. Sinclair at the earliest opportunity."

The colonel drew himself up as high as his swaying body would allow. Thrusting out his belly, he roared, "You do that, madam! I shall be happy to speak to Mrs. Sinclair myself. I shall at least then have the distinct pleasure of speaking to a proper lady."

Swinging around, he headed unsteadily for the hallway and disappeared down it, muttering something under his breath that Baxter was unable to catch.

Bracing himself, Baxter turned back to the group of women. "My apologies, ladies. I am afraid the colonel is not himself tonight."

The violinist sniffed. "I should be very much surprised if he is ever himself, whatever sad state of affair that might be." She gave Baxter a look that would have stopped a charging rhinoceros. "You have not answered my question, young man. Who are you?"

Baxter smoothed a hand over his hair. "I am the manager of this establishment, madam. Mr. Baxter is my name." He gave her a slight bow from the waist. "At your service."

"Well." Looking slightly appeased, the woman flicked a glance at the others, no doubt making sure they had noticed this little display of deference. "I am pleased to see that you have some manners, at least. Not like that pompous boor. He had the audacity to make a suggestive remark to one of my ladies. Disgusting oaf."

Baxter raised his eyebrows. "I most certainly apologize for the colonel," he murmured. "I shall have a word with him and make sure it doesn't happen again." He couldn't imagine why the old fool would be interested in any of the women. There wasn't one among them who could turn a blind man's head. Obviously the colonel was not functioning with both barrels, as usual.

"Yes, well, he's the least of our worries at the moment." The violinist looked pointedly at the clock as it began to chime the quarter past the hour. "I happen to be Mrs. Parsons, and these ladies are the members of my string quartet. We have been rehearsing in the ballroom, since we will be appearing at the St. George's Day ball."

"Ah, yes," Baxter said, rocking back on his heels. "Mrs. Sinclair mentioned to me that you would be here this afternoon."

"Yes, well, Mrs. Carter-Holmes promised us transportation to take us back to our homes this afternoon. I understand Mrs. Sinclair promised to take care of the matter. We have been waiting for over an hour in this lobby for the trap to arrive."

Baxter frowned. "I don't understand. I made the arrangements myself. The footman was supposed to be here at four o'clock to take you home."

"So I understand."

"I am most terribly sorry, Mrs. Parsons. I can't imagine what could have happened to him." The idiot was most likely still in the stables, having forgotten the appointment. Freddie Thompson had only recently been hired at the hotel. If he didn't have a damn good excuse for neglecting this duty, Baxter thought grimly, the new footman would be looking for some other employment.

"The point is, Mr. Baxter, we are all quite tired and rather peckish, this being so close to our dinner hour. We would be much obliged if you could arrange for us to be taken home immediately."

Baxter attempted to spread his most charming smile across his face. "Mrs. Parsons, I will do my best to arrange transportation for you as soon as possible. In the meantime, perhaps you would all like to retire to the drawing room, where I will be happy to arrange for a glass of sherry and some hors d'oeuvres to help temper your appetite."

A wary look crossed the pinched face of the woman. "That dreadful man will not be in there, I trust?"

"No, madam. The colonel is no doubt in his favorite seat in the bar."

The old bat had the grace to actually smile. "In that case, Mr. Baxter, we would be delighted to accept your most generous offer. That would be very nice indeed, wouldn't it, ladies?"

"Very nice," two of her companions chimed in together. The third woman, the tall one holding onto an enormous black case that bore the scars of numerous travels, merely stood silent without so much as a flicker of her eyelashes.

"Very well, then. If you'd care to follow me?" Deciding that he could only manage one of the instruments with any proficiency, Baxter took a step toward the bass player. "May I carry that for you?"

The musician's eyes narrowed, and her thin lips pinched together. Although she didn't speak, her swift rejection of his offer was apparent as she dragged the cumbersome case out of his reach.

Startled, Baxter pulled his hand back.

"Oh, thank you, Mr. Baxter," Mrs. Parsons said quickly, "but we always carry our own cases. It's a policy we have always found prudent. While I'm quite sure you would use the utmost care, some people do not know how to handle the delicate instruments."

Baxter nodded, still unsettled by the bass player's abrupt action. "I understand, Mrs. Parsons. This way, then."

He had to admit to himself, as he led the way down the narrow hallway, he was quite impressed with the way the bass player managed her burden. Awkward in size, and obviously heavy, the huge bass traveled quite swiftly to the drawing room in the arms of its owner.

Baxter very much doubted that he could have done any better. Which just went to prove, he told himself after he'd settled the four women in the lounge, that expertise counted for more than brawn.

In fact, he reflected, as he once more returned to the lobby, all of the women appeared to be quite sprightly indeed, in spite of their advanced age. Apparently the performing arts could be quite rejuvenating.

Wondering if perhaps he was in the wrong profession, Baxter headed for the stables to track down the elusive Freddie.

CHAPTER

❧ 5 ❧

"I haven't seen him, guv'nor," Samuel said, pausing to wipe the sweat from his brow. "I've been wondering meself what happened to him."

He'd left a streak across his forehead beneath the peak of his cap, Baxter noticed, trying not to let his irritation with the absent footman spill over onto his stable manager. Casting an impatient glance around the stalls, he took a moment to control his exasperation.

"When did you see Freddie last?" he demanded, inwardly vowing to chastise the young man severely when he did materialize.

Samuel leaned on his rake and frowned. "It must have been about half past two. He took the trap to pick up a bunch of fiddlers. Said as how they were going to rehearse in the ballroom this afternoon."

Baxter winced, wondering how the waspish Mrs. Parsons would appreciate her string quartet being referred to as a bunch of fiddlers. "Well, he arrived back at the hotel with the musicians, so he must be somewhere in the vicinity. He was supposed to take them all back again over an hour ago. The ladies are very upset at being kept waiting for so long, and I must say I don't blame them."

Samuel looked surprised. "They're still here? I wonder what Freddie did with the flipping trap, then."

"It isn't here?"

"No, guv'nor. It ain't." Samuel pushed his cap back on his head, leaving another streak of dirt on his forehead. "I was gone this afternoon. I finished storing the equipment for the tournament in the loft, so then I went down to the feed store to take the order in. Left about three o'clock, I reckon. Anyhow, when I got back, must have been about an hour, I sees as how the trap was missing. I thought Freddie had taken the fiddlers back home again. I was just wondering what was taking him so blinking long."

"I would like the answer to that myself." Baxter fumed inwardly, itching to get his hands on the wayward footman. "In any case, we must remove the musicians before the hotel guests arrive for the evening meal. Take the other trap, Samuel, and get them home as fast as possible. If you should see Freddie, send him to my office immediately."

"Will do, guv'nor." Samuel dropped the rake and straightened his cap.

"Please make sure you wash your face and hands first," Baxter said, heading back out into the yard. "I don't want to have to deal with another chorus of complaints from those ladies."

He left Samuel at the water pump and headed back to the hotel. He would wait until six o'clock, he decided, and if Freddie hadn't returned by then, he would have to tell Cecily. He knew how upset she would be.

It was becoming more and more difficult to find responsible people to staff the hotel. The youngsters nowadays were moving to the city, leaving only the lazy or incompetent behind.

Silently decrying the demise of the good old days, Baxter returned to the quiet peace of his office, hoping it would not be necessary to upset Cecily with this latest setback.

An hour later Cecily made her way to the drawing room to mingle with her visitors before the maid rang the gong announcing the dinner hour. Not that there were many guests at the hotel at present. The majority of them would arrive at the weekend for the St. George's Day celebration.

In fact, when Cecily entered the drawing room, much to her dismay the only person she saw was the colonel. He sat in front of the fireplace, an empty gin glass at his elbow, quietly dozing with the evening paper spread out on his lap.

Afraid that a sudden movement from the gentleman might knock the glass over, Cecily quietly crossed the room to pick it up. As she reached for it, however, the colonel stirred.

Opening sleepy, bloodshot eyes, he murmured, "Very nice of you, old girl. Don't mind if I do."

Realizing he had mistaken her action and assumed she had brought him another drink, Cecily said quietly, "It's almost time for dinner, Colonel. I'm sure you will enjoy the excellent French wine Michel has selected for the main course tonight." If the silly man had any more gin, she thought, he'd never make it to his dining table.

Revitalized at the prospect of French wine, the colonel sat up. "That sounds spiffing, old bean. Nothing like a glass of good wine to set up the appetite, what? What?"

Cecily smiled. "If you say so, Colonel."

His eyelids started blinking rapidly as he stared up at her. "I say, old girl, are those lady musicians going to be dining with us this evening?"

Startled, she shook her head. "Not as far as I know, Colonel. I imagine they left here at least two hours ago."

"You don't say. Could have sworn I saw them just a few minutes ago." He shook his head. "Must have dozed off there for a while."

"Indeed you did, Colonel."

"Yes, well, shame that." He gave his mustache a roguish twirl. "Rather took a fancy to one of them, you know."

Cecily wondered how she could make a hasty retreat without seeming rude. "How nice," she murmured, looking pointedly at the clock.

"Fine figure of a woman, that. Took my dashed breath away. Plays that oversized fiddle—what do you call it?"

"Cello?" Cecily suggested helpfully.

"No, no, no, old bean. Bigger than that." The colonel held up both hands and drew the shape of an hourglass in front of him. "Shaped like a dashed woman itself, by Jove," he commented.

"I think that's called a bass," Cecily said, hiding her irritation. Sometimes the colonel could be incredibly gauche.

"Whatever you say, m'dear. I was hoping to see the damsel again. I suppose I'll have to wait for the ball, though, what?"

"I'm afraid so," Cecily said, hoping the colonel wouldn't get wind of the rehearsals taking place in the ballroom. Fortescue nursed the fond delusion that he was irresistible to women. He could be extremely embarrassing at times.

"Oh, well, gives me something to look forward to, I daresay." The colonel shifted his weight, sending the newspaper on his knees to the floor.

Cecily bent to retrieve it and caught sight of the head-lines. She paused with the paper in her hands, distressed by the story. Several suffragettes had been imprisoned and were conducting a hunger strike. At least two of them were near death.

While Cecily thoroughly supported their cause, she couldn't help wondering how much the women hoped to achieve if they died in prison. According to some of the more lurid accounts, the protestors had been harshly treated while confined.

Very few men had any sympathy for them or their fight for equal rights. Indeed, many politicians were determined to stamp out the movement, deeming it a threat to the stability of the country.

Aware that the colonel was mumbling something, Cecily tore her attention away from the depressing story. "I'm sorry, Colonel. You were saying?"

"What?" He peered up at her, momentarily confused. "Oh, that. I was talking about the news, madam. All this chatter about war again. I shall have to sharpen my saber, what? Can't shirk my duty, by Jove. Have to jolly well give them what for, don't we."

Cecily could just imagine what would happen to the colonel if he tried to rejoin the army. "I sincerely hope it won't come to that, Colonel."

"Oh, bound to, old girl. Bound to." Fortescue shook his head mournfully. "Of course, it will be a very different war this time, take my word for it. All these explosives they use nowadays. Blow your blasted head clean off. Never know what hit you, by George. Damned heathen if you ask me. Doesn't give a man a chance to fight back. Not cricket, that."

Cecily felt a little squirm of uneasiness at his words. There was more than a glimmer of truth in them.

"No, sir. Don't know what you're up against anymore." He shook an unsteady finger at her. "All these dashed motorcars racing around. What's the matter with horses, that's what I want to know. Everything blasted mechanized nowadays, that's the trouble."

"A sign of progress, Colonel." Cecily's mind went back to the newspaper story. Progress was sometimes very dearly bought.

"Prefer a horse any day," the colonel mumbled, looking as if he were ready to doze off again. "Saw one today, haring up to the Downs pulling a trap without a driver. Dashed clever these horses are, you know. Think for themselves, some of them."

His chin fell forward onto his chest, and Cecily leaned over to pick up the glass. He was obviously rambling again. No doubt the colonel would awaken at the sound of the gong. Until then, she'd leave him to enjoy his snooze.

Halfway down the hallway she saw one of the twins hurrying back from the dining room. "Take this back to the kitchen with you, please, Doris," she said, handing the glass over.

"It's Daisy, mum," the housemaid said, bobbing a curtsy.

Cecily smiled. "I'm sorry, Daisy. You and Doris must both get awfully tired of being taken for each other."

Daisy shook her head. "We're used to it, mum. We answer to both names, anyway." She hurried off down the hallway, her long skirt swishing about her ankles as she turned the corner.

Cecily gave a wry shake of her head. There had been a time when she could tell the girls apart, more from their attitude than anything. Doris had always been somewhat subdued and far more congenial than her once surly sister.

Now that Daisy spent a great deal of her time taking care of Gertie's five-month-old twins, her disposition had gone through a transformation. Doris herself had also blossomed, gaining confidence as well as much needed weight, and it was almost impossible nowadays to tell the maids apart.

Half smiling at the thought, Cecily continued on her way to the dining room. Before she reached it, however, she was surprised to see Baxter waiting at the doors.

"I hoped I might catch you here," he said as she reached him. "I would like a word with you in my office, if you'll excuse me for delaying your meal."

She looked at him, concerned by his expression. "Something is wrong?"

"Nothing to be alarmed about, I'm sure, madam. I feel we should discuss the matter in private, however."

"Of course." Perhaps now, she thought as she followed him to his office, she would find out what it was that had been troubling him so much lately. She could only hope and pray that it wasn't anything serious.

Reaching the office, Baxter waited for her to sit down, his face, as always, giving her no hint of what was on his mind.

"Madam," he said once she was settled. "I'm afraid we might have a small problem on our hands."

She peered up at him, her concern making her voice sharp. "Nothing drastic, I hope?"

"Not at this point, as far as I know."

She waited, forgetting for a moment his exasperating habit of waiting to be prodded for information. "Then what is it?" she demanded finally, when it seemed he would remain silent forever.

"It's Freddie Thompson, madam."

"What about him?" She leaned forward, Madeline's warning returning forcibly to her mind.

"He neglected to pick up the musicians this afternoon."

"Oh, Lord." She leaned back, feeling a faint sense of relief that it was nothing worse. "Were they very upset?"

"Enraged, madam."

"How long were they kept waiting?"

"Over an hour, I'm afraid."

"I see. I trust you took care of the matter?"

"I had Samuel take them home."

Cecily nodded, wondering why Baxter had deemed this irritating oversight on Freddie's part important enough to interrupt her evening meal.

"I'm afraid that's not all."

Once more she felt a sense of disquiet. "What is it?"

"I'm afraid the colonel upset the musicians, madam."

"How did he manage to do that?"

Baxter's face remained inscrutable as he answered. "I believe he made an improper remark to one of them."

"Oh, dear, I was afraid of that," Cecily murmured. "He did mention something about it to me. We shall have to keep an eye on him, Baxter. We can't have him embarrassing the ladies."

"Yes, madam. I will do my best."

"I'm sure you will." She peered up at him, unsettled by the way he avoided her gaze. "What is it, Baxter? What is it you're not telling me?"

He hesitated just long enough to alarm her. "I'm afraid that Freddie has not returned with the trap as yet."

She narrowed her eyes, trying to make sense of his words. "Returned from where? I thought you said that Samuel took the ladies home."

"I did, madam."

She sat up, fixing him with as stern a look as she could manage. "Baxter, for heaven's sake, tell me it all. Where is Freddie?"

"I'm afraid I don't know. That is what concerns me." He paused, and for a moment she thought that was all he had to say. Then he added reluctantly, "By all accounts, Freddie brought the ladies here to the hotel this afternoon, then left again with the trap without a word to anyone. He has not returned."

Now she could hear Madeline's voice again inside her head. *Someone is in grave danger. More than one.* "Oh, dear Lord," she whispered.

Baxter held out a hand toward her, then dropped it again. "I beg you, madam, do not upset yourself. I am quite certain that the lad has merely taken the trap on some personal errand and has forgotten the time."

Cecily shook her head. "That isn't like him, Baxter. Freddie rarely leaves the hotel grounds, except on an errand for me. If you remember, he is new to the area and has no friends here."

"That may be, madam, but I see no need for concern. I am quite sure he will return in his own good time. When he does, I shall see that he is severely reprimanded. Perhaps a cut in his wages will remind him of his obligations."

Surprised, Cecily looked up at him. "That sounds unusually harsh, coming from you. I would expect you to be a little more concerned. If Freddie left after he delivered the quartet, then he has been gone several hours."

"I am not concerned, madam, because I know how easily a young man's head can be turned. He is most likely entertaining a young lady somewhere."

Cecily sighed. "I hope you are right. I can't help feeling worried, however." She rose, unaware that her appetite had vanished. "I would like to know the minute there is news of his whereabouts."

Baxter nodded. "I will inform you myself, just as soon as I hear anything."

She left the office, unable to rid herself of the uneasy feeling. Not only did Freddie's absence worry her, but Baxter's unconcern was a clear indication that all was not right with her manager. If only she knew what was troubling him, perhaps she could help in some way.

Until he chose to confide in her, however, she was helpless. It hurt her a great deal to know that he could not trust her with his problem. She had thought for some time that they had been drawing closer in their relationship. Apparently she had been mistaken. The thought depressed her no end.

She was about to pass through the doors of the dining room when once more she was interrupted. This time it was Mrs. Chubb who approached her, her round face lined with worry.

"Begging your pardon, mum, I am so sorry to interrupt your dinner, but I thought you should know the news," the housekeeper said, twisting a corner of her apron around in her chubby hands.

Cecily felt her throat tighten. "Is it Freddie?"

Mrs. Chubb looked startled for a moment. "Freddie? No, mum, it's Cynthia Chalmsford. I'm afraid she's missing, mum, and nobody can find her. Her father asked me to get some help in searching the grounds for her. He says she's been gone since early this afternoon."

A feeling of helplessness seemed to be crawling over Cecily's body. *Someone is in grave danger. More than one. I'm afraid for the child.*

CHAPTER
❈ 6 ❈

"I cannot imagine where Cynthia could be," Lady Chalmsford said, her voice trembling with suppressed emotion. "She has never stayed away this long. Why, she hasn't had her dinner yet. She never misses a meal."

Seated next to her in the sumptuous gold and green suite, Cecily touched the woman's arm in sympathy. "Try not to worry, Lady Chalmsford. Some of my staff are helping your husband search for her. I'm quite sure someone will find her before too long. Most likely she has fallen asleep somewhere."

The elegant woman rose swiftly to her feet and began pacing back and forth, her tea gown floating in a cloud of blue silk just above the ground.

Cecily's heart went out to the distraught mother. "I know

the agony you are feeling right now," she said gently. "I well remember how awful it is to be faced with the trauma of a lost child. When my eldest son Michael was only ten years old, he lost his way in the African jungle. He was missing all night."

Even now she shivered at the memory. "I was half out of my mind with gory visions of finding his remains after some wild animal had torn him apart. I'm happy to say, he was found the next morning, asleep in the tree in which he'd spent the night. The relief at seeing him alive and well was almost unbearable."

She paused, waiting for a response that failed to materialize. "It is amazing what unwarranted fears our minds can conjure up in such situations," she said after a moment.

Lady Chalmsford shook her head in a distracted way. "I dozed off but for a minute," she said, her voice so low Cecily could barely hear her. "Cynthia was playing with her dolls, right by my side. I simply cannot think how she could have left the room without disturbing me."

"Children can be very quiet when they put their minds to it." Cecily got up and crossed the room to the window. Drawing back the heavy velvet curtain, she saw the glow of the lamps moving across the lawn and among the shrubbery that bordered the fishpond. "At least it is a fairly warm evening for this time of year," she added. "Thank heaven we didn't have a late snowstorm."

The observation failed to comfort Lady Chalmsford. "I don't know what to do with the child," she said, her voice threatening to break at any moment. "The minute I turn my back, she is off on some adventure or other. I keep telling her that one day something dreadful will happen to her if she continues to disobey her parents. I shall have to resort to locking her in her room if she doesn't behave."

Cecily turned to see the other woman dab at her eyes with a lace-trimmed handkerchief. It was Cecily's private opinion that if the Chalmsfords paid more attention to the child, instead of leaving her to amuse herself a great deal of the time, the problem might not arise so frequently.

"She is a very intelligent child," she said in an effort to keep the poor woman's mind from dwelling on the situation. "Such children are naturally curious."

"Curiosity should be curbed in little girls. It isn't lady-like." Lady Chalmsford sniffed delicately as she dabbed at her nose. "Cynthia will marry well and will be taken care of by her husband for the rest of her life. Her father will see to that. She doesn't need to know anything beyond how to entertain, and to turn her hand at some fine needlework. Men do not appreciate intelligence in women. It is not considered to be feminine."

Which was why, Cecily thought fiercely, the affairs of women were in such a sorry state. She was beginning to feel extremely sorry for the child. No wonder Cynthia escaped at every given opportunity.

She turned back to the window, hoping to see some sign that the little girl had been found. The lanterns were still bobbing about the grounds, however. She could see the scattered light through the trees.

Lady Chalmsford appeared to have herself under control when Cecily turned back to the room. The aristocrat had seated herself on the ottoman and was gazing aimlessly at a sheet of paper in her hand.

Unable to bear the inactivity any longer, Cecily said quietly, "If you will excuse me, Lady Chalmsford, I think I will give my staff some assistance. Is there anything I can fetch for you before I leave?"

Lady Chalmsford looked up. "Thank you, no. I think I shall wait here for my husband to return with my daughter."

Cecily headed for the door, hoping that happy event would occur in the very near future. She could not get Madeline's warning out of her mind, and she would not rest easily until both Freddie and Cynthia Chalmsford were safely back inside the hotel where they belonged.

*   *   *

"Imagine that child wandering around all alone," Mrs. Chubb said, expertly cutting a huge slice of gooseberry pie. "Her parents must be fair out of their minds with worry." She lifted the piece from the pie plate and placed it carefully on the huge silver tray, which was already crowded with fruit flans and roly-poly puddings.

Gertie paused in the act of ladling brandied custard into the bone china jugs. "If you ask me, they don't bleeding well worry enough. How many times has Miss Cynthia been down here for hours before they even noticed she was bloody gone? That Lady Chalmsford is always bloody asleep, while her father goes off on his bleeding own somewhere. It's no blinking wonder the nipper's looking for someone to talk to all the time. Poor little bugger's lonely, that's what."

"Well, it's not for us to say how the gentry should treat their young, I'm sure." The housekeeper looked up at the clock on the mantlepiece. "Where is that Doris? She should have been back for the sweets ten minutes ago."

"Per'aps she's helping look for Cynthia," Gertie said, pouring custard into a jug. She didn't quite tilt the ladle quick enough, and the thick yellow cream spilled over the edge. After a quick glance to make sure Mrs. Chubb had her back to her, Gertie ran a finger up the side of the jug and scooped the little rivulet of custard into her mouth. It tasted wonderful, and she licked her lips. With any luck there'd be some left over after dinner. If so, she'd make bloody sure she'd be there to nab it.

"I certainly hope she isn't looking for her," Mrs. Chubb said, sounding irritated. "We can't have half the hotel staff running around searching for a naughty child. We have far too much to do."

"Well, I bleeding know one thing." Gertie finished filling the jugs and stood the empty pot back on the stove. "I'm not going to take my bloody eyes off my twins when they start walking around. If I have to bleeding chain them to me bloody belt, I'll do it."

Mrs. Chubb shook her head. "At the rate they're growing, it won't be long before they'll be into everything. That James is as strong as an ox."

"Don't I bleeding know it." Gertie stared gloomily at the tray of jugs. "Crawling all over the bloody place, he is. Not yet six months old, and already he can pull himself up to the bleeding window. I'm scared he's going to climb out one of these blinking days. Take his sister with him an' all, I wouldn't bloody wonder."

"Lillian knows better than to follow him. Girls always do. It's a good job you have Daisy to help you watch over them." The housekeeper looked up as the kitchen door opened.

The young girl who entered looked nervously at the clock. "Sorry, I'm late, Mrs. Chubb. That Colonel Fortescue kept me talking. It took me ages to get away from him."

"Daffy old buzzard," Gertie muttered. "Should be locked up, that one. He's bleeding dangerous, if you ask me. Always charging about and shouting his blinking head off. Everyone knows he's bleeding barmy."

"That's enough, Gertie," Mrs. Chubb said sharply. "The colonel is a guest in this hotel and, as such, must be treated with respect."

Gertie picked up the tray of custard and marched to the door. "Well, it's too bleeding bad he don't treat us with respect. I'm getting bloody tired of him pinching me bum every time I go past him. One of these bloody days I'm going to pinch him in the—"

"Gertay!"

"—hallway," Gertie said, winking at Doris. "Maybe he'll bleeding stay out of me way, then." She paused in the doorway and looked back at Doris. "Has Freddie turned up yet?"

Doris shook her head. "Mr. Baxter's right cross with him,

he is. Daisy heard him say that Freddie won't get no more time off for a month."

"Bloody twerp," Gertie muttered as she wedged the door open with her wide hip. "He should know better than to stay out all blinking afternoon. He knows he'll bleeding cop it when he comes back."

Mrs. Chubb thrust the tray of sweets into Doris's hands. "Here, take this back to the dining room and be quick about it. The guests will be wondering if they're going to get any afters at this rate."

Doris took the tray and followed Gertie out into the hallway. "It's sort of scary, isn't it, the way people keep disappearing? What if the gypsies are stealing them away and we'll never see them again? What if they steal us all away? I've heard as how they sell people to foreign countries. Nobody ever sees them again."

Gertie's harsh laugh echoed down the hallway. "They'd have a job getting anyone to buy any of us, that's for bleeding sure." She glanced at Doris's worried face. "'Ere, don't get your drawers in a knot. Freddie ain't disappeared. He's probably down the pub knocking back a few beers."

"Well, what about Miss Cynthia?"

Gertie grinned. "It wouldn't surprise me if she ain't bleeding with him, bugging everyone to death with her bloody questions."

For once she failed to get a return smile from Doris. Deciding to change the subject, she nudged Doris with her elbow. "'Ere, how'd the bloody rehearsal go this afternoon, then? I reckon you impressed them old biddies with your singing, didn't you?"

Doris shrugged. "Don't know about that. They gave me a song written in foreign words. I didn't understand them, and I couldn't say them right, neither."

"Aw, don't worry, luv. It'll be all right on the bleeding night, you'll see."

Doris looked unconvinced. "Them musicians are really

peculiar," she said, frowning. "Not one of them smiled. Not once. They seemed like they was scared of each other."

"Seems to me we have a lot of bleeding peculiar people running around here," Gertie said, thinking about the colonel.

"Like that Roland Young." Doris looked over her shoulder as if she expected to see that young man walking down it. "He is awfully strange. He always has such a funny look in his eyes."

"He's just bloody ignorant, that's all," Gertie said curtly. "He's not worth bothering with, that one."

"He's worth it if he can help me get what I want." Doris started as the clock began to chime in the lobby. "I'd better hurry and get this tray in the dining room, or Mrs. Chubb will cut off my tail. I just hope they find that little girl before something bad happens to her."

Watching the young maid hurrying down the hallway, Gertie had to admit to a twinge of uneasiness herself. She just hoped the little girl was all right. Much as the little pest irritated her, she wasn't a bad kid.

Taking a firm grip on the tray, Gertie followed Doris to the dining room, suddenly anxious to be off duty so she could get back to her twins and make sure they were safe for the night.

Reaching the lobby, Cecily glanced at the grandfather clock. Soon the dinner hour would be over, and the Chalmsfords had yet to dine. If this disappearance was nothing more than a childish prank, she thought as she headed for the front doors, she, for one, would have a serious talk with Cynthia Chalmsford.

Stepping through the door into the cool night air, she saw the tall figure of Lord Chalmsford hurrying up the steps, his dark hair ruffled by the brisk breeze from the ocean.

Baxter and Samuel followed closely behind, and she could tell by their faces that they had no news of Cynthia.

"She's not on the grounds?" she asked as Lord Chalmsford paused at the top of the steps.

He shook his head, brushing back his unruly locks with an impatient hand. "Not a sign of her. What about indoors? Has the hotel been thoroughly searched?"

"Every square foot of it. No one has seen your daughter since this afternoon." Cecily looked up at him, distressed by his agonized expression reflected in the glow of the lamps. "I'm sorry, Lord Chalmsford. I think we should contact the constabulary. They will be able to conduct a wider search than we could manage."

"I agree. Please ask them to begin searching right away. Tell them I will be happy to join them."

"I doubt if P.C. Northcott will allow that," Cecily said unhappily. "Perhaps it would be better if you stayed with your wife until we have news."

His mouth tightened, but he gave her a brief nod, then sent a hunted look left and right before hurrying through the door to the lobby.

Cecily looked at Baxter, whose own face was showing signs of strain. "Freddie hasn't returned, either," she said quietly.

"Freddie is old enough to take care of himself," Baxter said shortly. "It is the child who worries me." He turned to Samuel, who was hovering behind, holding a lamp in either hand. "Get down to the police station as fast as you can, Samuel, and report to the constable. Bring him back with you if possible. We must get started on this hunt right away."

"Yes, sir." Samuel bounded down the steps, light spilling crazily from the lanterns swinging in his hands.

Cecily felt the now-familiar ache as she met Baxter's impassive gaze. Once she would have sought comfort from him, and he would have given it. Now, however, she was wary of approaching him, afraid of asking for something he could no longer give.

"I suggest you go back indoors, madam," he said quietly.

"There is nothing more to be done out here until the constable arrives."

She nodded and turned away from him, drawing her stole closer about her shoulders. She felt cold and helpless and more alone than she had felt since that terrible day, more than three years ago, when her late husband had passed away.

It wasn't the fresh sea breeze that made her shiver as she entered the lobby again. Nor was it solely the thought of an eight-year-old child missing on this dark night. What disturbed her most of all was the cool detachment she had seen in Baxter's eyes.

Samuel struggled to harness the chestnut to the trap, cursing when the animal shied away from him. He would have ridden the horse down to the police station, except that for some strange reason the animal seemed unusually restless and frisky.

It took him longer than usual to tighten the straps as the chestnut kept stepping sideways, nostrils flared and eyes rolling back to reveal the whites of his eyes.

"What is the matter with you?" Samuel demanded, irritated by this unwarranted behavior. Normally the chestnut never gave him any trouble. Tonight of all nights, right when he was in a hurry, the blooming horse chose to play up.

Finally, after much cursing and shoving, Samuel drove the trap out onto the Esplanade. The minute he gave the chestnut his head, the animal cantered along the seafront as if the devil himself were after him.

Samuel had to keep a tight hold on the reins to remain in control. He was almost at the police station on the other side of Badgers End before the horse calmed down to a steady trot. Leaving him tied up to the rail, Samuel sprinted into the station.

Police Constable Stanley Northcott sat sprawled at his desk, his nose in a book, with a cup of steaming tea and a thick ham sandwich at his elbow. He looked up in disgust when Samuel burst into the office.

"'Ere, 'ere," he said, scratching his bushy red hair with his pencil, "what's your blooming hurry, then?"

"Mrs. Sinclair sent me," Samuel said, still out of breath from his tussle with the chestnut. "One of the guests is missing. A little girl. She's the daughter of Lord and Lady Chalmsford."

At the sound of such illustrious names, P.C. Northcott's expression changed. "Well, why didn't you say so?" He licked the end of his pencil and opened a grubby-looking notebook. Turning each page slowly, he came to a blank one and poised the pencil above it.

"The child's name?"

"What does it matter what her blooming name is?" Samuel said, wishing he could snatch the pencil out of the policeman's pudgy hand. "She's only eight years old, and she's out there somewhere all alone. We have to find her before something terrible happens to her."

"I 'ave to take down notes first," P.C. Northcott said, looking affronted. "It's procedure. I 'ave to h'ask questions and get some h'answers before I can go chasing off after missing persons."

Samuel held onto his temper. It wouldn't do any good to get angry. That would only slow the old fool down. He'd have to answer the stupid questions, then get the bumbling idiot back to the hotel.

Half an hour later Samuel was racing back along the Esplanade, ignoring the loud complaints of his irate passenger. After depositing the grumbling constable at the foot of the steps, Samuel led the chestnut back to the stables and unharnessed him.

Everything went fine until he tried to lead the horse back into his stall. The chestnut refused to go. Not only did he not want to go back in his stall, the animal seemed terrified, rearing and whinnying as if he'd seen some invisible enemy waiting to strike him down.

Thinking there might be a rat lurking about somewhere, Samuel tied the restless animal to a post and went inside the stall to take a closer look.

The far corner of the stable was in shadow, cast by the wooden divider. Squinting, Samuel stared at the mound that shouldn't be there. His heart started banging against his ribs, and his knees began to feel wobbly.

He didn't want to take a closer look; yet he knew he had to see what was there. He could only hope it wasn't what it appeared to be.

He lifted a lamp from the hook and quickly lit it. Holding it above his head, he took a step closer to the mound of hay. The light spilled across the rake standing in the middle of it, held upright by some invisible means.

Samuel drew closer, his eyes glued to the rake. As the light fell across it, he saw it wasn't a rake after all. It was one of the lances that had been delivered just that morning, a part of the equipment to be used in the jousting tournament.

Samuel felt sick as he drew closer. The lance leaned at an angle, caught in something half buried in the hay. One step closer and Samuel could see the entire mound now.

There in the straw the light from the lamp cast grotesque shadows across the body of a man. A little moan escaped from Samuel's frozen lips. He had found Freddie.

CHAPTER

7

Cecily sat at the long Jacobean table in the library trying to control her impatience as she watched P.C. Northcott fumbling with his notebook.

Across the room, Baxter stood by the fireplace, studiously avoiding her gaze. Even so, she could see his intense dislike of the police constable in the steely glint of his eyes.

Remembering the story that Baxter had told her of how the constable had stolen away his only true love many years earlier, Cecily felt a twinge of sympathy and more than a hint of jealousy.

She had always envied the woman who had commanded such emotion in her unyielding manager. What she wouldn't give, Cecily thought sadly, to have just a trace of that unfulfilled devotion that still had so much influence on

Baxter. Even after all these years, he could not forgive the man who had devastated his life.

"Now then, Mrs. Sinclair, perhaps you would be so kind as to fill the gaps for me," Northcott said, pulling his pencil from his pocket. "That there stable lad of yours was in such a hurry, he barely answered my questions."

"He was in a hurry, no doubt," Cecily said smoothly, "because he was concerned about the welfare of the child. As are we all."

"Quite so, quite so." Northcott licked the end of his pencil. "But I have to fill out my report, ma'am, as you well know, being as how you've seen me do it so many times."

This sly reference to her previous encounters with the constabulary smacked of a warning, arousing Cecily's resentment. She could almost hear Baxter gritting his teeth.

"May I suggest, Constable," she said quietly, "that we take care of the report after you have launched a search for the child? Surely the longer we delay, the greater the chance of some misfortune happening to her?"

"That's as may be, ma'am, begging your pardon." The constable slowly and deliberately turned the pages of his notebook. "But h'unless I know all the details, so to speak, I won't know where to start searching for her, now will I? I suppose you have already searched the grounds of this here hotel?"

"Both inside and out, Constable."

"Well, she can't have gone far by herself." The constable examined his notes long enough for Cecily to feel like screaming at him. Again she sought Baxter's gaze across the room, but her manager appeared to be intent on studying the bookshelves.

"Your lad said as how the young lady disappeared from her room early this afternoon."

"That's right. I believe Doris was the last person to see her." Cecily frowned. "And the musicians, I suppose, though I haven't spoken to them yet."

The constable looked up. "What musicians would that be, ma'am?"

"The string quartet, who were rehearsing in the ballroom this afternoon. One of my maids was also at the rehearsal. She mentioned that she saw Cynthia during that time."

"H'and what time would that be, Mrs. Sinclair?"

"Somewhere between three and four o'clock, I would imagine." Cecily's patience finally ran out. "Constable, far be it for me to tell you how to do your duty, but I do think we should commence with the search. Lord Chalmsford was most emphatic that we start right away."

The constable nodded with maddening deliberation. "Very well, ma'am. But I would like a word with the parents first, if I may? They might be able to shed some light as to where she might be."

"I think that—" Cecily broke off as a smart rap sounded on the door.

Baxter moved swiftly, pulling the door open to reveal Samuel. The stable manager's eyes were wide in his ashen face as he stood twisting his cap into a tight ball.

Cecily rose, the new-familiar feeling of dread rushing to full strength. "Come in, Samuel," she said while her mind protested violently. *No, not the child. What dreadful thing could have happened to her?* Dear Lord, she thought, let it not be related to anyone or anything in the Pennyfoot.

"Excuse me, mum," Samuel said, shooting a sidelong glance at the constable, who appeared to be absorbed in his scribbling. "I've got something to tell you."

His frantic gaze met hers, signaling clearly that he wanted to speak to her alone.

Cecily glanced at Baxter, who was staring intently at the stable manager. "Some crisis in the kitchen, no doubt," she murmured, trying to sound nonchalant. "Perhaps we should discuss this out in the hallway, Samuel, while the constable finishes his notes."

"Oh, don't mind me, ma'am," Northcott said, closing his notebook with a snap. "I'm finished for the moment." He sat back, gazing expectantly at Samuel, who sent another desperate look at Cecily.

Slowly Cecily sat down. There was no real point in avoiding the issue. The police would have to know eventually whatever it was that had happened.

"You may continue, Samuel," Cecily said with a sigh of resignation.

Samuel hesitated for so long that she knew it was the worst news possible. She sent a pleading look at Baxter and this time received an almost imperceptible nod. The gesture gave her little consolation.

She didn't know whether to feel relieved or concerned when Samuel blurted out, "It's Freddie, mum. I found him a little while ago."

"Where is he?" she asked carefully. Judging from Samuel's expression, she wasn't going to care for the answer.

"He's in the stable, mum." Samuel swallowed. "He's been murdered. Run through the chest with one of them lances they're using in the tournament."

Cecily shifted her gaze to the portrait of her late husband, which hung above the huge marble fireplace. Once it would have brought her reassurance. In the early days after his death, she would often talk out loud to the late James Sinclair, most times arriving at a conclusion or decision after gazing at length on his dearly remembered face.

Now she could find no solace in the painted image on the wall. The one person who could console her, the man who had faithfully promised her dying husband to take care of her, stood silent and emotionally removed from her. Baxter might just as well be on the other side of the moon for all the comfort he would give her now.

The constable had risen to his feet, excitement bringing beads of sweat to his brow. "H'oh my goodness, we 've got a busy evening, haven't we? Where is the body, then? I do hope no one has touched it?"

"I ain't touched it," Samuel said with a shudder, "and nobody knows about it except me." He looked back at

Cecily with apology written all over his face. "Now everyone here knows about it, too," he added miserably.

Cecily managed a bleak smile. "It's all right, Samuel, you did the right thing. Go down to the kitchen and ask Mrs. Chubb for a shot of brandy. Tell her I said it was all right."

"That sounds like a good idea," the constable said, his face brightening at the prospect of good French brandy. "I think I'll join him, if I may, Mrs. Sinclair?"

Cecily gave a brief nod as Baxter clicked his tongue.

P.C. Northcott appeared not to have heard the sound of irritation. "But first," he said, "I want to look at the body. And we have to send for Dr. Prestwick before I can remove the body."

"Constable." Cecily got to her feet again, wishing fervently that she could have a cigar. "I am devastated to hear this terrible news, of course, and I agree that you must look into the matter. Much as it grieves me to say it, poor Freddie is dead. No one can help him now. The child, however, is still missing, and one can only hope and pray that she is still alive. I therefore would suggest that our priority right now is to find Miss Cynthia Chalmsford and as quickly as possible."

Obviously reluctant to accept the advice of a mere woman, the constable nodded stiffly. "Perhaps you are right, ma'am. In which case, I must insist on speaking with the parents of the missing person immediately."

"I think that can be arranged."

To Cecily's utter relief, Baxter stepped forward. "I will send someone to notify the doctor, madam. I will then go down to the stable and await the constable there. I will make sure that no one interferes with the evidence."

She couldn't interpret the look in his eyes, but she could guess what was in his mind. This was one time when she would have to let the police take care of things. She could hardly keep Northcott out of it now.

"Thank you, Baxter," she said, moving around the table.

"In the meantime, I shall escort the constable to the Chalmsford suite."

Samuel looked relieved and barely waited for her to leave the room before bolting down the passageway toward the kitchen.

Baxter paused at her side, murmuring softly, "Will you be all right, madam?"

She smiled up at him, grateful for his concern. "I'll be quite all right, Baxter, thank you."

He nodded, then strode purposefully down the hallway with his coat tails flapping behind him.

She was aware of a faint sense of loss as she watched him go.

Lady Chalmsford appeared to have lost her self-control now that her husband had returned to her side. When Cecily and P.C. Northcott entered the room, the wealthy woman rocked back and forth on a platform rocker, clutching a wrinkled sheet of paper to her bosom.

Lord Chalmsford stood by the window, staring out onto the ocean with his lips tightly compressed. He turned as Cecily approached his wife, saying wearily, "I suppose it's too much to hope that you've found her."

"We haven't started looking as yet, Your Lordship," the constable said, stuttering slightly in his anxiety. "I need to ask some questions first."

"Good God, man," Lord Chalmsford muttered, "questions are not going to find my daughter."

"No, sir, but with due respect, the answers might help to narrow down the field, so to speak."

The aristocrat waved an irritable hand. "Very well, if you must. But make it quick, for pity's sake."

P.C. Northcott produced his shabby notebook and pencil. It was soon apparent that neither Lord nor Lady Chalmsford could shed much light on their child's disappearance. Cynthia had never wandered farther afield than the hotel to their knowledge. The last time either one of them had seen the child was earlier that afternoon. Other than that, they had nothing to add.

As the constable closed his notebook, Lady Chalmsford abruptly dissolved into tears. "My poor child, she must be so lonely and afraid. Please, you must find her soon."

"We'll do our best, milady," Northcott murmured.

The sheet of paper fluttered from Lady Chalmsford's hand, and Cecily stopped to retrieve it. Thick blotches of colored crayon covered the page, depicting a crudely drawn house.

"Did your daughter draw this?" she asked gently as she handed it back to the sobbing woman.

Lady Chalmsford nodded, pressing the paper once more to her breast. "It was my daughter's last gift to me," she said between sobs. "She gave it to me just two days ago, upon the occasion of our wedding anniversary."

"I'm so sorry," Cecily murmured. "I wish there was something I could say—"

The distraught woman clutched Cecily's hand, her tear-stained eyes peering beseechingly up at her. "Please, I implore you, find my daughter and bring her back to me."

In that moment Cecily knew that she was committed. "I will do my utmost to find her," she promised the sobbing woman.

Leaving the anxious parents to console each other, Cecily left the room with the constable, thankful that he had not seen fit to mention the murder of poor Freddie. She was very much afraid that the unfortunate footman's death and the missing child were connected in some way.

As yet P.C. Northcott had not voiced the possibility, but Cecily was certain it would be only a matter of time before the constable's ponderous mind reached the same conclusion.

All she could hope was that she could have time to form her own deductions before the constable brought in the disparaging Inspector Cranshaw, thereby crushing any opportunity to pursue the matter further.

She and the inspector had long battled over her so-called interference in police duties. The fact that she had more often than not been instrumental in uncovering the criminal had been dutifully ignored by the constabulary.

"I should like to question the kitchen staff after I view the body," Northcott said as they descended the stairs. "Also the musicians who were in the hotel this afternoon."

Cecily rolled her eyes at the ceiling. It seemed unlikely that the constable would get around to organizing a search before the night was over.

"I have a small suggestion to make," she said as they reached the lobby. "Perhaps, under the circumstances, it would be better if I question the staff at this late hour. I could also pay the musicians a visit. Lord Chalmsford is already most upset that the search has not been launched as yet. I'm sure you wouldn't want him complaining to Inspector Cranshaw. You know how the inspector feels about upsetting the gentry."

The constable nodded vigorously, a worried look on his face. "I do indeed, Mrs. Sinclair. Quite fanatical he is about it."

"Yes, well, I don't think that the ladies in the string quartet can be of much help in any case," Cecily said, pressing home her point. "I would be happy to talk to them and find out what little they might know. In the meantime, you can get on with the search. In the event that anyone tells me anything of value, I will see that the information is passed on to you immediately."

After a lot of hawing and humming, the constable reluctantly agreed. "I don't like it, Mrs. Sinclair, I don't mind telling you. I happen to think that a murder case is h'infinitely more important than a missing child. I don't want to upset Lord Chalmsford, however, so I'll wait for the doctor to examine the body and have it removed. Then I'll organize the search."

Relieved, Cecily watched him hurry out to the stables, then made her way to the kitchen.

She found the room in an uproar when she pushed the door open a minute or two later. Samuel sat in regal splendor at the head of the kitchen table, a large glass of brandy in his hand, while the rest of the staff crowded around him. Everybody appeared to be talking at once.

Silence fell dramatically over the group when the maids caught sight of her. Four pairs of eyes, which had been fixed on the stable manager's face, now regarded Cecily with a mixture of fear and excitement.

"Who do you think did it, mum? Who would want to kill poor Freddie?" Gertie asked, sending a nervous glance over her shoulder at the kitchen window. She had obviously been summoned from her room by the commotion, as she wore no cap and had thrown a lacy shawl over her daytime dress.

Daisy and Doris stood huddled together, looking so much alike that Cecily had no idea who was which. Mrs. Chubb, her buxom bosom heaving with agitation, stood by Samuel's chair, her face a deep red.

"I'm afraid that's impossible to say at this point," Cecily said quietly. "Gertie, I suggest you go back to your babies. There is nothing more to be learned tonight. If we have any news in the morning, I assure you everyone will be informed."

After a swift glance at Mrs. Chubb, Gertie mumbled a goodnight and left the kitchen.

Samuel, who had sprung to his feet as Cecily entered the room, looked guiltily down at the brandy still left in his glass.

"P.C. Northcott has gone to the stables," Cecily said, giving him a look that warned him not to say any more. "He will want to question you again, no doubt. It might be a good idea to go out there and talk to him."

Samuel nodded and grabbed up his cap from the table.

"If Mr. Baxter is still there, please tell him to meet me in the library, and as soon as the constable has finished with you, please harness up the trap."

"You'll be going out tonight?" Samuel said in surprise, glancing at the clock.

"Yes, but I'll have Mr. Baxter drive me, so you have no need to wait up for us. He will see that the horse is put back in the stalls."

"Yes, mum," Samuel said, looking disappointed. He reached the door and looked back. "I'd like to get me blinking hands on whoever did this to Freddie," he said fiercely.

"I'm sure you would, Samuel." Cecily glanced at the terrified faces of the twins. "I'm sure we all would like to know who is responsible for this dreadful thing." She looked back at Samuel. "By the way, I'd like to talk to you in the morning. Be in the library by nine o'clock, if you please."

"Yes, mum. I'll be there." With a nod, Samuel slipped out of the door.

"Can I get you a cup of tea, mum?" Mrs. Chubb asked anxiously, bustling forward.

"No, thank you." Cecily gave her a tired smile. "I'm sure you have plenty to do, and I really don't have time myself."

Mrs. Chubb nodded in agreement. "All this terrible upset has all our nerves in a dither. Thank goodness the dinner hour is over, though we still have to wash all the dishes."

"Don't let me stop you," Cecily said. "I just want a word with Doris, if you can spare her for a moment."

"Of course, mum." Mrs. Chubb looked at the two girls still huddled by the stove. "Look sharp, then, Doris. Don't keep madam waiting."

One of the twins stepped forward and bobbed a curtsey. She looked as if she were about to cry. "I don't know nothing, mum, honest I don't. I didn't see Freddie all day."

Cecily shook her head. "I don't want to talk about Freddie, Doris. I want to know exactly what happened this afternoon at the rehearsal when Cynthia was in the ballroom."

Doris looked startled, while behind her Mrs. Chubb gave

a little gasp. "The poor child is still missing? Oh, my, what a terrible day this has been." The housekeeper glared at Daisy, who appeared to be frozen to the spot. "Don't stand there gawking, girl, get with them dishes, or we'll be up all night."

Daisy shuffled over to the sink, rolling up the sleeves of her gray dress as she did so.

Doris sent a panic-stricken look at her sister, then back at Cecily. "I'm sorry, mum. With all the upset about Freddie, I'd forgotten about Miss Cynthia."

"I'm not surprised," Cecily said, wishing heartily that she had time for a cup of tea and a cigar. "Just tell me what you remember about the rehearsal this afternoon."

She listened while Doris described the scene in the ballroom. "Poor Cynthia," Doris added after she'd told Cecily how Esme Parsons had shouted at the child. "She got really upset and ran out of the room. I wonder if that's what made her run away. I was scared myself when I heard Mrs. Parsons carry on like that. She reminded me of my aunt, she did. She's got a real cruel voice and a terrible temper, just like my aunt."

Across the room Daisy made a guttural noise in her throat.

Ignoring her, Doris went on. "Anyway, I was glad to get off that stage meself. I don't like those ladies, mum, begging your pardon. I know they are performing for you at the ball, but there's something strange about the way they keep looking at each other. Like they're trying to hide something. They frighten me, they do."

"For heaven's sake, child," Mrs. Chubb said crossly. "You're letting your imagination run away with you. I know it's a terrible thing what happened to Freddie, but it isn't likely that four old ladies had anything to do with it."

"I didn't say as they did," Doris said, giving Cecily a troubled look. "I only said as how they were strange."

Cecily nodded. "Don't worry, Doris. I'm sure the musicians are harmless. Artists tend to act that way, you know. Creative people very often are considered odd."

Bidding everyone goodnight, she left the kitchen, deep in thought. Freddie presumably had been killed before four o'clock, or at least soon after, which was when he was supposed to have taken the musicians back to their homes.

According to Doris, Cynthia had been seen about half an hour before that and had then disappeared.

The more she thought about it, the more Cecily was convinced the two events were connected. She was very much afraid that Cynthia, with her interminable curiosity, might have seen whoever had killed Freddie, possibly even interrupting the deed to demand what was happening.

In which case, Cecily thought somberly, as she made her way to the library, the murderer would then have to make sure that Cynthia told no one until after he had disappeared from the scene.

There was also another prospect, one that she was most reluctant to consider. She could not avoid the possibility, however, that the murderer might well have found it necessary to silence the child permanently.

CHAPTER

❈ 8 ❈

The night had turned considerably cooler when Cecily
climbed into the trap at the foot of the hotel steps later that
evening. Baxter, she thought, looked most refined in his
homburg, and the white cravat he'd tucked into the neck of
his top coat was very becoming. She almost told him as
much, but somehow the words wouldn't come.

She felt strangely deserted when he closed the door of the
trap and climbed into the driver's seat. She would have
preferred to leave the canopy down, so that she could
converse with him, but the chill sea breezes would have
made the journey most uncomfortable. As it was, her hands
felt frozen in spite of her muff.

Baxter had offered surprisingly little resistance when
she'd told him she wanted to question the musicians. He'd

mentioned the lateness of the hour, but when she had shared her concerns about Cynthia's fate with him, to her immense satisfaction he had quickly agreed that they should pursue the matter with as much expediency as possible.

Cecily settled back against the cold leather seat and tried to allow the steady clop of the chestnut's hoofbeats to relax her. She tried not to think about Cynthia Chalmsford and what might have happened to her.

Her heart ached for Freddie. Such a tragedy to be cut down so early in his young life. His parents would have to be notified, of course. She sighed. They would take it very hard, no doubt. Life could be so very cruel.

Much as she missed her sons, she had the comfort of knowing they were alive and well. Though she couldn't be sure of that, she reminded herself. The sudden spasm of fear was quickly subdued. She had enough to worry about at the moment without weighing herself down with needless fears.

Do not trouble trouble until trouble troubles you, she told herself, smiling ruefully at the adage. How many times had she repeated those words to her sons? It was time she took heed of them herself. She was becoming far too morbid lately.

The steady beat of the horse's hooves slowed, and she peered through the tiny flap in the side of the canopy. They were traveling along the High Street now, which always looked so bleak at night with the shops closed and shuttered.

The trap jerked as the chestnut began the climb to the Downs, where the musicians lived in their modest cottages. They would pass by Madeline's house on the way.

Cecily would have dearly loved to talk to her friend about the tragic events of the day. After all, Madeline had foreseen the trouble. *Someone is in grave danger. More than one. I'm afraid for the child.*

Please, Cecily silently begged. *Not the child, too.*

The trap stopped with another sharp jerk, throwing her forward. Recovering herself, Cecily waited for Baxter to open the door for her, knowing how much he would resent it if she opened it herself.

"I'm sorry, madam," he said as he helped her down. "I'm afraid the horse is quite skittish tonight. He's a little difficult to control."

"Quite all right, Baxter," she murmured, removing her hand from his arm. "I imagine the horses must be very unsettled by what happened in the stables this afternoon. If only they had the ability to talk, they would no doubt solve this puzzle for us in no time."

"Yes, madam. No doubt they would." He glanced over his shoulder toward the cottage, which lay in the shadows of several trees. The windows were darkened, and his face wore a frown when he turned back to her.

"I must say, madam, I do not care for the task of questioning these ladies at this late hour."

"Neither do I, Baxter." Cecily paused at the gate and lifted the hem of her skirt clear of the muddy path. "Apart from the fact that they could well shed some light on Cynthia's disappearance, they might also provide a clue as to the identity of Freddie's murderer. Unfortunately it will be only a matter of time before the rest of our guests hear the news, if they haven't already. Under the circumstances, the sooner we apprehend this criminal, the better."

"I cannot imagine why anyone would want to kill Freddie," Baxter said as they trudged up the path to the front door. "He was a harmless young man, by all accounts. He kept himself to himself, so I understand from Samuel, and was completely inoffensive."

Cecily nodded. "I don't understand it either. I suppose we shall have to question anyone who might have come into contact with him. Did he spend any time at the George and Dragon, do you know? If so, it might be a good idea to talk to the new owner. I haven't met him yet, but Samuel mentioned that he is a very jolly man."

"I would imagine that the constable would include the

George and Dragon in his investigation," Baxter said not too subtly.

Cecily refrained from arguing. She would pursue that avenue later on, she decided. With or without Baxter's approval. The hotel would be crowded with guests by the weekend. She could not afford to have a murderer still on the loose by then.

The success of the Pennyfoot depended on its lack of notoriety. Many aristocrats used the secluded hotel to pursue their own dubious pleasures, assured that they were undetected by watchful eyes.

The card rooms in the cellar were among the popular amenities of the Pennyfoot, as were the luxurious boudoirs in which the gentlemen entertained their illicit lady friends.

Cecily provided a sanctuary for such goings-on, in lavish surroundings that enticed many a notable aristocrat. Her tight-lipped staff turned a deaf ear and a blind eye, aware that their employment depended on their silence.

So far Cecily had managed to keep several misfortunes out of the London newspapers, mostly because of her aptitude for being several steps ahead of the local constabulary. Usually the villagers of Badgers End were more apt to talk to her than the police, whom they mistrusted.

Cecily could only hope that would prove to be the case this time. With two tragedies on her hands and no notion of whether the events were connected, she faced a difficult road ahead. And this time she wasn't even sure she could count on Baxter to help her.

"This is the house of Mary Wainscott," Cecily whispered as Baxter lifted the door knocker and let it drop. The sound seemed to explode into the still night air.

Baxter nodded, his face illuminated by the moonlight that filtered through the scudding clouds. "I do hope she won't be alarmed by her late visitors," he murmured.

The door opened abruptly, spilling yellow light from the lantern swaying in the elderly lady's hand. Her other hand clutched the frilly collar of her pink flannel dressing gown tightly to her throat, and she wore a lace-trimmed nightcap pulled firmly down on her head.

"Who is it?" she demanded, her voice sounding quavery. "What do you want?"

Cecily stepped forward into the light from the lamp. "Miss Wainscott? I am Cecily Sinclair, the owner of the Pennyfoot Hotel. I believe you have met my manager, Mr. Baxter?"

Mary Wainscott looked from one to the other, obviously confused.

"I'm so sorry to disturb you at this late hour," Cecily said gently, "but I wonder if we might come inside and have a word with you?"

The woman looked over her shoulder at the room behind her. "I wasn't expecting visitors . . ."

"We won't stay but a minute or two," Cecily promised.

After another moment of hesitation, Mary Wainscott stepped back to let them in.

Walking into the cluttered living room, Cecily pretended not to see the knitting lying on the threadbare settee next to a half-eaten sandwich or the dirty dishes stacked on the sideboard.

Miss Wainscott scurried over to an armchair and shoved a sleeping cat off the cushion. "Please excuse the mess," she said, shooting an embarrassed glance at Baxter's stoic face. "As I said, I wasn't expecting any visitors. Won't you please sit down?"

Eyeing the layer of cat hairs on the seat, Cecily declined the offer. "I understand that you saw Miss Cynthia Chalmsford during the rehearsal this afternoon," she said, smiling at the jittery woman.

"Yes, I . . . we did." Mary Wainscott sent a desperate look at the cello leaning up in the corner of the room.

"I wonder if you can tell me what happened?"

"I . . . nothing happened. Nothing at all. The young lady came up on the stage, Esme asked her to leave, and she left. That is all that happened."

Cecily looked intently at the woman's face. Mary Wainscott seemed determined to avoid her gaze.

"My maid seems to think there was a disagreement between Miss Parsons and Cynthia," Cecily said, exchanging a quick glance with Baxter.

The other woman looked startled. "Disagreement? Oh, no, no. Not at all. Not that I could see, in any case."

"Well, perhaps you can tell me when you last saw the footman who brought you to the hotel?"

There was no mistaking the surprise on the elderly woman's face. "We last saw him when he left us in the lobby," she said, looking more confused than ever. "He didn't come back for us, you know."

"Yes," Cecily said slowly. "I know. And you didn't see him at all after he brought you to the hotel?"

Mary Wainscott shook her head so vigorously her cap fell sideways. Apparently unaware of it, she said in a plaintive voice, "Why are you asking me all these questions? Is something wrong?"

Cecily sighed. "I'm afraid that the footman didn't return for you this afternoon because he . . . met with an accident. In the meantime, it appears that Cynthia Chalmsford has wandered off and has not returned to the hotel. Mr. Baxter and I are naturally concerned, and we were hoping you or your fellow musicians would be able to help us."

"Oh, my." A fragile hand fluttered at the frightened woman's throat. "I do hope you are not going to disturb Beryl and Hilda tonight.. They are early sleepers, you know. They won't be at all happy to be woken up."

"I hope they will understand." Cecily caught Baxter's eye again. He looked exceedingly uncomfortable. "Well, we won't keep you any longer, Miss Wainscott. Thank you for being so gracious about our intrusion."

"Not at all, not at all," Miss Wainscott murmured. She stumbled to the door and dragged it open. "Please come again."

Cecily smiled. "We are all looking forward to your

performance at the ball. Mrs. Carter-Holmes tells me your music is quite spectacular."

"Thank you, ma'am. We will do our best, I'm sure." The door closed with a resounding thud, practically in Cecily's face.

"May I venture to say, madam, that our presence was most unwelcome," Baxter said as they tramped back to where they'd left the trap.

Cecily glanced up at his stern face. "Miss Wainscott was very nervous, I must say. I tend to agree with Doris's notion that the musicians have something to hide."

"In my opinion, the woman was merely embarrassed about the clutter in her house. After being summoned from her bed and confronted with questions for which she had no answer, I find it hardly surprising that she reacted with some restraint."

Cecily waited for him to open the door of the trap. "That's as may be," she murmured. "I do wonder, however, why she would deny that there was a confrontation between Miss Parsons and Cynthia."

"Isn't it possible that she simply didn't notice?"

Cecily stepped up into the cab and seated herself on the creaking leather seat. "Possible," she said quietly, "but not very likely."

Baxter shook his head and closed the door, leaving Cynthia to ponder Mary Wainscott's strange attitude.

Neither Hilda Barrett nor her sister Beryl seemed any more pleased to see them. Contrary to Miss Wainscott's warning, the sisters had not retired to bed when Cecily and Baxter arrived.

They appeared to accept Cecily's apology readily enough, though Beryl uttered not a word throughout the entire conversation. Neither of the sisters, it seemed, had paid much attention to the confrontation between Cynthia Chalmsford and Esme Parsons. Neither of them had anything to add to Mary Wainscott's assertion that the quartet had not seen Freddie after he left them in the lobby.

It wasn't until Cecily and Baxter were about to leave that Beryl showed any reaction. Cecily was intrigued by the gaunt-looking musician. She was not attractive by any means, though she did have quite beautiful eyes.

The colonel seemed to be quite smitten with the woman, for some reason, and Cecily wondered what it was about her that had caught that gentleman's attention. It certainly couldn't have been her sparkling conversation.

Cecily couldn't help mentioning something about it as she made ready to leave. "I understand Colonel Fortescue upset you this afternoon," she said, smiling at the sallow face of the bass player. "Don't let him alarm you. He is harmless enough, I promise you. If he becomes a nuisance, a sharp word or two is usually all that is necessary. He means well enough and just happens to admire you, that's all."

Beryl's face looked as if it were carved from stone, but Hilda, standing close to her sister's side, gave a start. "Oh, but—" she began. She cut off abruptly with a yelp as Beryl gave her a sharp jab in the ribs with her bony elbow.

After one anxious look at her sister's face, Hilda pinched her lips together.

It was obvious that Cecily would get no more out of the sisters that night. She left, wondering what it was that Hilda was about to say and why Beryl was so anxious to stop her.

After talking to Esme Parsons, however, Cecily had to admit that Doris might have been overreacting to the situation that afternoon, after all. Miss Parsons's manner would be enough to scare any child.

Naturally abrasive, the woman had a sharp tone and a cutting gaze that could chill even the impenetrable Baxter, judging by his expression.

The violinist was no further help, except to say that Cynthia had made a nuisance of herself that afternoon, and she had reprimanded her. She seemed genuinely concerned when Cecily informed her that the child was missing. She even volunteered the quartet's help, if needed in the search.

Thanking her, Cecily left with Baxter and returned to the hotel. She could hardly wait until they arrived, anxious as she was to discuss the visits with Baxter and learn his reaction.

In spite of his suggestion that they postpone the discussion until the morning, she waited for him to return the horse and trap to the stables. The clock was striking midnight as he entered the lobby, where she paced impatiently up and down.

"I thought you had retired to your suite for the night," he observed as she faced him expectantly.

"I rather thought we could share a cup of tea first."

A glimmer of his old self showed through as he said lightly, "And a cigar, no doubt?"

With a little lift of her heart, she smiled at him. "That would be very pleasant indeed."

Shaking his head, he accompanied her to the kitchen, where he brewed a pot of tea with an expert hand.

Sipping the hot liquid, Cecily reflected on how much better the tea tasted when made by her manager. Either he had a knack for the procedure, or perhaps it was simply that she enjoyed this personal attention.

She looked up at him as he hovered by the table, holding his cup and saucer. "For heaven's sake, Baxter, do please sit down. There is no one here to see us, and even if there were, I'm quite sure they would find nothing improper about sharing a cup of tea at the kitchen table. After all, we have enjoyed a meal or two together in the dining room." Smiling, she felt ridiculously close to tears as she added softly, "Why, I even remember you once danced with me alone in the ballroom."

For a moment she thought she saw pain in his eyes, but then it was quickly erased. "Happily no one saw us there, either."

She shook a reproving finger at him. "You worry far too much, Bax. Give me a cigar and sit down with me. I want to talk about our string quartet."

To her immense satisfaction, after a moment's hesitation he flipped his coattails back and sat down.

She waited until he had lit the cigar he'd handed her before asking, "What did you think of the lady musicians? Did you feel that they are hiding something, as Doris believes?"

"I think they were rather put out by our late visit."

"They would have been even more put out if P.C. Northcott had called on them," Cecily said mildly. She blew a stream of smoke through her pursed lips. "I thought they acted strangely, under the circumstances. They were certainly ill at ease. And yet I can quite see how Cynthia could be easily frightened by Esme Parsons's manner. And Doris as well, for that matter."

"I think Doris has entirely misconstrued the situation," Baxter said, leaning back in his chair. "She is young and inclined to be oversensitive."

"Well, the main point is that we have learned nothing." Cecily sighed. "As for Freddie, his death is still a complete mystery also. If only we knew a little more about his private life, we might have a clue as to who would want to kill him. There doesn't seem to be a motive as yet."

"It could have been an unprovoked attack." Baxter reached for his cup. "Perhaps an intruder out to steal the horses. Freddie could have surprised him in the act."

"Perhaps," Cecily agreed. "But I don't think so. I assume Samuel stored the tournament supplies before he left to go to the feed store?"

Baxter nodded. "So he told me."

"In that case, I hardly think that an intruder, caught in the act of stealing, would climb up the loft for a lance before facing his accuser."

"Unless he knocked Freddie unconscious and then looked around for something with which to finish him off."

"Why would he go to all that trouble? Unless Freddie knew him and could name him as a horse thief." Cecily thought about it for a long moment. "No, I think there's a lot more to this than we are seeing at present. I believe the murderer already had the lance in his hand when Freddie came along."

She drew on her cigar, then let the smoke drift from her mouth. "There's also the disappearance of Cynthia to consider. If, as I believe, the two are connected, and I think it's too much of a coincidence for them not to be, then why didn't Cynthia run away after Freddie was rendered unconscious? She would certainly have had the time."

Baxter gave her a brooding look. "Unless the murderer had already killed Cynthia."

Shocked, Cecily stared at him. "No, I can't believe that. Surely if he had killed the child, he would have left her body there with Freddie's."

"If he didn't kill her, then why did he take her with him?" Baxter countered. "She must be a burden to him."

"I agree, it doesn't make sense." Cecily shook her head. "None of it appears to make sense. I wish the musicians had been able to help us more."

Baxter hid a yawn behind his hand. "I think we can safely say that the ladies are not involved in Freddie's death. I find it a little difficult to envision any one of them climbing up into the hayloft to procure a lance, much less lying in wait for Freddie to come along in order to run him through with the thing."

Cecily nodded unhappily. "I have to agree, Baxter. It seems unlikely." She gave him a speculative glance. "What did you think of Beryl Barrett, the bass player? She seems the most remote of the ensemble. Yet she must possess some charm, since our colonel seems so smitten with her."

Baxter rolled his eyes toward the ceiling. "That old fool would romance a chicken if it paid enough attention to him."

Cecily smothered a laugh. "That's just it," she said, reaching for her cup. "Beryl Barrett doesn't exactly strike me as the sort of person who would pay attention to anyone, much less Colonel Fortescue."

"Ah, but you forget the colonel can't see farther than his nose. With all that heavy powder and rouge the woman piles on her face, she most likely looks quite ravishing to him. At least she had the good sense not to smother herself in that overpowering scent worn by the rest of her companions.'"

Cecily raised her eyebrows. "Why, Baxter," she said, amused by his comment, "how very observant of you. I wouldn't have imagined that you would notice such a thing."

He gave her an enigmatic look. "If I may say so, madam, I notice a great deal more than you realize."

Taken aback by his remark, she wondered if he was hiding a great deal more behind those words than he was willing to tell her.

CHAPTER

❈ 9 ❈

Some mornings it just wasn't worth getting up, Doris thought gloomily, as she stared at yet another widening puddle of milk at her feet. This was the third jug she'd dropped in the pantry in a month.

When she went out into the kitchen to fetch a bucket of water, Gertie wagged a finger at her, saying with mock severity, "You keep dropping those bleeding jugs, my girl, you'll cop it from the old battle-axe."

"I know," Doris muttered, heaving the bucket out of the sink. "It's those stupid cats. I sneeze as soon as I look at one of them."

She hurried back into the pantry to clean up the mess, sneezing violently as she mopped up the floor. Her heart sank when she heard Mrs. Chubb's strident voice demanding to know why the tables were not laid in the dining room.

"She's just filling the blinking jugs," Gertie said loudly, in an apparent effort to let Doris know that she had better get a move on.

"Well, it's time she was finished," Mrs. Chubb said, sounding closer. "If she didn't spend so much time daydreaming about the stage, she'd get her work done on time."

"Oh, Mrs. Chubb, have you heard anything about Miss Cynthia yet?"

"No, I haven't. I can't waste my time worrying about that now. We have a breakfast to get out."

"I reckon her parents must be bleeding beside themselves with worrying about her. Specially after what someone did to poor Freddie. Do you think the flipping murderer killed off Cynthia, too?"

"Good heavens, I sincerely hope not," Mrs. Chubb exclaimed. "Don't you dare mention such a thing to anyone, neither. We don't want to go around upsetting the guests. Or the staff, come to that."

"All right," Gertie muttered, "keep your bloody hair on. I was just asking."

Doris quickly wrung out the dishcloth, aware that Gertie was deliberately trying to delay the housekeeper from entering the pantry. She owed an awful lot to Gertie, Doris thought with a rush of gratitude. More than once the chief housemaid had come to her rescue.

Even so, it was impossible to escape Mrs. Chubb's eagle eyes. The minute Doris appeared in the doorway of the pantry, bucket in hand, the housekeeper pounced on her.

"Not another jug of milk? This one's coming out of your wages, young lady. You are costing this hotel a fortune with your carelessness."

"I couldn't help it, Mrs. Chubb," Doris said, near to tears. Already she owed a major portion of her wages for two tea plates and a brandy glass she'd broken earlier that week. "I sneeze every time I go into the pantry, and the jug just slips out of my hand."

"It's those bleeding cats that make her sneeze," Gertie muttered darkly. "Keep coming through the bloody window, they do. They come in at bloody night when no one's around, after the flipping food. I keep telling you we should close the bloody window at night."

"And I keep telling you that we have to leave the window open to keep the larder cool," Mrs. Chubb said with a trace of irritation. "Anyway, unless the cats can climb shelves, which I doubt, they won't be able to reach the food."

"They could reach the bleeding milk, though." Water hissed on the stove, and Gertie grabbed a wooden spoon and stirred the serviettes around in the tub of boiling water. "It's on the bloody floor, ain't it?"

"They'd have to pry the lid off the churns." The house-keeper clicked her tongue as Doris tipped the bucket over the sink, spilling a great deal of the contents on the floor as she did so.

"Now you'll have to clean that up, too," Mrs. Chubb said, looking pointedly at the clock.

Doris gazed down at her wet shoes, feeling more depressed by the minute. She was thankful when the house-keeper left the kitchen, muttering about the poor caliber of help nowadays.

"She makes me so nervous, she does," Doris said as Gertie lugged the huge tub of water over to the sink. "I wish I was tall like you, then I wouldn't spill when I poured it in the sink."

"Doris," Gertie said, puffing a little with the exertion, "you'd bleeding spill if you was ten feet tall. You're a proper bleeding butterfingers, you are. Nothing's blinking safe in your hands."

Doris felt even lower. "I can't help it," she said, beginning to whine. "I get jumpy when people shout and yell at me."

"Or when bloody cats are around."

"That's because they make me sneeze."

"Yeah, well you'd better bloody watch out. You get into

much more trouble with the bleeding old battle-axe and you'll be looking for another blinking job."

"She won't sack me," Doris said uncertainly. "It's too hard to find servants around here. I heard Mrs. Chubb say so. Besides, if she sacks me, then Daisy'll go, too."

"Well, don't get too bloody cocky about it," Gertie said, her voice straining as she tilted the heavy tub of water into the sink. A cloud of steam enveloped her head as the serviettes plopped into the sink. The kitchen reeked with the smell of linen boiled in bleach.

Doris wished she could handle the heavy pots as easily as Gertie seemed to manage them. It would make life a good deal easier.

"You going to the bleeding rehearsal again this afternoon?" Gertie asked as she carried the empty tub back to the stove.

Doris sighed. "I s'pose so. I wish I didn't have to, but madam would be upset with me if I didn't go."

"You have to go if you want to bloody sing on Saturday night." Gertie came back to the sink and ran cold water onto the serviettes.

"No, I don't." Doris finished mopping up the floor. "I'm not going to sing that stupid aria, am I."

Gertie's swung around to stare at her. "Go on! You're not?"

"No. I'm going to sing a song from the Variety. It's my afternoon off, so after the rehearsal I'm going to see Lydia Willoughby and ask her to rehearse with me."

"Blimey," Gertie said, obviously impressed. "I'd love to see Phoebe Carter-Holmes's flipping face when Lydia walks out on the bloody stage."

Doris looked up at her. "Do you think Lydia will play for me?"

Gertie let out an uproarious laugh. "Not half she will. She fancies herself as a proper bleeding piano player, does our Lydia. Give her the bloody chance to play at the Pennyfoot?

Strewth, she'll bleeding carry the flipping piano on her back to get here."

"Well, she won't have to do that," Doris said, feeling immensely relieved. "There's one here already."

"Oh, Gawd, can you imagine Lydia Willoughby playing a bleeding grand piano? In front of all those toffs?" Gertie laughed so hard she bent double at the waist.

Alarmed now, Doris scrambled to her feet. "She can play, can't she?"

Gertie stopped laughing and eyed her warily. "How loud can you sing?"

"Loud enough."

"Well, you should be able to drown her out if she makes a mistake, shouldn't you?"

"I s'pose so," Doris said doubtfully.

"Then you ain't got bleeding nothing to worry about, have you, luv." Chuckling, Gertie turned back to rinsing out her serviettes.

Doris wasn't exactly sure about that, but she had no time to worry about it then. Already she was late for the dining room, and the last thing she needed was more scolding from Mrs. Chubb. Picking up her skirts, she hurtled down the hallway and up the stairs.

She saw the man with the funny accent a second before she plowed into him, but by then it was too late to stop. He let out a noise that sounded like air escaping from a balloon as her head collided with his stomach.

"I'm sorry, sir," Doris stammered, gasping for breath. "I didn't see you coming around the corner."

"That's okay. I'll survive." The gentleman smoothed his hands down his jacket. "You must be in a great hurry this morning, Miss Hoggins."

"Yes, sir, I am. I have to lay the tables for the breakfast, and if I don't get on . . ." She couldn't remember the name he'd called out to her the day before. It was Jeremy something or other.

"Do you have a second or two to chat?" the man asked,

giving her a very pleasant smile. "There's something I'd like to talk to you about."

Doris shook her head in a decisive way that left no room for argument. "I'm sorry, sir. I must run. I'm late already, you see . . ." She was backing off as she spoke, gathering herself for flight.

"Perhaps we could meet later—"

She didn't wait to hear the rest of the sentence. Gertie had warned her about talking too much to the guests. Madam didn't like it, she'd said.

She was in enough trouble as it was, Doris thought, scuttling down the hallway to the dining room. Besides, he wasn't the kind of man she'd waste her time on.

She was only interested in toffs or someone who could help her get on the stage to meet one. Because that was the only way a toff would be interested in meeting her. He certainly wasn't going to take any notice of a lowly kitchen maid.

Thinking of the man she'd just left reminded her of Roland Young. If she had time this day, she vowed, she'd try again to talk to him. Perhaps he'd be in a better mood today. Only this time she'd try to make sure there were other people at least within earshot.

She didn't trust that young man at all, she told herself as she wandered into the dining room. In fact, if it weren't for the fact that he might be able to help her meet someone on the stage, she wouldn't go within an inch of him.

There was something very strange about Roland Young. Doris didn't know what it was. She only knew that he gave her the creeps. Still, sometimes she would have to do things she didn't like to become a star. She might as well get used to it.

Suppressing a shiver of apprehension, Doris went to work on the tables.

Cecily had barely stepped out of her suite when Roland Young strode past her, whistling a tuneless melody that grated on her ears.

She called out after him, and he halted, turning to face her with obvious reluctance. "Yes, ma'am?"

"I was just wondering how the repairs are coming along," she said, walking toward him. "Do you have enough supplies? If not, I can have Samuel pick up some more for you."

"I've got plenty right now."

He turned to go, but she forestalled him by saying, "I wonder if you could give me a minute, Roland? I have some questions I'd like to ask you."

Hunching his shoulders, Roland gave a surly nod.

"I was wondering if you are acquainted with Lord and Lady Chalmsford's daughter Cynthia."

"She's been about a bit."

"Can you remember when you saw her last?"

He narrowed his strange eyes, in a way that made her feel most uncomfortable. "Nah, I can't remember. I fink it were yesterday or the day before. Me mind ain't working good. I didn't have no sleep last night."

Cecily peered at him in concern. "Are you sick?"

Roland startled her by throwing back his head and letting out a hoarse guffaw. "Nah, not sick. Me bleeding bird kept me awake, didn't she? Couldn't keep her hands to herself, that's her problem. All over me, she was."

"I see," Cecily said cooly. "I suppose you have heard about Freddie's tragic death?"

Roland shrugged. "I heard as how he ran into the wrong end of a spear. Must have stung a bit." He grinned, much to Cecily's disgust.

"I hardly thing it's a matter to smile about," she said in a voice of reprimand. "The young man is dead and deserves some respect."

"Pardon me, ma'am, I'm sure." Roland Young gave her an elaborate and contemptuous bow from the waist. "I have to get on wiv me work now." With an insolent wave at her, he spun around and sauntered down the hallway.

For two pins, Cecily told herself, she'd get rid of the

unpleasant oaf on the spot. The repairs needed doing, however, and before the weekend if she were to fill the rooms. She would just have to bear with him for the next day or two.

Hurrying down to the library a few minutes later, she saw Samuel waiting for her by the door, his cap clutched tightly in his hands.

He touched his forehead as she approached and bade her a polite good morning. The contrast between her stable manager and the uncouth young man she had just left upstairs was so refreshing that Cecily gave Samuel a wide smile.

"Come in, Samuel," she said, pushing open the doors to the library. "I won't keep you long, but I need to ask you some questions."

"Yes, ma'am." Samuel followed obediently behind her and stood in front of the fireplace, looking as if he wished he were anywhere but there.

Seating herself at the end of the table, Cecily folded her hands and stared at her intertwined fingers for a moment or two. "I know this can't be pleasant for you, Samuel," she said when the silence had gone on a little too long. "But I do need to know every detail you can remember about the discovery of Freddie's body yesterday."

"Yes, mum. I thought that might be what you wanted." Samuel drew in a deep breath. "I don't mind telling you, mum, it has fair knocked me for a loop. I didn't know Freddie very well like. I don't think anybody did. But he was a nice kid. I liked him."

Under any other circumstances, Cecily would have smiled at Samuel referring to Freddie as a kid, since the footman couldn't have been more than a year or two younger than her stable manager.

"I did, too, Samuel. It is very sad that someone of such a tender age had to die in that horrible manner."

"You'll find who did it, mum. I know you will. You and

Mr. Baxter are good at that. Better than the police, I say. Everybody says so."

Cecily heaved a rueful sigh. "Thank you, Samuel, but I hope you didn't say as much to P.C. Northcott. I'm afraid he and Inspector Cranshaw would not share your view."

Samuel managed a small grin. "I didn't say nothing to them, mum. Though I'd like to."

"Very well. Now perhaps you can tell me exactly what you saw when you found Freddie's body."

"Well, it was really strange, mum, the way he was laid out." Samuel lifted his chin and looked at the ceiling. "Like I told the constable, the horse was making such a fuss, I thought maybe there was a rat in the stall. So I went in there to have a look."

He gave a slight shudder, and Cecily felt a pang of sympathy. The discovery must have been a great shock for the young man.

"I saw the rake first," Samuel said, his voice quite hushed now. "At least I thought it was a rake. There was a mound of hay there, and it was sort of sticking up out of it. It looked a bit funny to me, so I went and took a closer look. And that's when I found him."

He looked back at Cecily, the horror of it still lingering in his eyes. "It was a strange sight," he said in a near whisper. "There he was, lying flat on his back with his eyes open, staring at the ceiling. I could see then that it wasn't a rake at all, but one of the lances, stuck right through the middle of his chest. There was blood all over him and . . ."

His voice trailed away, and Cecily nodded in sympathy. "Go on," she said gently.

"He had his hands crossed on his chest above the hole." Samuel swallowed. "The straw was tucked all around him, just like he was Jesus lying in a manger. I felt as if I was looking at one of them ceremonial things you see in books, like in Africa when they offer a sacrifice to the gods."

A momentary picture of her daughter-in-law, Simani, popped into Cecily's mind. Michael's wife was the daughter of an African chief, and Michael had talked about such ceremonies.

Aware that the stable manager had said something else, she dragged her attention back to the present. "I'm sorry, Samuel," she said quickly. "What did you say?"

"I said that this is the second body I've found in three months. I'm beginning to think someone put a hex on me."

"Just unfortunate, that's all," Cecily said, wishing she could take that distressed look out of his eyes.

"Well, at least this one smelled better." Samuel made a weak attempt at a smile.

Cecily frowned. "I'm not sure I understand."

"Well, the last one was in the butcher's shop, and everything smelled bad down there." Samuel wrinkled his nose in disgust. "Freddie smelled like he was lying on a bed of flowers. Though I couldn't see any flowers lying around him anywhere."

"Flowers? How interesting," Cecily murmured.

"I don't know as how you're going to find out who did it, mum," Samuel said, looking worried. "But if I can be of any use, I'd really like to help look for him. Freddie was a friend of mine, and I don't think he had many friends. I want to see the bugger who killed him in jail."

"Thank you, Samuel. I'll keep that in mind." Cecily rose to her feet. "I don't suppose you happened to see Cynthia yesterday?"

Samuel shook his head. "No, mum. I was gone for a good bit yesterday afternoon. I had to go down to the feed store."

"Yes, so Mr. Baxter told me."

"I hope the murderer didn't kill her, too," Samuel said, looking as if he'd just thought of the possibility.

"I really don't think so," Cecily said firmly. "I would prefer that you don't discuss this with anyone, Samuel, except the police, of course. Things tend to get blown out of proportion when rumors start spreading around."

"The girls downstairs are frightened." Samuel shot an uneasy glance at the French windows. "Can't say as how I blame them. I'm a bit nervous myself now, especially after dark. I keep looking in the corners, expecting someone to jump out on me."

"I really don't think you have to worry," Cecily said, praying she was right. "Whoever killed Freddie is most likely far away from here now."

"Yeah," Samuel murmured as he turned toward the door. "But where is Miss Cynthia Chalmsford? That's what I'd like to know."

Would that she knew, Cecily thought, as the door closed quietly behind him. She had a strong hunch that wherever the murderer happened to be, that's where they would find Cynthia. She could only hope that the child was still alive.

CHAPTER

❖10❖

When the tap sounded on the library door a minute or two later, Cecily thought it might be Samuel returning with something he'd forgotten to tell her.

It was Daisy, however, or maybe Doris, who poked her head around the door and announced, "Police Constable Northcott wishes to speak with you, mum."

Cecily rose swiftly to her feet. "Where is he?"

"He's in the kitchen, mum, having a sausage roll and a mug of tea."

"Tell him to meet me here in the library as soon as he is finished, please, Daisy. I'll wait for him here."

"Yes, mum." Daisy bobbed a curtesy and turned to go.

"Oh, and Daisy? Please ask Mr. Baxter if he could meet me here, also."

"Yes, mum." Daisy looked as if she wanted to smile, then thought better of it. Very quietly she closed the door.

If that was Daisy, Cecily thought, things had certainly improved with the child. There was a time when Daisy went around with a permanent scowl on her face, as if she had the troubles of the world on her shoulders.

Of course, considering the twins' background, it was no wonder, after the way they had been treated by their abusive aunt. Beaten and deprived of food, kept virtual prisoners in the house and considered little more than slaves, the girls had had a miserable life until they had finally run away.

Seating herself again, Cecily smiled, remembering the moment when she had learned that there were two new maids. Only one had been hired, but the girls had shared a room and the work until their little deception had been uncovered.

It would appear that things were working well for the girls after all, and she was glad that she'd had the where-withal to hire them both. Good help was hard to find, and in spite of Doris's unfortunate habit of dropping things, the twins were a great asset to the Pennyfoot.

Cecily glanced up at the portrait of her late husband. James had been a handsome man, especially when dressed in his uniform, as he was in the painting.

Once it had been so hard to look upon his face, but now it was as if he had never really existed in person. He was a shadowy figure, living only in her memory, and sometimes weeks went by without her giving him a single thought.

There was really no need for a woman to have a man in her life in order to be happy, Cecily assured herself. In fact, a man could be quite bothersome, especially when he refused to explain the reason for his disturbing behavior.

If she ever returned to this life, she had often told herself, it would be as a man. Men, it seemed, were blithely unconcerned with the feelings of others.

The tap on the door disturbed her thoughts. Almost immediately the source of her irritation stalked into the room. "You wanted to see me, madam? There is news of the child?"

"I am waiting to find that out, Baxter." Cecily eyed her manager with a critical eye. Baxter always looked impeccable. There was not a speck of fluff anywhere on his black morning coat and striped gray trousers.

Even under duress, he managed to keep his hair smoothed down and his bow tie straight. It had long intrigued her as to what it would take to see the man rumpled and . . . human. At that moment he looked a little like a mannequin in Savile Row.

He was not entirely unaffected by their scrutiny, however. "I certainly hope that you do not have to wait too long for news, madam," he said stiffly. "Judging from your pained expression, it would appear that the suspense is giving you acute indigestion."

It was on the tip of her tongue to retort that *he* gave her an unpleasant ache in her stomach. It would serve no purpose, however, other than to arouse his indignation. Right now she needed his support, especially if the constable had brought adverse news.

"I am quite well, thank you, Baxter," she said, giving him a soothing smile. "I am, however, rather anxious to hear what the constable has to say. Since he will be here at any second, I thought you might like to be present."

Baxter's expression changed at once. "He has news?"

"I don't know." She sighed, leaning back in her chair to ease her back. "Daisy didn't appear to know anything, but then I doubt if Northcott would say anything to the kitchen staff. We shall simply have to wait until he gets here."

Baxter's face now registered disapproval. "If the man is in the kitchen, I doubt very much if we shall see him before noon," he muttered.

As if echoing his words, three raps sounded on the door. Cecily smiled, saying lightly, "It would seem as if you have misjudged our good constable."

With a low growl in his throat, Baxter moved to the door and opened it.

With barely a nod at her manager, the constable strutted into the room and stood close to the table with his helmet tucked under his arm. "I 'ave to say, Mrs. Sinclair, that there cook of yours makes the best sausage rolls I ever tasted in me life, so help me. Could hardly tear meself away from them, and that's a fact."

"I have to agree. Mrs. Chubb is an excellent pastry chef," Cecily said, raising her voice to cover the low mutter coming from the fireplace, where Baxter stood scowling at the constable's back.

"Yes, indeed, madam. Never met one like it, I do declare. Wish my wife could cook like that. Mebbe then I'd stay home a lot more."

The constable's loud chuckle made Cecily wince. Avoiding Baxter's glare of disgust, she said quickly, "Do you have any news of Cynthia Chalmsford, Constable?"

She wasn't sure how she felt when the policeman shook his head. "No, ma'am, I 'ave not. Been out all night, me men have. Searched the Downs from one end to the other, combed the woods, even went up to Lord Withersgill's h'estate, they did. No one ain't seen hide nor hair of the little nipper."

"Oh, dear," Cecily murmured. "I wonder where she could be."

"We did find something h'of interest, however," the constable said with maddening pomposity. He paused, obviously enjoying the suspense he was creating.

Baxter shifted his weight, his neck beginning to turn red.

Cecily gave him a warning look to hold his temper. "And what's that, Constable?"

"We found the missing horse and trap, madam. Running loose it were, up there on the Downs. Reckon whoever murdered your stable lad took the trap to make his h' escape, so to speak. Might well have taken the child with him, I'm thinking. She might have seen what happened, got in his way, like. He'd have to keep her quiet until he got clean away, I should think."

The constable's buttons strained on his jacket as he puffed out his chest, looking inordinately pleased with himself.

"How very clever of you, Constable," Cecily murmured. "I wonder why I didn't think of that."

In the background, Baxter rolled his eyes to the ceiling.

"Ho, well, Mrs. Sinclair, we policemen are paid for our superior h'intelligence. It's all part of the job, you know."

"And I'm sure you do it very well." Cecily could almost see the fire coming from Baxter's nostrils. "I wonder, Constable, if it might be better not to mention the possibility to Lord and Lady Chalmsford at this point? They have been secluded in their room since their daughter's disappearance and may not know about Freddie's murder as yet. I would like to keep that from them if possible, until we have more information on the child's whereabouts."

The constable looked disappointed but reluctantly nodded. "You may be right, ma'am. I have to go and make my report to them, but I won't mention nothing about the horse and trap, nor the murder, h'unless they ask, of course."

"Thank you, Constable. I appreciate that very much. In the meantime, please keep us informed of any new development, if possible, and do stop by the kitchen on your way out. Mrs. Chubb is baking her famous Dundee cakes today, and I'm sure she will be happy to give you a slice with a cup of cocoa."

"Much obliged, ma'am, I'm sure. Rest assured, I will h'inform you as soon as we have any news at all. Good day to you, Mrs. Sinclair." He backed away from her, bobbing his head up and down as he went.

Baxter's outraged expression as the man disappeared through the door was almost comical. "It is no wonder we have a problem with our finances, when gluttons like that are encouraged to fill their vast stomachs from our kitchen. He has already had one meal there today. Surely that should be enough?"

Knowing full well that Baxter's wrath stemmed more from his personal feud with the constable than with her deferential attitude toward him, Cecily said mildly, "It's always wise to gratify the constabulary, Baxter. They have resources unavailable to us, and in certain cases we must rely on them to do what we cannot. In which case we need to know what they know."

"I agree, madam. But is it really necessary to fawn over the man?"

She lifted an eyebrow. "Fawn? I wasn't aware that I was fawning, Baxter. I'm not sure I would know how to fawn. Over anyone." Including you, her tone implied.

Baxter's cheeks turned a pale shade of pink. "Perhaps that was not the correct word to use, madam. I apologize."

"Apology accepted." She regarded his unhappy face for a long moment, then added quietly, "As long as P.C. Northcott can eat his fill of Mrs. Chubb's wonderful baking, he will use any excuse to pay us a visit. There is a method in my madness, Baxter."

"Yes, madam."

Once more he had retreated behind his rigid role of manager. She tried to suppress the rising tide of despair. These days he seemed more and more remote. Would they never regain the fragile familiarity they had once enjoyed?

"I feel that there is some small reason for hope in the constable's report," she said, concentrating on the problem at hand. "Since the police did not find Cynthia's body, it is possible that she is still alive. Perhaps the murderer took the trap in order to take her somewhere she could not tell any-one what she had seen."

"In which case it would seem that he has found an impregnable hiding place," Baxter said, reverting to his normal placid tone.

"We shall just have to hope that the child can be found before she starves to death." Cecily shook her head. "The poor little girl must be terrified. I only hope that if she survives this terrible trauma, she will not be permanently affected by the experience."

"I wager she will curb her curiosity in future," Baxter murmured. "This is one very good case in point of curiosity killing the cat."

Cecily brought up her chin. "Cynthia Chalmsford is not dead yet," she said stubbornly. "I refuse to believe anything other than that she is alive and well, and someone will find her before too long."

"I was merely quoting the proverb, madam. I did not expect you to take it literally."

She sighed. "I'm sorry, Baxter. I suppose all of our nerves are on edge over this dreadful situation. Poor Freddie dead and the child missing. This has to be the worst disaster to befall the Pennyfoot."

He moved swiftly, striding down the table to reach her side. "Please, madam, try not to distress yourself. The Pennyfoot has seen disasters before, and each time you have managed to conquer them admirably. I see no reason why you should not do so this time."

She felt close to tears for some silly reason. "Always with your help, Baxter. You have always been there to advise and support me."

"As I am now, madam. That has not changed."

"Then what has, Bax?" She looked up at him, pleading silently for some reason for his attitude.

He stretched his neck above the stiff white collar, as he always did when uncomfortable. "I wasn't aware of any change, madam."

"You have been . . . preoccupied," she finished, uncertain whether that was the word she wanted.

"Perhaps." He hesitated, and for a moment she thought he might enlighten her as to what troubled him, but then he cleared his throat. "If you are finished with me, madam, I have to inspect the repair work in the upstairs suites. Roland is waiting for my approval before starting on the next room."

She hid her acute disappointment behind a brief nod. "Very well. I think I will take a look at the stables, just in case the constable might have missed something."

"You will take care, madam? You will not do anything rash without my presence?"

Her smile held no humor. "No, Baxter. I will not do anything rash. You heed my late husband's promise very well."

The look he gave her was full of hidden meaning. "If I do so, madam, it is of my own choosing. Major Sinclair, I am certain, was fully aware that his wife is quite capable of taking care of herself. I believe now that he was merely asking me to lend my sympathy and support during the difficult months after his death."

She could not believe the bitterly cold sensation his words had created. "You no longer feel obligated, is that it, Baxter?"

The pain in his eyes cut her like a sharp blade. "I prefer to think that my concern for your safety is a personal matter, not a contractual one. Now, if you will excuse me, madam, I have a matter that needs my immediate attention."

He turned abruptly and strode for the door, passing through it without a backward glance.

Now what was she supposed to make of that? Cecily thought miserably.

Staring up at James's portrait, she whispered aloud, "I'm not certain that you did either one of us a favor, James, by appointing Baxter to watch over me. It appears that the task has become too much for him. I don't know what to do about it. I suppose my penchant for becoming involved in police business has taken a toll on him, but what am I to do? The Pennyfoot must be protected."

James's painted eyes stared back at her. The Pennyfoot must be protected. Baxter wasn't the only person who had given James Sinclair a promise on his deathbed. She had promised her dying husband that the Pennyfoot would remain in the family. She must adhere to that promise.

Slowly she rose, her heart heavy. If that promise meant the end of her relationship with her manager, then it had cost her dearly indeed.

"I just want to talk to you for a minute," Doris said, standing in the doorway of suite eleven.

Roland Young, squatting in front of a paint pot, scowled up at her. "Why do you keep pestering me, kid? Why don't you find someone else to play with?"

"I'm not a kid, so there. I'm fifteen years old."

"Fifteen." He rose to his feet, an odd light gleaming in his eyes. "All grown up, are you? I wonder if you really know what that means? Maybe I should teach you a thing or two, little lady. All about the dangers of playing with fire." He uttered an unpleasant laugh and started toward her.

Doris took one look at his face and fled for the stairs, her heart hammering like a steam engine. His wild laughter followed her, echoing in her ears all the way down to the lobby.

Cecily crossed the yard to the stables, making sure to watch where she trod as she lifted her skirts clear of the ground. Samuel was outside the stalls, washing down the missing trap, which had apparently been returned by the police.

She wondered whether P.C. Northcott had inspected the vehicle for clues. It seemed an obvious course of action, though one never knew with the local constabulary.

Pausing by the trap, she asked Samuel if he'd cleaned the inside as yet.

"Not yet, mum." Samuel wrung out the chamois leather and flapped it open. "Just getting the mud off the sides for now."

"I'd like to take a look." She waited for him to open the door. "I don't suppose I'll find anything, if the police have already gone over it."

Samuel uttered a scornful laugh. "Wouldn't be surprised

if they've missed all sorts of clues," he said, offering his arm to help her inside.

"Now, Samuel, you should have more faith in your local constabulary," Cecily said facetiously.

"And pigs should fly." Samuel coughed. "Begging your pardon, mum."

"Certainly, Samuel." Cecily peered into the corners of the seats and ran her fingers between the cushions. "There doesn't appear to be anything useful here. Was the canopy down when the police found it, do you know? If so, anything of use would likely have been blown away by the wind."

"The constable didn't mention anything about it." Samuel ran his hand along the edge of the door. "It must have been driven into the woods, though, judging by all the scratches on the side. The bay had a couple of scratches on his flanks, too. Caked in mud he was. I reckon he'd come pretty close to Deep Willow Pond to get that filthy."

"Oh, dear." Cecily scrambled down from the trap. "I do hope that Cynthia is not in the pond. If so, we'll never find her."

Samuel gave her a gloomy look. "They've looked everywhere else, mum."

"No," Cecily said firmly. "I won't believe that. I have my own theory as to what happened to Cynthia Chalmsford, and the more I think about it, the more convinced I am that I'm right."

Taking hold of her skirt, she headed for the stable. The corner stall, where Freddie had been found, was in deep shadow, and she paused to light a lamp before going inside.

The shadows flickered over the bloodstained ground, and a chill touched the back of her neck. She reached for the whip hanging on the back wall and poked it into the straw, moving it back and forth while she peered intently into the scattered pieces.

"Can I help you look for something, mum?" Samuel said behind her.

"Thank you, Samuel. I was looking for pieces of broken glass. Did you happen to notice anything like that when you discovered Freddie's body?"

"No, mum," Samuel said, sounding mystified. "I didn't see no broken glass anywhere. Do you think Freddie was drinking?"

"No." Cecily poked a little further into the straw. "I was wondering if perhaps there might have been pieces of a broken bottle of scent lying around. It would certainly explain the smell of flowers that you mentioned."

"Scent?" Samuel's voice rose in astonishment. "What would Freddie be doing with scent?"

"That I don't know," Cecily said quietly.

"Who would want to kill him, anyway? That's what I'd like to know."

"And why." Cecily straightened, staring thoughtfully at the ground. "That's the puzzle, Samuel. Unless . . ."

She paused, her mind working on the problem.

"Unless what, mum, if I may ask?"

"Unless," Cecily said slowly, "we have this murder around the wrong way. Instead of the murderer kidnapping Cynthia in order to keep her quiet, he might well have killed Freddie to keep *him* quiet."

"I don't understand, mum," Samuel said, rubbing his forehead in bewilderment.

"Neither do I, as yet," Cecily admitted. "But if I am right, I have a strong suspicion that we will soon find out the truth of the matter. If so, heaven help those poor parents."

CHAPTER

❖ 11 ❖

When Cecily went down to dinner that evening, to her dismay she was waylaid by Colonel Fortescue, who had just staggered out of the bar with a lopsided gait that quite alarmed her.

"I say, old bean," he muttered when he caught sight of her. "Don't suppose you know the name of that fiddle player, do you? Dashed if I can remember it."

Cecily frowned. "I wasn't aware that you knew her name, Colonel."

He swayed, his bloodshot eyes staring at her through wildly flapping lids. "What? Well, bless my soul! That would account for me not remembering it, what?"

"It might," Cecily agreed cautiously. She wondered whether perhaps the colonel had succeeded in attracting the bass player's attention after all. "Have you had occasion to speak with Miss Barrett?"

"Miss Barrett?" The colonel blinked, reaching out a hand to steady himself against the wall. "Who the devil is Miss Barrett? Do I know her?"

"The bass player," Cecily said, wishing she had been a little more discreet. "Her name is Miss Beryl Barrett."

"Is it, by Jove!" The colonel uttered a loud burp and, letting go of his hold on the wall, waved a hand in front of his face. The effort threatened to unbalance him, and he grabbed the wall again.

"Perhaps you should take your seat at your table," Cecily said, hoping the colonel wouldn't fall on the floor before he got there.

"Table? Why, is she there?" He peered short-sightedly down the hallway.

"No, Colonel. I'm afraid you won't be able to see Miss Barrett until the concert on Saturday night."

"Concert? What concert? Nobody told me about any blasted concert."

Taking a deep breath, Cecily took hold of his arm. "The string quartet, Colonel. They will be playing at the ball on Saturday night."

"Dashed decent of them, I must say." The colonel once more relinquished his grip on the wall and allowed Cecily to lead him to the dining room.

"Will that fiddle player be at the ball?" he asked as Cecily guided him to his table.

"The lady will be playing with the quartet," Cecily assured him.

"Suppose I'll have to wait until then to have a go at charming her, what?"

"I'm afraid so, Colonel."

"Playing cat and mouse, that's what she's doing." He picked up the empty wineglass by his plate and peered inside it. "Women love men to chase after them. That's why they wear skirts, you know. Hampers their progress so the men can catch up with them."

"No, I didn't know," Cecily said evenly.

The colonel peered up at her. "What? By George, madam, you should know. After all, old bean, you are a woman and all that rot. What?"

"I am indeed, Colonel. Some of us, however, do not follow the conventional customs of an outdated society. We have progressed beyond that, fortunately."

The colonel shook his head in confusion. "Sorry, old girl. I'm afraid I haven't the faintest idea what you're talking about."

"That's quite all right, Colonel. Enjoy your dinner." She escaped before she succumbed to the temptation to give him a lecture on women's rights. Not that he'd understand any of it, of course.

She could only hope that Beryl Barrett was smart enough to stay out of the colonel's way. Judging by that woman's austere demeanor, however, Cecily had no doubt that she could probably wipe that good gentleman from the face of the earth with one well-delivered comment.

Smiling at the thought, Cecily made her way to her own table. She was anxious to be done with her meal. She wanted to present her theory to Baxter and obtain his opinion.

Her smile faded as she remembered their last exchange. Although he had promised her his help as usual, she was well aware of his reluctance to do so.

Accepting the fact that she no longer had his undying support, she felt a very keen sense of loss. Without his help and advice, the excitement would go out of the challenge. The Pennyfoot would then become a cumbersome burden, a weight that would have to be borne, rather than enjoyed, until the end of her days. It was a depressing thought.

To her surprise, Baxter seemed quite accommodating when she cornered him in his office later. He appeared to have forgotten their differences and actually seemed pleased to see her. Hoping that she had simply been overreacting to his earlier remarks, Cecily seated herself and told him about her theory.

"Since there is no apparent motive for Freddie's death," she said, beginning to feel much better, "I wonder if perhaps we are looking at the murder from the wrong angle. Up until now, we have assumed that Cynthia disturbed the murderer in some way while he was attacking Freddie and that she had been kidnapped to prevent her from alerting anyone."

"That seems the most likely explanation," Baxter said, giving her a wary look. "You have discovered evidence to the contrary?"

She shook her head. "It's more a lack of evidence," she said. "As we have said, if the murderer wanted Cynthia's silence, why didn't he kill her also?"

"Perhaps he has an aversion to killing children?"

"Perhaps. I tend to think, however, that anyone who was prepared to kill a young man in cold blood in that way would have no compunction about killing anyone else who threatened him."

"Then what do you suppose he did with her?"

Cecily tapped her fingernails on the desk. "I don't believe he would take her with him if he was intent on running somewhere, and if he lives in the village and is hoping to escape detection, one has to wonder what he is going to do with a witness who can identify him."

"Precisely." Baxter paused, rocking back and forth on his feet for a moment before adding, "Have you considered the possibility that Cynthia Chalmsford could be at the bottom of Deep Willow Pond?"

"I have, and I have rejected the idea."

"For what reason?"

"For the reason I have already mentioned. According to everyone I have talked to, Freddie had precious few friends and no known enemies. There simply is no motive for such a brutal, cold-blooded murder."

Baxter frowned. "I'm not sure that I follow your reasoning."

Cecily leaned forward. "Baxter, supposing that someone had already planned to kidnap Cynthia for ransom. Freddie could have walked in as the killer was seizing the child. Therefore the murderer might have actually killed Freddie to hide his identity until the ransom has been paid."

Baxter stared at her for a long moment. "That would certainly establish a motive."

"Yes," Cecily said with quiet satisfaction. "It would."

"There's just one flaw in that deduction." Baxter looked apologetic.

"Yes, I know. The ransom note." Cecily leaned back in the chair. "I've thought of that. But let's suppose the murderer had planned to kidnap Cynthia. Freddie's murder was an unexpected complication. That would be a setback. He would have to give things time to settle down before he dared to return with a ransom note, wouldn't he?"

"I imagine so." Baxter frowned. "But how does that explain the peculiar way Freddie was arranged after his death? Someone had gone to a great deal of trouble to lay him out. That doesn't sound much like an inadvertent incident."

"I have to admit that has me puzzled also," Cecily said with a sigh. "This entire situation is so bizarre. For some reason, I just cannot convince myself that Cynthia Chalmsford is dead—thought all I have to go on at the moment is intuition."

"You have relied on that before now," Baxter reminded her quietly.

"Yes, I have." She looked up, giving him a rueful smile. "Either way, I'm afraid that things do not bode well for Miss Cynthia Chalmsford."

Baxter's nod of agreement only deepened her anxiety. "I agree, madam. I feel that it is entirely possible we shall never see the poor child again."

*   *   *

Belowstairs in the kitchen, the topic of conversation was also the disappearance of Cynthia Chalmsford. Samuel was once more holding court, while Gertie and Mrs. Chubb hung onto his ever word.

"Anyhow," he finished, closing his fist around a mug of hot cocoa, "that's what they reckon now, that Miss Cynthia has been kidnapped, and the killer is holding her until the Chalmsfords hand over the money."

"Blimey," Gertie muttered. "Poor kid. She must be bleeding scared to death."

Mrs. Chubb clicked her tongue. "Shouldn't wonder if she has nightmares for the rest of her life."

"That's if she lives," Samuel said mournfully.

"Watcha mean?" Gertie looked shocked. "The killer will let her go once he gets what he wants from the toffs, won't he?"

Samuel shrugged. "He might. Then again, he might not. After all, she might have seen him kill Freddie. She could identify him to the bobbies. It's likely he'd kill her off, too, once he's got the money.

"Oh, my," Mrs. Chubb said, fanning her face with her hand. "That poor, poor child."

"Well, I think he'd let her go," Gertie said stoutly. "Once he's got the bleeding money, he can get clean away. Even go to America, he could. Strewth, I wish I could go to America. They have bloody everything there, they do. Machines that sweep the flipping floors and wash clothes—they don't have to heave those dirty great tubs of steaming hot water to the sink every day like we do."

"If we had machines to do the work," Mrs. Chubb said, picking up Samuel's empty mug from the table, "we wouldn't have no use for housemaids, now would we."

Gertie watched the plump housekeeper take the mug to the sink. Somehow her words disturbed her even more than what Samuel had been talking about. What would happen to her twins, she thought uneasily, if by the time they grew up everyone had machines to do the work?

It might not be too bad for Lillian. Being a girl, she could find a bloody husband to take care of her. But what about James? How would he take care of himself, much less a bleeding wife and kids of his own? Didn't bloody bear thinking about, it didn't.

Mrs. Chubb startled her by turning sharply around. "Did you hear that?"

Gertie felt goosebumps rising up her arms as she saw the housekeeper staring at the pantry door. "I never heard nothing," she said nervously.

"It's those darn cats again, I reckon," Mrs. Chubb said, marching across the room primed for battle.

Samuel darted ahead of her and barred the way. "Better let me take a look," he said in a creepy way that made Gertie's goosebumps spread all the way down her back.

Both women watched as Samuel slowly pushed the door open and peered inside. Gertie held her breath when he disappeared into the pantry. A moment or two later he reappeared, shaking his head.

"Couldn't see nothing," he said, "but it's dark in there. I could light the lamp and take a look if you want."

"Never mind," Mrs. Chubb said, wiping her hands on her apron. "You've probably frightened him off by now."

Samuel grinned. "Reckon I did, at that. He should know better than to mess about with me, I tell you."

"Cor, bleeding hark at him," Gertie said in disgust. "You wouldn't be so bloody cocky if there'd been a murderer lurking in there, that's for sure."

"If he had've been, he would've had a fight on his hands," Samuel said, looking fierce. "I'd love to get my hands on the bastard who killed Freddie."

"Especially if he's got Cynthia, poor little mite," Mrs. Chubb murmured. "Monsters like that should be hung, drawn, and quartered, that's what I say."

"In front of the entire village," Samuel agreed with relish.

"I'm off," Gertie said, heading for the door. Strewth, she thought, as she hurried down the hallway, listening to that lot was enough to give anyone bleeding nightmares. All she hoped was that they were all wrong about Cynthia being kidnapped. Though the longer the kid was missing, the more likely it seemed.

Reaching her room, Gertie looked down on the sleeping faces of her babies. She didn't like leaving them alone anymore, even if she was just down the hallway. One never knew, nowadays, what might happen to them.

Shivering, she undressed and crawled into bed, trying not to think of a terrified little girl out there in the darkness somewhere, with only a monster for company.

When Doris entered the kitchen the next morning, Mrs. Chubb pounced on her the minute she set eyes on her. "Have you been taking food from the pantry?" she demanded, digging her fists into her wide hips.

Doris lifted her chin in indignation. "No, I have not. I don't steal nothing from nobody."

"Well, somebody has," Mrs. Chubb said, whirling around to look at Daisy, who stood at the sink peeling potatoes.

"It ain't me," Daisy muttered. "I don't eat all my meals now."

"But then you get hungry late at night," the housekeeper said darkly. "I don't mind anyone taking something to eat if she's hungry, as long as she asks. I can't abide someone taking things behind my back."

"I keep telling you, Mrs. Chubb," Gertie said, emerging from the pantry, "it's those bleeding cats again. Remember you heard them last night. I told you they come in the bloody window if it's left open."

"And I tell you that even if one of those cats could climb up three shelves, it would have a hard job carting off a whole joint of roast beef and a jar of pickle." She glared across the room at Gertie. "How do you suppose it planned to open the lid of the pickle jar?"

"It could bloody well drop it and smash it," Gertie said without much conviction.

"And I suppose it twisted the lid off the milk churn with its paws," Mrs. Chubb said, her voice heavy with sarcasm.

"Well, who do you bleeding think it was, then?" Gertie said defiantly. "The flipping murderer?"

"I don't know who it was, but you can mark my words, I'll find out." The housekeeper marched across the polished brick floor and paused at the door. "And when I get my hands on whoever took that joint of meat, they'll pay double what it's worth out of their wages, that's what."

So saying, she stalked out of the door, letting it swing to behind her.

"Bloody flipping hell," Gertie muttered. "What got into her wig this morning?"

"She's cross because she had to promise P.C. Northcott a roast beef sandwich when he came back today," Daisy said, plopping another potato into the pot of water at her elbow.

"Blimey, he's beginning to bleeding live here," Gertie muttered.

"Who do you think took the food?" Doris looked nervously at the pantry. "Do you think it could have been the murderer?"

"Don't be bleeding daft," Gertie said, taking the poker to stoke the fire. "It was more likely to be one of the staff. Always thieving from the kitchen, they are. It was probably Michel. He's always taking food home to his landlady on his night off, 'cause he hates her bleeding cooking."

She poked the coals, sending red-hot sparks flying up the chimney. "It was his night off and all last night. I bet he took the meat. He never asks, he don't. Too bleeding stuck up, that's his problem. You'd think he owned the bloody hotel, the way he carries on sometimes."

"Well, all I know," Doris said as she started sorting out the silverware, "it weren't me. I wasn't even in the kitchen after lunchtime. It was me afternoon off."

"Did you see Lydia Willoughby yesterday, then?" Gertie

asked, lifting coal out of the scuttle with a small flat shovel.

"Yes," Doris said, remembering the visit with a small quiver of apprehension. "She said she'd love to play for me on Saturday."

"Bloody hell," Gertie muttered. "I pity them poor buggers what have to listen to her."

"I thought you were singing with the string quartet," Daisy said in surprise.

"I tried, but it sounds awful. You know I'd rather sing Variety, anyway." Doris lifted a fork and pretended to be examining it. She didn't want to say so, but she had serious qualms about Lydia's performance. She would just have to take Gertie's advice and sing loud enough to drown her out.

She would have liked to ask madam's permission first, but she knew that Mrs. Carter-Holmes was in charge of the entertainment. Doris also knew full well that the vicar's mother would have a pink fit if she so much as mentioned Variety.

No, Doris thought as she laid down the fork, the only way she was going to be able to sing what she wanted to sing at the ball was to take everyone by surprise. She'd worry about what everyone said later. All she hoped was that Lydia sounded better than she had in rehearsal yesterday. She certainly couldn't sound any worse.

Telling herself that everything would be all right on the night, she went on sorting the silverware. It was too late now to change things, anyhow. Like it or not, the guests at the ball were going to hear one of the latest songs from the Variety shows. She just hoped she wouldn't end up in too much trouble, that's all.

CHAPTER

❖ 12 ❖

Cecily stood in the drawing room, pleasantly chatting with some of the guests who were awaiting the breakfast gong, when Samuel appeared in the doorway, his face burning with suppressed excitement.

His eyes signaled that he wanted to talk to her. Quite desperately, by all accounts.

Excusing herself, Cecily joined him in the hallway. "Come along to the library," she said, already anticipating a new turn of events. Her biggest concern was for Lord and Lady Chalmsford. Whatever had happened, she would have to be the one to break the news to them.

She wasn't even sure how much they knew about the situation. Except for accepting their meals in their suite, the anguished couple had not been seen elsewhere in the hotel.

Samuel, it seemed, was positively bursting to tell her the news. The minute the library door closed behind him, he fished a piece of torn paper from his pocket and handed it to her. "You was right, mum," he said a trifle breathlessly. "That there's the ransom note."

"Good gracious," Cecily exclaimed, studying the poorly scrawled words. "Where did you find it?"

"It was stuck in the gate of one of the stalls," Samuel said, thrusting his hands into the pockets of his breeches. "I saw it the minute I stepped inside the stable. I guessed what it was even before I read it."

Cecily stared at the words written in thick crayon on the back of a torn poster announcing the tournament. The spelling was atrocious. *I have kidnap the child,* the note read. *Plees place five hundrid pound and the dimund and emrald necklas that lady chalmsford wares in the hollo trunk of the big tree at the end of deep willo pond.*

"That must be the elm," Cecily murmured. "If I remember, it has a large hollow in the trunk."

"That would be the one, mum, I reckon," Samuel said, nodding his head. "It's the only big tree next to the pond. We can catch the bastard now, begging your pardon. All we have to do is watch for him to come and get the money. Then we can nab him."

"I think we shall have to let the police constables take care of that," Cecily said, sympathizing with Samuel's obvious disappointment. She would rather have liked to be there herself when they made the arrest.

"I s'pose so," Samuel said gloomily. "I just hope they don't botch the job, that's all."

"I'm sure they know what they are doing." Cecily glanced at the clock. "I will take this note to show the Chalmsfords while you take the trap and fetch the constable. I am quite sure that Lady Chalmsford will want to meet the demands, and I daresay the constable will want to talk with them."

"Right you are, mum. I'll be back before you know it."

Samuel turned to leave, then paused, looking back over his shoulder at her. "Do you think the little girl is still alive, mum?"

"Yes," Cecily said firmly, "I do."

It made her feel better to say it out loud, she thought as she climbed the stairs to the Chalmsfords' suite a few minutes later. She was not looking forward to her task. It would seem, however, that any news of the child would be better than the agony of not knowing what had happened to her. At least the note offered some hope that Cynthia was still alive.

Apparently Lady Chalmsford agreed, as the second she read the note her hands were at her throat, fumbling with the clasp of her necklace. "Take it to him," she said, thrusting the sparkling jewels at her husband. "Whatever he asks. I would give him our entire fortune if it meant having our only child back in our arms."

Lord Chalmsford ran the glittering pendant through his fingers. "I'm sorry, my dear," he said quietly. "I know how much this necklace means to you."

"It is one of my most treasured possessions," Lady Chalmsford said in a broken voice. She looked up at Cecily, who stood silently by, her heart aching for the tormented parents. "My dear husband gave me this beautiful necklace just three days ago."

"It was our anniversary," Lord Chalmsford said, holding onto his wife's trembling hand. "The very first night we arrived at the Pennyfoot, I gave the necklace to my wife. Now we have to hand it over to a despicable scum who can't even spell the word correctly."

"If it means our daughter's safe return," his wife said tearfully, "he can have all my jewelry. It means nothing to me if I have lost my child."

She sobbed, and Lord Chalmsford wrapped an arm about her shoulders. "There, there, my dear. We'll give the bastard what he wants, and Cynthia will be back with us in no time. I promise."

A rather rash promise, Cecily thought despondently as she descended the stairs to the lobby. There was absolutely no guarantee that the kidnapper would return his hostage. He had killed once in cold blood. He would not hesitate to do so again if it served his purpose. If he hadn't already.

Tapping on Baxter's office door a moment or two later, she was relieved to hear his voice bidding her to enter. She had no wish to hunt all over the hotel for him. She was too anxious to tell him about the latest news.

He rose from his desk as she opened the door, scrambling into his jacket, as usual. He was always so upset if she happened to catch him without his full attire, though personally she couldn't possibly imagine what difference it made whether or not he wore his jacket in his own office.

He listened gravely while she repeated the message on the poster. "Both the writing and the spelling were extremely poor," she told him after she had settled herself on a chair. "Obviously the handiwork of an uneducated person."

"It could be that the murderer deliberately misspelled the words in order to throw the constable off the scent," he remarked.

Cecily thought about that for a moment or two. "That's possible, I suppose," she said at length.

He narrowed his eyes as he looked down at her. "I'm quite sure I don't have to remind you that this is a police matter, madam. I trust you are not going to do your best to outwit them again?"

She raised her eyebrows at him. "Why, Baxter, whatever do you mean?"

"I mean," he said carefully, "that I sincerely hope you are not planning on being at the pond in the hopes of apprehending this criminal yourself."

"Ah." She nodded her head. "Could I have one of your wonderful cigars, do you think?"

He straightened his back. "Cecily, I will not be sidetracked from this issue of your propensity for police work. I really cannot allow—"

"Cannot allow?" she interrupted, overjoyed to hear him speak her Christian name again.

"I will not allow you to put yourself in such danger again," he finished as she continued to stare at him with studied innocence.

She was tempted to remind him of his implication that he no longer was bound by his promise to James but thought better of it. Besides, if that were true, by his own admission his apprehension arose from his personal concern, a fact that went a long way toward easing the ache she had suffered lately on his behalf.

"Please, Baxter, do not worry that I should interfere in police business at this point. I have no intention of being at Deep Willow Pond, either now or in the immediate future. Now, can I please have a cigar?"

He lit one for her without commenting on her detestable smoking habit. In spite of his relaxed manner, he still seemed somewhat withdrawn, even a little sad. She couldn't imagine the reason, nor was she likely to find out. He had made it very clear that he had no wish to discuss whatever it was that ailed him. She would respect that wish, no matter how frustrated she became.

"I do have one tiny thought to add to what we already know," she said as she watched the fragrant smoke drift toward the ceiling.

"And what is that?"

"I do believe that the murderer is either a guest at this hotel or one of the staff."

She had thoroughly dismayed him, she could see. "How in the world did you arrive at that conclusion?" he muttered, smoothing a hand over his hair.

Baxter always made that familiar gesture when he was deeply disturbed. She knew how he felt. She felt the same distress herself at the thought of someone close to them being involved in such terrible crimes as murder and kidnapping. It didn't bear thinking about.

She heaved a long sigh. "Lord Chalmsford told me that he had given his wife the necklace on the first night they had arrived at the hotel. How else would the kidnapper know about the necklace, unless he had seen it for himself?"

"He could have seen it the day he came here to kidnap Cynthia," Baxter said, none too convincingly.

"Lady Chalmsford was asleep in her room all afternoon," Cecily said, shaking her head. "I doubt very much if the murderer would have time to see the necklace then. He must have seen it at some time before that, while he was here in this hotel."

"Then who in heaven could it be?" Baxter said, looking aghast.

Cecily nodded her head. "Who, indeed? That is something we would all very dearly like to know."

P.C. Northcott reached the Pennyfoot a short while later and was taking some refreshment in the kitchen according to Samuel, who informed Cecily of the constable's arrival as she crossed the lobby.

"I told him about the note," Samuel said, "and where I found it. He wanted to take a look at that first, before he spoke to the Chalmsfords."

"Very well. I would like to have a word with him before he goes up to their suite, however. I'll wait for him in the library."

"Yes, mum."

He was about to leave, and on impulse she came to a decision. "I'd like you to take me out later this afternoon, Samuel. I'll be calling on Dr. Prestwick. Two o'clock will be a good time."

"Yes, mum." Samuel hesitated. "Begging your pardon, mum, but what about the lady fiddlers? I was supposed to fetch them this afternoon."

"Oh, yes, I had forgotten." Cecily wrinkled her brow.

"Have one of the other footmen fetch them, if you please, Samuel."

"Very well, mum." Samuel touched his forehead and then headed for the kitchen stairs.

Deep in thought, Cecily made her way to the library. She wasn't sure whether Dr. Prestwick would be able to help her or not. She didn't know what he could tell that she didn't already know. But if the murderer was someone connected to the hotel in some way, she had to explore every avenue.

As for Baxter, well, she would tell him about her visit afterward. She had no wish to argue the point with him at the moment.

She was surprised a few minutes later when her next visitor turned out to be not the constable, but Madeline. The vibrant-looking woman swept into the library, seemingly filling the room with the scent of wildflowers and damp mossy meadows.

With her loose, flowing locks and soft, simple gowns, she was the essence of all things growing wild and free. Sometimes, Cecily thought, looking at her friend was like looking at Mother Nature herself. If there were such a tangible, earthly image, that lady would surely resemble Madeline.

"I came to tell you that the flowers for the ball will arrive on Saturday morning, and I will be here around noontime to set up the arrangements." Madeline flung herself down in the chair next to Cecily. "I've also acquired the colored streamers to hang from the balcony. It should look quite effective, I think."

Cecily eyed her companion with a speculative look. "I suppose you have heard about Freddie's death?"

Madeline nodded. "It's all over the village, of course. Such a dreadful thing to happen, a violent death like that. His parents are inconsolable, so I hear. He was their only son, you know."

"Yes, I know," Cecily murmured, her thoughts flying to

her own sons. No matter how many sons one had, one still worried just as much over each one.

"Is there any news of the missing child?" Madeline asked, flipping back a length of dark hair with a languid hand.

Cecily sighed. "She has been kidnapped, it seems. We believe it could be Freddie's murderer who has taken her, though we can't be sure, of course."

"Oh, my stars, how absolutely dreadful." Madeline shot up in her chair. "Has there been a ransom note?"

"Yes, there has. Samuel found it this morning."

"What did it say?"

Cecily repeated the demands written on the note.

"The old elm tree," Madeline murmured. "Let me know when the ransom has been picked up. I might be able to help with vibrations."

"We are hoping the police will be able to arrest the kidnapper when he arrives to collect the ransom." Cecily shook her head. "I must admit, it all sounds too simple. I can't believe that anyone intelligent enough to plan a kidnapping would walk into such an obvious trap."

"Then again," Madeline said, rising to her feet, "who can tell what goes on in the twisted mind of a murderer? It could well be that he considers himself invincible against our local constabulary. Heaven knows, he wouldn't be the first one to think so."

"I hope you're right." Cecily got to her feet, prepared to walk with her friend to the door. "In any case, we are all praying for Cynthia's safe return."

"Oh, speaking of Cynthia." Madeline unfastened a small cotton sack she had tied around her waist. "I almost forgot. I brought you some of my potpourri. I intended to give you the bag I had with me the last time I was here, but I gave it to Cynthia instead."

"Why, thank you, Madeline. I shall enjoy this," Cecily said, genuinely pleased.

Madeline shook her head. "It is so hard to believe that only two days ago I was talking to the child. Now she is helpless in the hands of a murderer. I felt it, you know. I felt the danger." She paused, standing at the door with her head at an odd angle. "It's strange," she murmured. "I can feel nothing now. Nothing at all."

Cecily watched her go with a cold feeling of dread.

A few minutes later P.C. Northcott arrived at the library door, apologizing profusely for his unexpected delay. "I was taking a look at where Samuel found the ransom note," he said, huffing importantly. "I haven't, as yet, spoken to Lord and Lady Chalmsford."

Cecily was more inclined to think that the constable had spent the major portion of his morning in the kitchen but refrained from saying so.

Inviting him in, she seated herself at the head of the table again.

"Well, then, Mrs. Sinclair," P.C. Northcott said, pulling his notebook from his pocket. "In view of this further h'evidence, I have come to the conclusion that it would seem as if Freddie might have been killed trying to stop the kidnapper from taking Miss Cynthia away."

"How very astute of you, Constable." Cecily gave him a smile of approval. "It is certainly something to consider, I agree."

Northcott puffed out his belly. "Yes, well, if I could just take a look at the note?"

"I don't have the note," she told him. "I left it with the Chalmsfords."

"Perhaps you can tell me what was in the note, then, Mrs. Sinclair?" the constable said, studying his notebook. "Samuel has already given me his version of it, but I want to make sure he got it right."

Cecily repeated the message one more time.

"Word for word," the constable pronounced, shutting his notebook with a snap. "Funny thing is, the note doesn't mention anything about not informing the police. Most unusual that. I would say that this is not a very h'experienced criminal, by all accounts."

"I tend to agree with you, Constable."

"Makes our job easier, that does." Northcott's florid face registered his satisfaction. "Now all we have to do is post a couple of constables in the woods within sight of the elm, and Bob's your uncle."

"Quite." Again Cecily had the distinct feeling that the procedure seemed far too simple. They were all missing something, she was sure. Yet she could not think what that could be.

She should mention the fact that she suspected someone in the hotel of being involved in the kidnapping. Yet somehow she couldn't bring herself to say the words. That would open up all sorts of unpleasant situations. No doubt P.C. Northcott would insist on questioning everyone, and they would all be under suspicion.

She would just have to keep quiet about it for now and hope that the murderer would be caught when he collected the ransom. Even so, she couldn't help feeling guilty as she watched the constable leave.

CHAPTER

❊ 13 ❊

It really was most pleasant to be out in the fresh air on such a day, Cecily thought as the trap jogged along the Esplanade. Deciding it was warm enough that afternoon to ride with the canopy down, she'd anchored her hat with a yellow chiffon scarf. She needed the fresh salty breeze from the ocean to clear the cobwebs from her head.

Although it was still early in the season, Cecily noticed a nanny watching her charges play happily along the beach. The children chased balls and dragged kite strings while a small dog yapped playfully at the waves gently washing to shore.

Cecily settled back in her seat with a sigh. Soon it would be summer again, with visitors swarming the sands and crowding the narrow High Street. The bell on Dolly's tea

shop would soon be ringing constantly, and the village of
Badgers End would give up its quiet serenity for three
months or so, until the long summer days dwindled and
autumn brought back the night frost.

The years seemed to be passing by so very quickly.
Before long she would be old and unable to keep up the
hectic pace of running the big hotel. What would become of
her then?

Cecily watched a young boy peddle his bicycle furiously up
the slope to the High Street. A bright yellow motorcar chugged
and banged in a cloud of black smoke as it struggled past
him.

She could go back to the tropics and live with one of
the boys, Cecily thought gloomily. The prospect gave her
little pleasure. As yet, Andrew was unmarried, and much as
she loved Michael, she didn't think she could live with him
and Simani.

Giving herself a mental shake, she straightened her back.
It wasn't like her to be depressed. This was such a beautiful
day, she told herself firmly. With so much tragedy going on
around her, she should be thankful for her health and good
fortune. If only she could have news of her boys, she would
be a contented woman.

She refused to even consider that Baxter might be the
cause of her depression. It was time she stopped yearning
for something she couldn't have. She had to make the most
of her blessings, she told herself as the trap pulled up in
front of Dr. Prestwick's surgery.

Telling the footman to wait for her, Cecily made her way
up the path to the door. The doctor's regular visiting hours
were mornings only, but since his office was in his cottage,
he could usually be found there in the afternoons unless he
were called out on an emergency.

Judging by the rather luxurious carriage waiting outside
the gate, it would appear the doctor had a visitor. Cecily
glanced curiously at the padded leather seats and gleaming
ornate brass lamps of the carriage as she passed.

She waited some time after she'd tapped on the door for it to open. Charlotte Phillips, the doctor's new housekeeper, apologized for the delay. "I was just taking buns out of the oven," she explained as she ushered Cecily inside.

"That's quite all right, Charlotte," Cecily assured her. "I came to pay a social call on the doctor. Is he available?"

"He's with a visitor at the moment, Mrs. Sinclair." Charlotte glanced at the clock on the wall. "But I'm sure he won't be long if you would care to wait."

"I'll be happy to wait," Cecily assured the pleasant young woman. "It will give me a chance to catch up on my reading."

"We have the latest edition of *The Tatler*," Charlotte said helpfully.

"Wonderful. I haven't read it yet." Sighing with pleasure, Cecily settled herself in the corner of the deserted waiting room and picked up the popular magazine.

Colonel Fortescue was feeling particularly pleased with life that afternoon. In the first place, he had enjoyed an excellent lunch, beginning with Michel's fine lobster bisque, followed by ptarmigan pie, spring greens, and the delightful tiny round new potatoes that were his favorite.

He couldn't quite remember what he'd had for dessert, because by then he had enjoyed more than one glass of French cognac. He just knew that his stomach was full, his head pleasantly fuzzy, and the pleasurable afternoon loomed ahead with the promise of a lengthy snooze before his dinnertime tipple.

Dashed fine way to spend his days, he reflected hazily as he tottered along the passageway. He had almost reached the stairs when the front door opened to admit a group of women.

To his immense delight, he spotted the tall figure of the bass fiddler—the alluring woman he'd had his eye on lately. She lagged behind the other three ladies. Not surprising really, considering she was carrying that massive case.

Deciding to act like the gentleman he was, Fortescue stumbled across the lobby toward the woman. All four of them stopped short at the sight of him.

"Jolly good afternoon, what?" the colonel roared.

The little one with the scraggly hair jumped in the air as if he'd shot at her. Blinking his eyes at her, Fortescue announced with as much dignity as he could muster, "I have come to offer my services, madam."

"We do not need your services, sir," the bossy one with the face like a ferret screeched at him.

This was not going as well as he'd planned, the colonel thought, swaying unsteadily on his feet. He was not one to give up, however. Once presented with a mission, he saw it through to the bitter end, by Jove.

Stepping around the ferret-woman, who seemed determined to stand in his way, he sidled up to the bass player. Peering shortsightedly at her, he stammered, "I would be most happy to lighten your load. It would be an honor if you would permit me to assist you in carrying your instrument to the ballroom."

Dashed fine figure of a woman, he thought. He wouldn't mind spending a few evening hours with the likes of her, damned if he wouldn't.

"Will you please leave us alone?" Ferretface shrieked, as he stood smiling sheepishly at the object of his affection.

Annoyed at this unwarranted intrusion into his personal affairs, the colonel fixed the shrew with a wildly flapping eye. "Madam, will you kindly do me the courtesy of remaining quiet? Your voice goes through me like a blasted banshee. Never heard such an abominable noise in my life."

"If you do not leave us alone this minute," Ferretface snarled, "I will report you to the local constable for harassment."

Thoroughly incensed by now, the colonel threw back his head and roared, "Will you, by Jove! Well, do you worst, madam. It means nothing to me. All I ask is a moment alone with this ravishing beauty here. I suggest you allow her to speak for herself."

He was happy to see that he had made an impression. The two women who had remained quiet throughout this interchange were edging toward the passageway, while Ferretface drew herself up as if to launch an attack.

Staring straight into the face of his beloved, she said harshly, "Tell him, Beryl."

Beryl—that was it, the colonel thought, groping in his mind for some forgotten memory. He'd heard the name somewhere before, but dashed if he could remember now. Not that it mattered. He knew her name now, and he wasn't about to forget it again, by George.

Doing his best to focus his blurry gaze on her face, he said in his most seductive voice, "Beryl, my dear. Let us steal some time away this evening to share in some hanky-panky, what?"

His heart leapt as Beryl leaned toward him. Breathlessly he waited for the light of his life to answer.

"Bugger off," Beryl said.

Astounded, the colonel jerked backward, almost toppling over. In a haze of confusion, he watched the four women march down the passageway, each of them holding their damned instrument cases like weapons in front of them. His gaze remained on Beryl until she had disappeared.

The sun felt pleasantly warm on Cecily's back through the leaded pane windows as she turned the pages of the magazine. She was engrossed in a delicious piece of gossip about an American heiress who had recently married an English lord. The woman, it seemed, was fond of throwing elaborate, if somewhat strange, parties.

Milady's latest effort was a "dog's dinner," in which several canine guests had been invited to sit at the dining table, dressed in their best jeweled collars. The dogs were fed paté, among other delicacies, and were entertained by a musician.

Cecily's enjoyment of the story was interrupted when the door to the doctor's office opened, and she heard Dr. Prestwick exclaim, "Why, Cecily, my dear, what a very great pleasure it is to see you."

She looked up with a smile and laid the magazine down before rising to her feet. Dr. Prestwick's visitor stood at his side, an expectant look on his face.

He was a tall man, taller even than the doctor and quite a bit younger, if Cecily was any judge. His finely etched features were perfectly arranged and complemented his dark good looks. A striking man, his bearing suggested a certain arrogance, tempered by a quite charming smile.

"Cecily," Dr. Prestwick said, sounding almost reluctant, "I would like you to meet our newest resident of Badgers End. This is the late Lord Withersgill's grandson, the new Lord Withersgill. Milord, may I present Mrs. Sinclair, the present owner of the Pennyfoot Hotel on the Esplanade."

Cecily offered her hand and watched the young man draw it to his lips.

"I am most charmed to meet you, madam," he murmured when he raised his head again. "I have heard wonderful things about your hotel. In fact, I intend to visit it myself, just as soon as my affairs are in order."

"That would be a very great pleasure, Lord Withersgill." Cecily withdrew her hand under the watchful eye of the doctor. "Please accept my sincere condolences on the death of your grandfather. He was a great man who performed many good deeds for the village."

"Thank you, madam. I appreciate your kind comments." Lord Withersgill's shrewd dark eyes regarded her intently. "I only hope I can follow in his footsteps. There is much that can be done in the village."

"You may find the villagers resistant to change," Cecily warned him. "Not everyone takes kindly to the rapid progress of the modern world."

"Rest assured that I shall take that into account, madam," Lord Withersgill said, bending low over her hand again. "Now, if you will excuse me, I must return to my arduous duties."

Cecily waited in the waiting room while Dr. Prestwick ushered the new lord of the manor out of the door. She felt rather bemused by the man. His appearance hardly matched the intense purpose she had seen in his eyes.

He was not a man to be taken lightly, she thought uneasily. Whether he would be an asset to the village or a fascinating, but critical antagonist remained to be seen.

"Well," Dr. Prestwick said, rubbing his hands together as he reentered the room. "What did you think of our new lord and master?"

"I thought he was charming," Cecily said cautiously.

The doctor gave an exaggerated sigh and wiped his brow with his forearm in a dramatic gesture of despair. "I was afraid of that. My life lies in ruins at your feet, my dear. You have shattered my heart by preferring another younger, richer, more handsome man than I. I shall never recover from this mortal wound."

Cecily laughed. "I can see I have chosen the right person to govern the jousting tournament on Saturday. Your speech is just flowery enough to sound authentic."

"You mock me, my dear, but there is a grain of truth in my words." Kevin Prestwick moved to his desk and gathered up the scattered papers lying on it. "You must be aware of how much I admire you. It would sadden me to see you swept off your feet by such a man."

Again Cecily laughed. "You have no fear of that, Kevin. Lord Withersgill is far too young to be interested in an old woman like me, and I am far too old to be taken in by youthful charm and good looks."

"You do yourself a disservice, madam." The doctor gave her an appraising look that warmed her cheeks. "You carry your age very well. Any man would be proud to have you walk by his side."

"Thank you, Kevin. You always do know the right words to lighten my mood. No wonder all the ladies in the village swoon over you."

"Ah, but only one has captured my heart."

Cecily was beginning to feel uncomfortable. She was never quite sure if the doctor was joking or not. Deliberately changing the subject, she asked, "Do you think the new Lord Withersgill will be beneficial to the village?"

Kevin Prestwick shrugged. "Only time will tell. The chap seems sincere enough. I find it difficult to trust someone who looks like a Greek god, but that's my personal phobia. I never did take kindly to men who threatened my standing with the ladies."

"You are incorrigible, Kevin," Cecily murmured.

He grinned. "But irresistibly charming, am I not?"

"Perhaps. But I didn't come here to discuss your prowess with women."

His smile faded at once. "You are not ill, I trust?"

"No," she assured him, "I am quite well, thank you."

His face cleared. "Aha! Then you have come to ply me with questions about the recent murder, knowing full well I cannot supply you with the answers. At least until the investigation is over."

"I just wanted to discuss it with you," Cecily said, glancing at the clock above his head. The footman was still waiting outside for her, she remembered.

"I'm sorry, Cecily, you know my hands are tied. It was a tragedy. Such a young man and so well liked."

"Yes, he was. Were you aware that Miss Cynthia Chalmsford has been kidnapped?"

"Good Lord!" The doctor's eyes widened in surprise. "I had heard that she was missing, but I assumed she had been found."

"We received a ransom note this morning." She fixed the doctor with an intent stare. "We believe it was Freddie's murderer who took her. We think that Freddie was killed because he disturbed the kidnapping."

Dr. Prestwick pursed his lips. "We, I presume, meaning you and the constable?"

"Yes. I spoke with P.C. Northcott this morning."

"I see."

"Kevin"—Cecily leaned forward and peered earnestly at his face—"if there is anything that you can tell me, I would greatly appreciate it. That little girl's life could depend on the speed with which we identify her kidnapper. While I'm sure the constable will do his very best, sometimes his methods are a little slow."

Kevin Prestwick nodded. "I'm afraid there is little I can tell you, except that there appeared to be no signs of a struggle. Whoever ran that lance through Freddie's chest had to be quite tall, judging from the angle it entered his body. Standing directly in front of him, I would say."

"But you cannot tell me anything else about the killer?"

The doctor looked genuinely sorry. "I might be able to tell more when I have done a thorough autopsy. Unfortunately those findings will remain under lock and key with the constabulary."

"Yes, I know." Cecily rose to her feet. "Well, thank you, Kevin. I appreciate your help."

"I wish it could have been more."

He came with her to the door, where she bid Charlotte goodbye. Following her out to the gate, he said lightly, "I am so happy I had the good sense to hire a housekeeper. It is so much more pleasant talking to you inside my home rather than outside on the doorstep."

"I heartily agree," Cecily murmured, remembering more than once standing in the bitter cold, rather than jeopardize her reputation by being alone with the doctor in his cottage.

"I shall look forward to seeing you at the tournament, Cecily," Kevin Prestwick said as he opened the gate for her. "I only hope this matter of the murder can be cleared up before then."

"I hope so, too." Passing through the gate, she saw the footman waiting patiently for her. He stood by the head of the chestnut, his gaze directed discreetly ahead at the street.

"Thank you again, Kevin," she said after he had handed her into the trap. "I shall look forward to seeing you at the tournament, then."

"Certainly, my dear. My one hope is that this year the contenders will refrain from consuming an excessive amount of alcohol before the tournament. Half of them barely remained seated even before they reached their opponent."

"It's all part of the fun," Cecily said, settling herself in her seat. "We should be thankful there have been no broken bones so far."

"Well, that's the one advantage of imbibing so heavily. Those idiots are so relaxed, they're not even aware of hitting the ground."

"I agree, it is rather a barbaric practice," Cecily shook her head. "The villagers won't hear of abolishing it, however. Every time the suggestion is brought up, there is a public outcry. I suppose if it were not for the tournament, the men would find some other way to demonstrate their strength and daring."

"Indubitably," the doctor said with a twinkle in his eye. "We men must have our chance to show off our superiority now and again."

Rising to the bait, Cecily answered crisply, "Thank goodness women are far too sensible to feel the need to prove their worth. They demonstrate it every day, in everything they do, without expecting or receiving constant praise and encouragement. It is our misfortune that men so easily take us for granted."

The doctor threw back his head and laughed. "Ah, Cecily, I do so enjoy our little debates. One of these days, when we both have more time, we shall have to indulge in a lengthy discussion of the foibles of men."

"I should enjoy that very much." She relented enough to give him a smile. "I shall see you soon, Kevin."

"You shall indeed, my dear." He gave her a slight bow as the trap pulled away, leaving her unsettled by his remarks.

Concentrating on their earlier conversation, she thought about his contention that there had been no struggle. That would indeed suggest that Freddie knew the person who had attacked him and that he not anticipated the attack.

Where was Cynthia while this was going on? Cecily wondered. Bound and gagged, perhaps? The child must have been terrified. Who in the world would have gone to such great lengths for such a paltry sum? Five hundred pounds hardly constituted a fortune, and while the necklace was a very pretty piece, it was also recognizable and would not be easy to sell.

There was also the matter of the ransom and the way it was to be delivered. No instructions as to who should deliver it or, as the constable pointed out, no threats if the police were notified. It would seem, as the constable had said, that the kidnapper was not an experienced criminal.

Cecily leaned back and idly watched the shops as she passed by. Some of them were opening up for the early season. The owners had been sprucing up the windows and adding a coat of paint to the weather-beaten exteriors, she noticed.

Her mind drifted back to the doctor's words. A tall person, she mused. That description could fit many people. Thinking about tall persons brought her mind back to the new Lord Withersgill. He was bound to make a stir in the village, no matter what actions he took.

The villagers had become somewhat complacent, lulled by the inactivity of the old Lord Withersgill. The newcomer could easily shake up a sleepy little village like Badgers End.

In spite of Cecily's enthusiasm for progress, she couldn't help hoping that the new lord of the manor wouldn't change things too drastically.

The countryside as she had always known it was fast changing and disappearing with the loss of farmland and farmers to work it. It would be a great pity if some of the picturesque villages would suffer the same fate.

Arriving back at the hotel a few minutes later, Cecily happened to meet her American guest in the lobby. The polite young man reminded her of his name, for which she was thankful, since she had forgotten it.

"I was wondering, Mrs. Sinclair," he said, after exchanging comments on the pleasurable weather, "when the workman will be finished in the suite next to mine."

"I'm sorry, Mr. Kern," Cecily said, full of concern. "Has the noise disturbed you?"

"It's not so much the noise of the actual work," Jerome Kern said, looking apologetic, "as the dreadful caterwauling of the workman. While I have nothing against a man singing—I happen to be extremely fond of music myself—this man apparently believes that the louder he sings, the better he will sound. Unfortunately this is not the case."

"Oh, dear," Cecily murmured, making a mental note to have a word with Roland Young. "I'm am so very sorry he has disturbed you."

"I wouldn't complain unless it was a severe problem," the American said. "Yesterday afternoon I was trying to work in my room. It became quite impossible, I'm afraid. For the entire afternoon I was treated to this terrible racket until I was about to wring his neck. I tried asking to keep the noise down, but he completely ignored me."

"Oh, my." Cecily paused, staring at Jerome Kern as a thought occurred to her. "What time would you say this happened, Mr. Kern?"

"Well, let's see." He paused with a look of concentration on his face. "I returned to my room shortly after two, and I finally gave up trying to work about five. I left to go for a walk soon after that to try and clear my head. It's impossible to create when my mind is being tortured by such lousy singing."

"I do apologize for the young man," Cecily said, "and I assure you he will be severely reprimanded. I don't think you will be disturbed again, however, as he has completed the work in that particular suite. Nevertheless, I shall make sure that he doesn't disturb anyone else. I thank you for bringing this to my attention."

"My pleasure," Mr. Kern said, giving her a slight bow. "I'm sure my complaint must seem frivolous, taking into account the misfortunes that have occurred here lately."

Cecily's heart sank. So the news was circulating after all. It was only to be expected, of course. Nevertheless, it was unpleasant to have it confirmed.

"Has there been any news of the missing child? Or who was responsible for the young man's death?"

"I'm afraid not," Cecily said, unwilling to discuss the matter further. "The constabulary are working on the cases, however, and we hope to have news soon."

The American nodded. "This is a wonderful place you have here. It's unfortunate that these calamities had to happen. It must be a great worry for you."

"It is indeed," Cecily agreed.

"Otherwise everything in this hotel is delightful. I am looking forward to the ball this weekend."

"I hope you will enjoy the evening, Mr. Kern." She bid him goodbye, wondering if anyone would be able to enjoy the festivities with a kidnapper and murderer lurking about. It seemed extremely unlikely at this point.

Until Freddie's murderer was apprehended and Cynthia was returned to her frantic parents, a very large cloud hung over the Pennyfoot.

Everything depended on the kidnapper picking up the ransom, and the police being on the spot to capture the man. Until then, there seemed little else to do but wait.

CHAPTER

❖ 14 ❖

"I thought you were finished for the day," Doris said that evening when she saw Gertie striding into the kitchen.

"I was. I came in for some bloody bread and milk." Gertie headed for the pantry without stopping. "Those greedy buggers of mine are never bleeding satisfied. I never knew babies could be so bloody hungry all the time." She disappeared, her words muffled by the door.

Doris looked across at her sister, who was shoveling ashes from the stove into a cast-iron bucket. "I'll be glad when we're finished tonight, that I will. My feet are killing me."

Daisy looked up with a frown. "You should tell madam that those shoes hurt your feet."

"I don't like to complain. It was my fault for telling Mrs.

146

Chubb they fit all right. I was so glad to have a new pair of shoes when we first came, I was frightened that if I said they didn't fit, I might have to do without." Doris looked down at her black oxfords. "I'll wait until the season when there's more people in the hotel. Madam will have more money then."

"You might not be able to walk by then," Daisy said, lifting the bucket with both hands. "You'd better tell her now."

Doris watched her twin march to the back door with the bucket swinging in her hands. She envied Daisy's strength. The two of them might look like each other, but she was the weaker one, no doubt about it.

"I'm going to empty this," Daisy said. "Then I'm going for a walk along the seafront to get some fresh air. My head feels like cotton wool inside." She glanced back at her sister. "You want to come with me?"

Doris shook her head. "Can't. I still have to polish the silverware before I can go to bed." She glanced at the window. "You ain't going out there on your own, are you? It's dark outside."

"It usually is after the sun's gone down," Daisy said, opening the door with one hand while she held onto the bucket with the other. "The lamps will be lit along the Esplanade, though. I'll be all right."

"What if the murderer is creeping around out there?" Doris said fearfully. "He could stick one of them lances in you like he did poor Freddie."

"I'd like to see him try," Daisy said scornfully. "Besides, there's plenty of people what walk along the seafront now that it's warmer. It's not like I'll be all alone in the woods, now, is it?"

"Well, if you're not back by the time I've finished polishing the silver," Doris said, a little put out that Daisy would go out without her, "I'm going to bed."

"Suit yourself. I'll see you in the morning, then." The door closed behind her with a snap.

"Who was that?" Gertie demanded, emerging from the pantry with a large bowl of bread cubes soaked in milk.

"Daisy." Doris stared gloomily at the pile of silverware waiting to be polished. "She's gone for a walk."

"Oh, I thought it was that bastard Roland Young." Gertie sniffed and wiped her nose on her sleeve. "I saw him in the lobby talking to madam a little while ago. I'll be bleeding glad when he's been and gone, that I will. Gives me the blinking willies, he does."

"Me, too." Doris was about to tell Gertie about the way he'd frightened her that morning, but the door opened just then, and Roland Young himself strolled in, whistling something shrill and tuneless.

"Bloody hell, talk of the bleeding devil," Gertie muttered.

"What's the matter with you, then?" Roland demanded, leering at Gertie while his eyes raked her up and down.

"Looking at you, that's what's the bloody matter with me." Gertie lifted her chin in a belligerent gesture. "Fair turns me blinking stomach, it does."

"Oh, yeah?" The young man swaggered across the floor toward her. "Go on, I know what you're really thinking. You fancy me, you do. I seen you looking at me out the corner of your eye."

"Cor, bleeding hark at him," Gertie said in disgust. "Who'd want to bloody look twice at someone like you, that's what I want to know."

Doris, who had been watching the exchange, decided that this was her chance to jump in. She'd never have a better opportunity to corner Roland Young.

"I was wondering, Mr. Young," she began, her face heating up when he spun around to look at her.

"Mr. Young now, is it? Well, well, what 'ave I done to deserve this dubious honor?"

He grinned at her with yellowed teeth, and Doris's stomach did a nervous flip.

"'Ere, you bleeding leave her alone," Gertie said sharply. "She's only a flipping kid, she is."

"Yeah? Well, then, she should behave like one, shouldn't she, instead of chasing after men twice her age."

"I wasn't chasing after you, honest," Doris protested. Twisting a corner of her apron in her hands. "I wanted to ask you a question, that's all."

"Well, why didn't you say so? I'm always happy to share my vast experience." Roland sauntered across to the table and sat on the edge of it.

"Keep your bleeding bum off the bloody table," Gertie said, her dark eyes flashing fire. "I scrubbed that down for the blinking night already."

Ignoring her, Roland gave Doris a sly look. "What's the question, then, sweetheart?"

Doris didn't care for his tone at all, but now she'd started, she wasn't going to give up. Taking the plunge, she said breathlessly, "I was just wondering if you knew any of them performers at the Hippodrome. I'd like to meet one of them."

Roland gave her an unpleasant smile. "Which one, ducky?"

Doris shrugged, her heart beginning to pound at the thought of such a momentous event. "Any one of them." She took a step closer to him. "I want to be on the stage, see, singing in the Variety. I thought if I could meet one of the performers, they might be able to help me . . ." Her voice trailed off as Roland let out a harsh shout of laughter.

"You? For Chrissake, what makes you think you could sing at the Hippodrome? Variety ain't for kids like you. It's for real singers, grown-ups, who know what they're bloody doing."

He pushed himself away from the table and shook his head at her. "Strewth, kid, forget it. You ain't never going to make it in Variety. You ain't got the bloody nerve." Still laughing, he strode out through the back door and into the night.

Doris watched him go, then promptly burst into tears.

Choking on her sobs, she felt Gertie's arm land clumsily on her shoulders.

"'Ere, 'ere," Gertie said, sounding awkward, "don't let that little twit upset you. What does he know, anyhow?"

"I hate him." Doris sniffled and dug into her apron pocket for her handkerchief. "I *can* be a singer on the stage, I can."

"Of course you bleeding can." Gertie took the handkerchief from her and pinched Doris's nose with it. "Here," she said gruffly, "give it a bloody good blow."

Doris obediently blew.

"There, that's better." Gertie tucked the handkerchief back in Doris's pocket. "Now, you blinking listen to me. You're going to be on the bleeding stage here at the Pennyfoot on Saturday, aren't you?"

Doris nodded tearfully.

"All right, then. You go out there, and you sing your bloody heart out. Give them the bleeding performance of your life. You never know who might be watching. Some blinking toff from London might hear you and offer you a bloody job right on the spot. You never know. And even if they bleeding don't, it will be a flipping experience for you, won't it. You got to start somewhere, haven't you?"

Again Doris nodded, feeling a good deal more cheerful.

"All right, then. I've heard you sing, we all have, and everyone what's bleeding heard you thinks you sing like a bloomin' angel. So piss on bloody Roland bleeding Young, that's what I say. Go out there and show him what you're bloody made of. All right?"

Doris actually felt a smile peeking through her tears. "All right," she whispered. "I will."

"Good for you." Gertie gave her a hearty slap than rattled her teeth. "Now I have to get back to me bleeding babies before they wake up screaming their flipping heads off for more grub. I'll see you in the morning, all right?"

Doris nodded. "Thanks, Gertie. You're really nice. I won't forget you when I'm famous and have pots of money."

Gertie nodded, wagging a finger. "You'd better not," she said sternly. "I'm going to need all the bleeding help I can get when my little'uns grow bigger. Gawd help me, then, that's what I say."

With a cheery nod, she closed the door behind her, leaving a grateful Doris to dream about being spotted by some toff in the audience on Saturday.

"It is late, madam. I should have thought you would have retired for the night." Baxter sent a disapproving look at the clock as Cecily poked her head around his office door.

"I wanted a word with you before I went upstairs." She glanced at the pile of papers in front of him. "Am I interrupting anything?"

"Not at all, madam." He swept up the sheaf of papers in his hand and laid them in the basket. "I was merely looking over a few papers, that all."

"You are working late yourself tonight," Cecily said, studying him intently. "That's doesn't seem like you, Baxter. You are usually so particular about getting enough rest. Had I not seen the glow of your lamp from the passageway, I would have assumed you were in bed already."

"I did not feel like sleeping yet," Baxter murmured, avoiding her gaze. "What was it you wanted to ask me?"

She moved over to the desk and sat herself down in the chair, earning another reproving glance from him. "It's not so much ask you as tell you something. I met the new Lord Withersgill today. He is an interesting man, very charming and quite becoming to look at, but I'm not altogether sure I like him."

Baxter's eyebrows lifted. "You met him? Where?"

"At Dr. Prestwick's house. I went there this afternoon to ask him a question or two about the murder."

"I see." Baxter's gaze turned frosty. "You certainly do appear to have your fill of charming men surrounding you, madam. I congratulate you on your popularity."

Shocked, Cecily stared at him in disbelief. "And what, pray, is that supposed to mean?"

For a long moment he stared at her while she struggled to contain her temper. Then he said quietly, "My remark was unwarranted and highly offensive. I can only offer my sincerest and humble apology. I am not myself this evening."

"It is my considered opinion," Cecily said huffily, "that you have not been yourself for quite some time. Since you refuse to discuss what ails you, I must ask you to please consider my sensibilities when you feel the need to strike out at the world."

She rose and marched to the door, where she paused long enough to look back at him. "I shall do my utmost to forget your unfortunate remark, Baxter. I trust you will do the same. I suggest you go to bed and get a good night's rest. It might well put you in a better frame of mind tomorrow."

He gave her a look of such misery that she felt quite alarmed. Had she not been so affronted by his thoughtless remark, she might have attempted once more to learn what it was that troubled him so deeply.

She hesitated, drawn by that lost expression, but then Baxter said brusquely, "If you will excuse me, madam, I think I will take a stroll along the seafront. Perhaps the night air will clear my mind long enough for me to sleep."

There didn't seem to be any answer to that. She gave him a brief nod and left him, knowing that it would be a long time before she herself fell asleep that night.

The lamps cast an eerie light along the Esplanade, their orange glow shimmering like huge Chinese lanterns in the thick sea mist that had rolled in.

Baxter shivered, wishing he'd stopped to put on his top coat. After the warm day, the contrast in the temperature was quite remarkable.

He strode along the promenade at a brisk pace, hoping to

increase his circulation enough to stay warm. He needed this time, alone in the dark night, to think more clearly.

His footsteps echoed eerily on the empty pavement, the only sound other than the ceaseless splash of the waves on the deserted sands. This late at night, he had the entire street to himself.

The dark and shuttered windows of the shops were veiled in the swirling mist. Above them, their owners slept peacefully behind drawn curtains. Baxter envied them their restful state. He couldn't remember when he had last slept through an entire night.

His heart ached when he remembered Cecily's hurt expression earlier. Whatever had possessed him to say such a thing? He could not go on like this, he told himself. Something had to be done, and soon, before he destroyed whatever relationship they might have.

He hunched his shoulders in an uncharacteristic gesture of despair. Taking advantage of the absence of spectators, he thrust his hands into the pockets of his trousers. He was tired of fighting the new, relaxed principles of society. All around him age-old customs and standards were being abolished, giving way to new thinking, new behavior, new morals.

There were times when he longed to be able to accept the new way of thinking. Times when he wished he understood them. There were certainly times when he wished with all his heart that he was not the manager of the Pennyfoot Hotel.

So many of his ideals were tied up securely in the old morals, when everyone knew his place and what was expected of him. He sensed danger in this bold, new way, a loss of discipline, a lack of respect, mass confusion, perhaps, on the unknown roads ahead.

Yet deep inside him he knew that in order to find the happiness that so far had eluded him, he would have to accept and change. He would have to set foot on that strange new ground and meet whatever challenge awaited him.

The thought terrified him; yet he could not deny a certain

sense of excitement in the prospect of such an enormous venture. He quickened his step, as if subconsciously anxious for this metamorphosis to begin. As he did so, he heard a distinct echo of footsteps—faster, less sure than his own.

The mist had thickened, coiling about his face so that it was difficult to see into the dark shadows that lay ahead. The lamplights dimmed as they stretched away from him, and he could not see the town that he knew lay ahead.

He could not even see the sweep of Putney Downs rising high above the bay or the lights of the tiny thatched cottages that nestled in the hills. He could, however, hear the footsteps coming toward him. And now he heard something else. The quiet, plaintive whimpering of a child.

Baxter was not a particularly religious man. He did not believe in spirits, angels, or any of those other unearthly creatures that Cecily and her strange friend, Miss Pengrath, held so dear.

At that moment, however, as he watched the ethereal shape of the child approaching him through the damp, writhing mist, he was almost convinced that it was, indeed, a ghost.

He paused, unwilling to accept what his senses told him. He was acutely conscious of the salty sea air, thick with the aroma of wet sand. The chill had now penetrated his bones, and he felt unable to move a step or draw his hands from his pockets.

He could only stand and stare as the shape materialized, then vanished, then reappeared, ever closer, while the dreadful sound of its whimpering grew increasingly louder.

The figure was almost upon him before he regained his senses. Blinking, he strained to see in the shifting light. As he did so, he saw without a doubt that it was not a ghost who stumbled toward him. It was a flesh-and-blood child. It was a child he recognized. He was, in fact, staring at Miss Cynthia Chalmsford.

With a muffled exclamation, Baxter darted forward and

swept the weeping girl up into his arms. "Hush, now," he told her, "you are quite safe now. Are you hurt?"

She shook her head, though the sobbing increased.

Without another word, Baxter turned and headed back to the hotel.

CHAPTER

❈15❈

Cecily awoke to the sound of tapping on the door of her suite. Instantly alert, she reached for her dressing gown and wrapped it about her. Without waiting to put anything on her feet, she hurried across her drawing room, a dozen thoughts tumbling through her mind.

Her first concern, engulfing her in a rush of cold fear, was that something had happened to Michael or Andrew. Almost immediately her common sense told her it was unlikely that news of her son would be brought to her door in the middle of the night.

Pulling open the door, she was amazed to see Baxter standing there, his gaze studiously averted as he muttered, "Forgive me for disturbing you at this hour, madam. I thought you should know . . ."

"What is it?" she demanded, her anxiety overriding any thoughts of propriety. It had to be serious for Baxter to awaken her. Could it be news of Michael after all?

Her relief was twofold when Baxter murmured, "It's the child, madam. She has returned."

"Cynthia Chalmsford? Thank heavens!" Cecily uttered a silent prayer of thanks. "Where is she? Is she hurt? Where has she been?"

Baxter cleared his throat and stared fixedly down the hallway. "I happened to meet the child on the Esplanade. She appears to be unharmed, though she is thoroughly shaken. I took her to her parents. She is with them now in their suite. I know nothing beyond that."

"I want to talk to her," Cecily exclaimed, already closing the door. "Please wait for me until I am dressed."

"Perhaps it might be better to wait until morning?" Baxter suggested in a tone that indicated he knew he was wasting his breath.

"Undoubtedly," Cecily said, "but all the same I want to talk to her now. If she has news of the murderer, I want to know it as soon as possible. Time could make all the difference whether or not we can catch him. Wait there, Baxter. I shan't be but a minute."

She shut the door on his resigned, "Yes, madam." She had no time to stand on ceremony. At last she had a chance to learn more about Freddie's murderer, and she wasn't about to wait until P.C. Northcott appeared on the scene.

Hastily dragging on a crisp white blouse, she wondered if the killer had found the ransom and had allowed the child to leave. If so, why hadn't the police captured him and returned the child themselves? What was Cynthia doing by herself on the Esplanade?

Cecily buttoned the lace cuffs and collar of her blouse. She hated to disturb Lord and Lady Chalmsford at this time of night, though it was doubtful they had settled down again as yet. They must be ecstatic over the return of their child, unharmed by all accounts.

Ready at last, Cecily opened the door to find Baxter standing patiently in the hallway. "You wish me to accompany you to the Chalmsfords' suite?" he asked when he saw her.

"Yes, Baxter, I do." Cecily hurried ahead of him to the stairs. "I want you to listen to what the child has to say. Just in case I should miss something."

"Very well, madam."

She could tell by his tone that he wasn't happy at the prospect, but she couldn't worry about that now. All she could hope was that Cynthia could tell her something that would lead them to the identity of Freddie's murderer, and as soon as possible.

Pausing outside the Chalmsfords' suite, she could hear the commotion going on inside. Cynthia's voice was raised in tearful protest, while her father apparently bombarded her with impatient questions.

Cecily had to rap quite hard before her summons was answered.

When he opened the door, Lord Chalmsford appeared flustered. Both he and Lady Chalmsford were fully attired, though somewhat hurriedly, judging by the lack of tie at Lord Chalmsford throat and the crumpled tea gown Lady Chalmsford wore.

"Oh, Mrs. Sinclair," Lord Chalmsford said, throwing an enigmatic glance at his wife, "as you can see, our dear daughter has been returned to us. We can't tell you how relieved and happy we are to have her back."

"I am quite sure you are beyond words," Cecily said, sending his wife an apologetic smile. "While I truly hate to disturb your happy reunion, I wonder if I might be permitted to ask Miss Cynthia a few questions, if she is able to talk with me?"

Lord Chalmsford looked as if he would refuse, but his wife called out, "Ask them in, Geoffrey. We should get to the bottom of this as soon as possible."

Lord Chalmsford stepped back, allowing Cecily to enter.

Baxter followed her, wearing his uncomfortable expression.

Cynthia Chalmsford sat on the green velvet settee with Lady Chalmsford's arm tightly encircling her. The child looked as if she had indulged in a great deal of crying. Even now her shoulders heaved with dry sobs every once in a while.

She appeared to be very disheveled and grubby. Little white trails streaked her face, where her tears had washed through the dust. Dark circles ringed her eyes, and her face sagged with exhaustion.

Feeling sorry for the child, Cecily knelt in front of her. "I'm sorry you were so frightened," she said softly. "Do you feel like telling me what happened?

Cynthia nodded. "I'm hungry," she said, tears spilling from her eyes once more.

"Mr. Baxter will get you something to eat, just as soon as you've told us what happened to you," Cecily said, reaching for a small, cold hand. "He'll fix you a sandwich and hot cocoa and a large slice of Mrs. Chubb's cherry cake."

Cecily was relieved to see a flicker of interest in the little girl's eyes. If she was hungry enough to feel like eating, then there couldn't be too much harm done to her.

"I saw Freddie get hurt . . ." Cynthia paused as her throat worked on a sob.

"Just take your time," Cecily said gently. She rose and sat herself on the settee next to the child and her mother. "Where were you when you saw Freddie get hurt?"

Cynthia drew in a shuddering breath. "I was playing in the loft, and I saw Freddie come in. There was a man with him. A big man, and he had one of those things over his face that the knights wear."

"A visor?" Cecily exchanged glances with Baxter. "He wore a knight's helmet and visor?".

Cynthia nodded. "I couldn't see his face, not at all."

"I see." Cecily's hopes faded. "So then what happened?"

"I saw the man take one of the spears and lift it in the air."

Cynthia raised her arm holding an imaginary lance. "Then he threw it, and it went right into Freddie's chest."

"Oh, dear," Cecily said, patting the child's trembling shoulder. "That must have been dreadfully frightening."

"It was." Cynthia swallowed back a sob. "I was so scared, I screamed, and the man saw me and came up the ladder after me." She turned to her mother and buried her face in Lady Chalmsford's bosom.

Cecily waited a moment, then asked quietly, "What happened when he caught you, Cynthia?"

The child didn't answer, and her mother gave her a gentle shake. "Come, Cynthia, answer Mrs. Sinclair now."

"The child is exhausted," Lord Chalmsford said, starting forward. "Can't this wait until tomorrow?"

"I'm sorry," Cecily said. "I'll be as brief as I can, but I feel we should know anything at all that might possibly help us to apprehend this criminal."

"By all means," Lady Chalmsford agreed. "The despicable man must be found and severely punished for what he has done. In any case, he has my necklace. I want it back."

"The constables will do their best to recover it, my dear, I'm sure," Lord Chalmsford murmured.

"I am not concerned about the money," his wife said, giving him a direct look, "but I do want my necklace returned. It is of great sentimental value to me."

"I agree with Lord Chalmsford," Cecily said. "The constables will be working very hard to apprehend this criminal. I doubt if he can sell your necklace to anyone, as it is so recognizable. I'm quite sure you will have it back eventually."

Looking unconvinced, Lady Chalmsford put a hand under her daughter's chin. "Now, Cynthia, tell Mrs. Sinclair what happened after the man caught you."

"He put me in the trap," Cynthia said, her voice quavering. "He took me all the way up to the Downs." Her eyelids drooped, and she uttered a long sigh.

Cecily looked up at Baxter, who hovered by the door with

a worried expression on his face. "Perhaps we should get some food for her," she said. "I dare say there will be soup in the pantry."

"I'll see to it right away, madam," Baxter said. He left, closing the door quietly behind him.

"He won't forget the cake, will he?" Cynthia said sleepily.

Cecily smiled. "I'm sure he won't. Now can you tell me where the man took you on the Downs?"

Cynthia nodded. "To a cave under the cliffs."

"A cave? Was it a big cave?"

Cynthia nodded again. "It had a passageway that went a long way in the dark. I was afraid to go down it, though."

The only cave Cecily knew of with a passageway was the one that ran underneath the hotel. The entrance to it was originally in the library, but after it had been sealed up, someone opened up another entrance in one of the card rooms. That, too, had been sealed up, but now she wondered if someone had perhaps opened it again. The very thought of it filled her with dread.

"Did the man tie you up?" she asked as Cynthia's eyelids fluttered.

"No." The little girl jerked her eyes open. "I mean, yes, he did, when he went to get the money and the necklace. That's when I ran away."

"You managed to untie yourself, then," Cecily said, hoping that Baxter would return with the food before the child fell asleep.

"He didn't tie me up very good," Cynthia said, leaning against her mother. Her mouth opened in a wide yawn.

"He didn't tie you up very well," Lady Chalmsford corrected softly. She looked up at Cecily. "I don't think she is going to be much more help tonight, Mrs. Sinclair. Perhaps we should continue this in the morning."

"Of course," Cecily said, rising to her feet. "Just one more question before I leave." Once again she knelt in front of Cynthia. "Tell me," she said gently, "was there any time, any time at all, when you saw this man's face?"

Cynthia shook her head emphatically, sending her matted curls bouncing to and fro. "He wore that thing on his head the whole time. I never saw him."

"Was he a tall person?" Cecily asked.

"A very tall person," Cynthia said solemnly, holding her hand above her head. "He was much taller than this."

Cecily nodded as she stood. "Thank you, milady. You have all been most patient. Thank you, too, Cynthia. You have been extremely helpful. Don't worry, we shall catch this man. He will pay for frightening you so badly."

Cynthia nodded sleepily, her eyes closed, and her cheek pressed against her mother's shoulder.

Cecily crossed the room to the door. "I'm sure Baxter will be here at any moment with the food. I trust that you will all have a good rest the remainder of the night. I will inform P.C. Northcott of the child's return. He will most likely want to talk with her tomorrow if she is up to it."

"I'm sure she will be," Lord Chalmsford said, opening the door for her.

Thanking him, she passed through and looked down the passageway. Baxter had just reached the top of the stairs with a loaded tray in his hands. "Ah," she said, "here is the food now. I'm sure your daughter will feel a great deal better once she has some sustenance."

"Thank you, Mrs. Sinclair," Lord Chalmsford said gravely. "You've been most kind."

Cecily waited for Baxter to hand over the tray before bidding the weary parents a good night.

"Well, this has been an interesting night," she said as he followed her down the stairs to the second floor.

"It has indeed, madam. I'm afraid there isn't much of the night left for you to rest."

"Ah, well, I shall just have to catch up with my sleep tomorrow night," Cecily said, stealing a glance at her manager's face. He seemed a little more relaxed than when she'd left him in his office earlier that evening.

"Did you have time to enjoy your walk?" she asked lightly.

"I hadn't gone too far before I saw the child," Baxter said without looking at her.

Realizing that she would get no further comment about his disgruntled mood, Cecily decided to change the subject. "What did you make of Cynthia's story?"

"I find it puzzling. It appears that Freddie was killed before Cynthia was kidnapped. Therefore our theory that he was killed disturbing the kidnapping would seem incorrect."

"Not necessarily," Cecily said thoughtfully. "The killer could have planned to kidnap the child, perhaps followed her to the stable. It's possible that Freddie came in before the kidnapper could seize the child."

Baxter frowned. "If I remember, madam, the child said that the man came into the stables with Freddie."

"So she did." Cecily sighed. "Perhaps he saw Freddie arrive with the trap, decided he would need it, and followed Freddie into the stables, where he killed him."

"That is a possibility."

She reached the landing and paused in front of her door. "Though I still don't understand when he armed himself with the lance and the helmet. He must have done that before Cynthia went into the stables, which means that he must have been there earlier in the afternoon."

"But after Samuel had left to go into town."

"Presumably, since Samuel stored the equipment." She rubbed a hand across her forehead, aware of a headache gaining strength. "I wonder why he would arm himself that way in order to capture a small child, unless he expected a confrontation with someone."

"The puzzle has become even more complicated," Baxter murmured, barely managing to contain a yawn.

"Go to bed, Baxter," Cecily said, giving him a sleepy

smile. "At least we shall have an hour or two before we have to get up again."

"Yes, madam." He looked at her, and she had the odd feeling that he desperately wanted to say something to her.

"What is it, Baxter?" she asked urgently. "Whatever it is, you can tell me. We are friends, are we not? I would hope that you could trust me with a confidence."

"I would trust you with my life, madam. I would hope that you are well aware of that." His face looked drawn in the dim light from the gas lamps.

A pang of apprehension touched her, and she laid a hand on his arm. "If you are not well, my dear friend, I beg you to tell me."

To her relief, he gave a decisive shake of his head. "I promise you, madam, as I have many times, my problem has nothing to do with my health."

He hesitated for a moment while Cecily held her breath. Perhaps, at last, she thought with a rush of apprehension, she would learn the nature of his problem.

For some reason she felt a jolt of dismay when he added, "I am wrestling with a major decision—a very difficult decision. It has been disturbing me for some time, but I think I am finally approaching the resolution."

She knew full well, by his set expression, that he intended to say no more than that. "And you will not tell me what it is?" she asked without too much hope.

"Not at this point."

"Very well, I will respect your privacy. I will not ask again." She turned abruptly away and fitted the key into the lock.

"I am sorry, madam. I can only say that I will confide in you in due time."

She would have to curb her impatience, she thought in frustration. She could only hope that she wouldn't have to wait too long to discover what it was that had him so confused and indecisive.

"Goodnight, then, Baxter," she murmured. "I hope you sleep well."

He inclined his head and answered softly, "Goodnight, madam."

She watched him walk to the stairs and disappear down them before opening her door and going inside. A major decision, she thought, as she climbed once more into her frigid bed. Whatever could that be? She couldn't help wondering if his resolution would affect her and in what way.

The only thing she could be certain of was that she wouldn't know the answers to those questions until Baxter was good and ready to tell her. Heaven only knew how long that would be.

Cursing the capricious disposition of men in general, and one man in particular, Cecily drew the eiderdown over her shoulders and tried to sleep.

She dozed fitfully, only to be woken up with sunlight streaming into the room and the sound of insistent tapping on her door.

Not again, she thought wearily as she pulled on her dressing gown once more. This was the second urgent summons in the space of a few hours. Surely there couldn't be another calamity.

Mrs. Chubb stood on the doorstep, her round face creased with deep worry lines. She held a large jug of steaming water in her hands, much to Cecily's surprise. No matter the circumstances, it certainly wasn't the housekeeper's place to bring the hot water to the rooms.

"Here's your wash water, mum," Mrs. Chubb said, handing Cecily the jug. "I thought I'd better bring it myself this morning."

"What has happened now?" Cecily asked, sensing at once that something was dreadfully amiss.

"I'm afraid it's more bad news, mum," Mrs. Chubb said, looking as if she were about to burst into tears.

Cecily grasped the edge of the door with cold fingers. "Michael?"

She felt quite light-headed with relief when the housekeeper hastened to reassure her. "Oh, bless you, mum, no. It's not Mr. Michael. It's Daisy."

"What has happened? Is she ill? An accident?"

"That's just it, mum. We don't really know." The housekeeper bit her trembling lip. "Daisy went out last night to empty the ashes. She told her sister she was going for a walk, so Doris tells me. Well, she didn't come back all night. Her bed hasn't been slept in. It looks as if she's missing now, mum."

Cecily rubbed her chilled arms. "Oh, good Lord," she muttered. "Not Daisy, too."

"Doris is in such a state, mum, I don't know what to do with her. She keeps saying that the killer has got her sister, and it was her fault because she didn't go with her. She's terrified that he'll come back for her, too."

"Oh, dear, the poor child." Cecily made an effort to collect her thoughts. Her head felt fuzzy, and she couldn't seem to find the right words to say.

"The breakfast is all behind because of this," Mrs. Chubb went on, "and the visitors will all be arriving today for the weekend. I don't know what we shall do without Daisy, mum. I really don't."

Cecily took a deep breath. "Try to relax, Mrs. Chubb. Give me time to get dressed and I will come down to the kitchen. I'll talk to Doris, and please make sure Samuel is there, too. He will have to go and fetch the constable again."

"Yes, mum. I'm sorry I had to wake you up with such bad news, I am that."

The housekeeper turned to go, and Cecily said quickly, "Oh, there is one piece of good news. Cynthia Chalmsford returned to the hotel last night. Baxter found her wandering down the Esplanade."

"Oh, mum, that is good news indeed. Is the poor child all

right? What happened to the man who kidnapped her? Did they catch him?"

"That we don't know, I'm afraid. As for Cynthia, she seems unharmed. I'm afraid she couldn't tell us much, however."

"Did she see him kill Freddie, mum?" Mrs. Chubb asked fearfully.

"She saw him," Cecily said, "but she couldn't recognize him. He wore a knight's helmet and visor on his head."

"He's still lurking around, then," Mrs. Chubb murmured. "What if he's got hold of our Daisy, mum? She doesn't have any rich parents to hold to ransom. He wouldn't have any reason to keep her alive."

"Let's not jump to any conclusions," Cecily said quickly. "It could be that Daisy went to visit someone and decided to stay the night. I'll come down and talk to Doris just as soon as I am washed and dressed."

"Thank you, mum." Mrs. Chubb looked a little more relaxed. "I only hope you can do some good. As I said, it's going to be hard enough to manage without Daisy. If Doris can't work neither, we'll never get all the chores done. Gertie can't do it all by herself, and there's no one to watch the babies."

"Don't worry, Mrs. Chubb," Cecily said, doing her best to reassure the anxious woman. "I'm sure Daisy will return at any minute, and if needs be, I'll watch Gertie's twins myself. It's been a while since I've taken care of babies, but I'm sure I'll remember how."

The housekeeper actually smiled at that. "Gertie would be real honored, mum, that she would."

Cecily closed the door as Mrs. Chubb hurried down the hallway. She wished she could feel as optimistic as she'd sounded. She couldn't imagine why Daisy would stay out all night without a word to anyone, not even her sister.

It seemed more than likely that something had happened to her. Something that Cecily preferred not to dwell upon right then.

CHAPTER

❈ 16 ❈

To Cecily's dismay, Colonel Fortescue waylaid her as she reached the bottom of the stairs.

"Good morning, madam! Dashed nice day out there today, I must say. Hope it holds for the jolly old tournament, what?"

"Quite, Colonel," Cecily said as she tried to pass him. "If you will excuse me, I'm in a hurry—"

"Oh, won't keep you, old bean. Just wanted to tell you I had a word with her yesterday."

Cecily stared as the colonel laid a finger on his cheek and gave her an elaborate wink, followed immediately by a furious flapping of his lids.

"With whom, Colonel?" she inquired cautiously.

"Why, Betty . . . Bella . . . whatever her name is. The fiddle player, madam. You know the one."

Cecily wasn't quite sure whether he was winking or blinking. "Oh, you mean Miss Barrett," she said. For a moment she'd actually wondered if he could possibly know something important about the murder.

"Yes, old bean, Beryl Barrett, that's her name. Dashed if I know why I have trouble remembering that. Such a spiffing name, what?"

"Very," Cecily agreed. She hoped fervently that the colonel had not made a nuisance of himself again. She would have to ask Baxter to have a stern word with the lusty gentleman.

"Got a voice like a foghorn, though," the colonel said, absently twirling the end of his mustache. "Pity that. Be a bit of an earthshaker first thing in the morning, I'll be bound."

"I'm sorry, Colonel," Cecily said hastily, "I really must fly. I have something very important to take care of in the kitchen."

"In the kitchen?" Colonel Fortescue blinked at her. "Oh, don't let me keep you, old girl."

She slipped past him but had barely gone two steps before he called out after her. "I say, old bean, you don't happen to have something to cure bad breath, do you?"

Cecily paused, to look back at him. "I've heard that mint leaves work very well, Colonel. I'll ask Mrs. Chubb. She'll know how to help you."

"Oh, it's not for me, old girl. Dashed clean breath, I have, if I say so myself. No, it's for my fiddle player, Bella whatever her name is. Breath strong enough to fell a blasted elephant at five feet, by Jove. Have to cure that before I slap one on the old kisser, what?"

Cecily curbed her tongue. "I'll see what I can do, Colonel," she said quietly, then fled across the lobby before he could delay her any longer.

When she approached the kitchen a few minutes later, she

could hear Michel crashing pots about while Mrs. Chubb raised her voice to be heard above the din. Doris's voice could be plainly heard, sounding close to hysteria.

Pushing open the door, Cecily saw the young housemaid cowering by the stove while the housekeeper did her best to console the girl.

Catching sight of Cecily, Mrs. Chubb said firmly, "Madam's here now, Doris, so you'd better pull yourself together this minute. She needs to know exactly what happened last night."

Doris's eyes looked puffy, and dark red blotches covered her face. She managed a wobbly curtsey and held a hand over her mouth to stifle her sobs.

"Come and sit down at the table, Doris," Cecily said kindly. "Mrs. Chubb, please warm up some milk and put a large spoonful of brandy into it."

"Yes, mum." The housekeeper flew into the pantry while Michel busied himself at the stove, taking a good deal more care with the pots now that madam was in the kitchen.

Doris moved to the table and sat on the edge of a chair. "I don't know what I shall do without Daisy, mum," she said between sobs. "She's in terrible danger, I know it. I can feel it. I'll never be able to sing at the ball tomorrow night, knowing she could be dead."

Cecily waited for yet another storm of tears to pass before saying quietly, "What time did Daisy go out, Doris?"

"It were about half past eight, mum, if I remember rightly. It was dark, I know. Daisy was just going to walk along the seafront. I had to polish the silver, so I couldn't go with her." Doris uttered a shuddering sigh. "I wish I had now. He wouldn't have been able to grab us both, would he?"

"Doris," Cecily said, trying to sound convincing, "I doubt very much if the killer has your sister. Cynthia Chalmsford escaped from him last night, but it was past midnight when she reached the Esplanade. If Daisy had been kidnapped by him, Cynthia would have known it."

Doris sniffed, looking doubtfully at Cecily. "Do you really think so?"

"I really think so." Cecily patted the girl's arm. "Now tell me, does Daisy know anyone in the village she might have gone to visit?"

Doris shook her head, tears spurting from her eyes again. "No one, mum. That's what has me so worried."

Cecily looked up as Mrs. Chubb set a cup of milk in front of Doris.

"I don't know what's keeping Samuel," the housekeeper said worriedly. "I sent word that he was to come here right away."

"I'm sure he'll be here any minute," Cecily assured her. "You can get on with your work, Mrs. Chubb. Doris will be feeling better in a minute or two, I'm sure."

"Yes, mum, I will," Doris said, looking as if she would fall in a dead faint at the slightest provocation.

"Very well, mum. I'll get up to the rooms and make sure they're ready for the visitors." The housekeeper hurried to the door. "You will let me know if there's any news of Daisy?"

"Of course," Cecily promised. She turned back to Doris as the housekeeper left. "Drink your milk," she ordered the girl. "It will make you feel better."

Doris obediently sipped, pulling a face as she did so. "It burns," she said, putting down the cup.

"That is my best cognac," Michel said from the stove. "It does not burn, it warms ze cockles of ze heart, that ees all."

"Try it again." Cecily glanced at the clock on the mantelpiece above the fireplace. "It will make you feel better, I promise."

The door opened abruptly just then, and Cecily turned her head to see Samuel rush in.

"Oh, good morning, mum," he said, sounding flustered. "Sorry I'm late. Had a bit of trouble with the horses this morning."

"Nothing serious, I hope?" That's all she needed, Cecily thought.

"No, mum." Samuel dragged his cap off his head with a sheepish smile. "Just frisky, that's all. They haven't been the same since Freddie died."

At that Doris uttered a moan of anguish.

Samuel looked at her in surprise. "What's the matter with her, then?"

"Daisy didn't come home last night," Cecily said, giving Samuel a look that warned him to be careful what he said.

"Strewth," Samuel muttered.

"Cynthia Chalmsford did, however, return to us. I want you to fetch the constable, Samuel, as soon as possible, please. You will have to hurry, as you will have to be back in time to meet the London train."

"Yes, mum." Samuel hesitated, obviously longing to ask questions, then thought better of it. Without another word, he spun around and hurried out of the door.

Cecily turned back to Doris, who had drained her cup. She was relieved to see a faint color returning to the young housemaid's cheeks.

"I must pay Cynthia another visit," she said, rising to her feet. "I want you to get on with your work now, Doris. It will help to keep your mind off things. Just do your very best not to worry. I know it's hard, but Mrs. Chubb really needs your help right now."

"Yes, mum." Doris got up from her chair, dashing a hand across her eyes. "I'll do me best, mum."

Cecily left her at the sink, half-heartedly peeling potatoes. She felt sorry for the girl. It would be tragic indeed if some harm had befallen Daisy. She doubted that Doris would ever recover from the loss.

Giving herself a mental shake, Cecily hurried up the stairs to the Chalmsfords' suite. There was no point in borrowing trouble. She would just have to wait and hope that, like Cynthia, Daisy would return unscathed.

Lady Chalmsford looked quite rested when Cecily saw

her a few minutes later in spite of the traumatic events of the
night before. Upon hearing that Cecily wished to question
her daughter further, she invited her into the suite without
hesitation.

Cynthia sat on the window seat, gazing out at the ocean,
when Cecily entered the room. She turned her face as Cecily
spoke her name and looked at her with huge, fearful eyes.

Although her color had returned, the child still appeared
to be fighting some inner horror, and Cecily had the distinct
feeling that she hadn't heard the entire story as yet.

"How are you feeling this morning, Cynthia?" she asked
as the child continued to stare at her with an odd look of
panic in her eyes.

"I am quite well, thank you," Cynthia said nervously.

Cecily gave her a reassuring smile. "I have one or two
more questions for you," she said, "and then I'll let you
rest."

"Actually, we plan to meet my husband in the gardens in
a short while," Lady Chalmsford said. "We thought it would
do her good to play outside for a while, rather than be
cooped up in this room."

"I'm sure it will," Cecily said, watching the child closely.
"Cynthia, all I want to know is whether you remember
seeing anyone else before you escaped from the bad man."

Cynthia shook her head.

"No one at all? You didn't see a young girl with light
brown hair?"

"May I ask what this is all about?" Lady Chalmsford sat
down next to her daughter and put a protective arm about
her shoulders.

"One of our housemaids, Daisy, failed to return home last
night," Cecily said, taking her gaze from Cynthia for a
moment. "We were wondering if Cynthia might have seen
her."

To her dismay, Cynthia abruptly burst into tears. "I don't
know," she kept repeating, her voice getting more and more
shrill. "I don't know. I don't know."

"Hush, child," Lady Chalmsford murmured. "It's all right. No one is going to hurt you now." She looked back at Cecily. "I'm sorry, Mrs. Sinclair. I'm afraid she is still very upset. I really don't think she can tolerate any more questions."

The child certainly seemed agitated, almost to the point of hysteria. Cecily reluctantly left them alone together, after expressing the hope that Cynthia would feel well enough to speak with the constable when he arrived.

She would have liked to ask a few more questions, Cecily thought as she made her way downstairs. She couldn't escape the conviction that Cynthia Chalmsford knew a great deal more than she had told anyone.

It was doubtful that P. C. Northcott would get any more out of the child. Cecily would have given a great deal to know what was going on in Cynthia's mind right then.

She was still pondering the problem when she reached the lobby. Head down, deep in thought, she almost ran into Roland Young, who had halted in front of her, barring her way.

"I'm going to need some more paint to finish the outside," he announced as she pulled up with a start of surprise.

"I'll let Mr. Baxter know," she said, nettled by his tone. "Have you finished with the rooms?"

"Yes, ma'am. All done, they are."

"Well, I'm happy to hear that. As a matter of fact, I've been meaning to have a word with you."

Roland Young gave her an ugly look. "What about?"

"About your singing. I received a complaint from one of the guests. It might be as well to refrain from singing while you work, since the noise could disturb other people."

"I ain't going to disturb no one but the birds outside now, am I?" Roland Young said nastily. He turned away, then looked back at her, adding as an afterthought, "Ma'am."

She watched him cross the lobby to the door and made a

firm promise to herself that he would never set foot inside the hotel again.

She couldn't imagine why Baxter should see fit to hire such a young ruffian, but she was going to find out. Thinking about Baxter, she wondered whether he'd heard the news about Daisy yet.

She must let him know at once, she thought, hurrying down the passageway to his office. P. C. Northcott would likely arrive shortly, and it wouldn't do for Baxter to be unaware that one of his staff was missing.

She found him in his office, studying a ledger sheet covered with figures. Judging by the frown on his face, the hotel's financial picture had not improved greatly of late.

He received the news about Daisy with well-controlled apprehension. "I suppose we shall have to send for that simpleton of a constable again," he muttered.

"I have already done so," Cecily assured him. "Samuel left a short while ago to fetch him."

As always, he had insisted on remaining on his feet. Seated on a chair in front of his desk, she watched him rest the fingers of one hand against his eyelids for a moment. "I hope to God nothing has happened to that young girl," he said with such feeling that her heart went out to him.

"We are all praying she is unharmed." No matter what his inner anguish was about, she longed to go to him and offer him the comfort of her arms. "There is something else I wanted to ask you," she said, forcing her mind back to a less hazardous topic.

He lowered his hand and looked down at her, his face weary. "I trust it is not more questions about my health?"

"No," she said with just a trace of resentment, "it is not. I wanted to ask you why you hired such an unpleasant young man to do the repair work on the hotel. Whatever happened to that nice young man who mended the wall in the roof garden?"

"He went the way of most of the young men in this

village," Baxter said wearily. "He has moved to the city to find work."

"Ah." Cecily nodded. "So you are saying that Roland Young was the only person you could find to do the job?"

"No, I was explaining what happened to Ben Parkinson."

Cecily frowned. "Ben Parkinson?"

"The young man who mended the wall."

She gave him a look of exasperation. "Baxter, sometimes you can be quite trying."

"Yes, madam."

"Well, I certainly hope that Roland Young is not the only laborer available next time we need some work done. I really don't want him in this hotel again. He is arrogant, rude, and a little threatening. In fact, if that nice Mr. Kern hadn't furnished him with an alibi the afternoon Freddie was murdered, I might well have suspected him of being the culprit."

She was quite taken aback when Baxter said, "I quite agree, madam. I have to admit to letting my personal feelings interfere with my good judgment."

She stared at him for a moment in silence. "Your personal feelings?" she said at last. "You are personally acquainted with this young man?"

"In a manner of speaking," Baxter said, absently shuffling through the papers on his desk.

Cecily sighed, knowing full well that if she wanted to know the entire story, she would have to drag it out of him piece by piece.

She was tempted to forget it, except that now she was burning with curiosity. Maybe, just maybe, this could be the answer to the questions that had been plaguing her lately. Perhaps she would learn what it was that demanded such a momentous decision from him.

"I do trust I haven't insulted a member of your family," she said, hazarding a wild guess.

"No, madam. Roland Young is not a member of my

family. As a matter of fact, it was his father with whom I was acquainted."

"Was?"

"He died a few months ago."

She was immediately contrite. "Oh, Baxter, I am sorry. I didn't mean to pry—"

"No apology is necessary, madam. Raymond Young was not a particular friend of mine."

"I see," she said, not seeing at all.

"I felt sorry for the young man," Baxter said after a lengthy pause.

"Because his father died?"

"Because the young man is in desperate need of money."

"He has to support a wife and children?" For some reason she couldn't imagine Roland Young as a father.

"No, he is supporting his ailing mother. He has trouble finding enough work in the village, and he doesn't like to work too far away from home in case his mother should need him."

"Well," Cecily said in amazement, "it would seem as if I have misjudged the young man."

"He has an unfortunate attitude," Baxter said, apparently finding what he was looking for among the scattered papers. He lifted the sheet and studied it intently.

"He does, indeed," Cecily said feelingly. "It's no wonder he can't find enough work. Someone should set that young man down and explain a few things about manners to him."

"I have a strong suspicion it wouldn't be of much use," Baxter moved over to the filing cabinet and tucked the paper inside one of the drawers.

"I have to agree." Cecily thought about asking for a cigar, then changed her mind. This was the first time in days that she'd had a relaxed conversation with Baxter, in spite of the subject matter. She wasn't about to risk interrupting that quite yet. "I do feel for him, though. It is a terrible thing to lose a parent. Almost as bad as losing a child."

She felt a stab of pain at the thought of Freddie. She

thought of each of her staff as a member of her family. To lose one of them was like losing a relative. Now Daisy was missing. Already the twins had earned a place in her heart. She couldn't bear the thought of losing one of them.

"It was rather a bizarre accident," Baxter said, almost as if he were talking to himself.

For a moment she had lost the thread of the conversation, her mind wandering to Michael and the absence of news. She realized now that he was still talking about Roland Young's father. "How did he die, then?" she asked, her mind still dwelling on the whereabouts of Daisy.

"He was walking through the woods alone, as he often did," Baxter said, gathering up the rest of the papers into a neat pile. "It was shortly after that violent thunderstorm we had late last year."

"Yes, I remember," Cecily said with a shudder. "It was during that time those poor gypsy girls were being so brutally murdered."

"Yes, well, the storm apparently damaged the branches of several trees. Raymond Young was walking through the woods the following morning, when one of the branches, weakened by the storm, snapped clean off and plunged to the ground."

"Oh, dear. The branch hit the poor man, I suppose."

"Raymond Young looked up at the sound," Baxter continued as if she hadn't spoken. "The branch hit him square in the chest, piercing his heart. He died instantly."

Cecily sat very still. There it was. All this time she'd had the feeling that she had the clues, and now they had all fallen into place. The last little piece, delivered straight into her lap, so to speak.

Staring up at her manager, she said quietly, "Baxter, I do believe I know who killed Freddie."

CHAPTER
❖ 17 ❖

"I must talk to Cynthia again right away," Cecily told a startled Baxter as she rose to her feet. "Before P.C. Northcott gets here. If he should arrive before I am finished with the child, please do your best to delay him until I return."

"I trust you are going to tell me the name of the murderer, madam," Baxter said plaintively as she hurried to the door.

"Not until I am absolutely certain." Cecily looked back at him. "Don't worry, Baxter. If I'm right, we shall have the culprit under lock and key very soon now."

"You will take care, madam?"

She smiled at him, warmed by his concern. "Of course. I shall be perfectly safe. Please don't worry." She left him, wishing she could share her suspicions with him. It was not her practice, however, to accuse someone without positive proof. Though in this case, proof might be difficult to obtain. It would more likely have to be a confession.

Reaching the lobby, she cast an anxious eye about. P.C. Northcott, it seemed, had not as yet arrived, unless he was in the kitchen. She could only hope that she could accomplish her mission before he came in search of her or attempted to speak with Cynthia.

The long climb up the stairs seemed endless, but at last she reached the third landing. As she had hoped, Doris was in one of the suites, laying the fire. After quickly explaining what she wanted, Cecily waited in a fever of impatience for the girl to finish the task before leading her to the Chalmsfords' suite.

She tapped several times on the door before accepting the fact that the suite was empty. Cynthia had to be in the gardens with her parents already.

Heart sinking, Cecily once more headed for the stairs, with Doris trailing behind her. Her chances of forestalling the constable were diminishing by the minute.

Reaching the bottom of the stairs, Cecily had to wait with mounting frustration until Doris caught up with her.

"I'm sorry to be so slow, mum," Doris said, panting a little. "It's me feet what's to blame."

Cecily looked down at the girl's shoes. "What's wrong with your feet?"

"Me shoes don't fit very good," Doris said, looking sheepish. "They pinch me toes."

Taking the girl's arm, Cecily hurried her to the door. "They fit you when you first had them, didn't they?"

"No, mum. I was scared to say anything, in case Mrs. Chubb took them back and I wouldn't get no more."

Cecily rolled her eyes heavenward. "Good gracious, child, you can't walk around all day in shoes that pinch. I'll have a word with Mrs. Chubb and make sure you have the right shoes."

"Yes, mum," Doris said breathlessly. "Thank you, mum."

Cecily paused at the front door and looked cautiously out.

The Esplanade was quite busy that morning. A pair of nannies, pushing perambulators side by side, were chatting together as they propelled their tiny charges along the seafront.

Three motorcars, one behind the other, chugged majestically down the street while a young man took his life in his hands darting among them.

Farther down the street, coming toward them at a brisk pace, was a chestnut drawing a trap. Even from that distance, Cecily recognized Samuel's straight back and the jaunty angle of his cap.

"Quickly," she said to Doris, "we must hurry and find Cynthia and her parents before Samuel gets here."

"Do you really think Cynthia knows where Daisy is, mum?" Doris asked as she huffed and puffed alongside Cecily.

"I really think she does," Cecily answered, her gaze scanning the lush lawns that tomorrow would be torn and churned up by the sharp hooves of the horses. "We must be very careful to do exactly as I told you, however, if we are to find out anything. She is a very frightened little girl, and unless we take care, she could refuse to utter a word."

"Yes, mum," Doris said, stepping up her pace. "Don't worry, mum, I know what to do. I just hope she tells us, that's all."

Cecily silently echoed that sentiment as she strode across the bowling green to the fishpond. Pausing at the edge of the rock garden, she held up her hand. In the distance the soft sound of a child's high-pitched voice carried on the morning breeze.

"The pavilion, I think," Cecily announced, setting off in that direction. "I should have thought of that. They will be sheltered from the wind there."

Making sure Doris was close behind her, Cecily hurried across the grass. The damp hem of her skirt flapped about her ankles, but she ignored the discomfort in her haste to reach the child.

As she drew near, she could see Cynthia tossing a ball in the air, while Lord and Lady Chalmsford, seated side by side inside the pavilion, watched her without speaking.

Cecily paused, giving Doris time to catch up with her. Then together they approached the little girl.

Cynthia looked up as they drew closer, her eyes widening as she stared at Doris.

"Hello, Cynthia," Cecily said cheerfully. "I found Daisy after all, and I brought her to meet you. She wants to talk to you, don't you, Daisy?"

Doris nodded and took a step toward the child. She opened her mouth to speak, but at that moment Cynthia uttered an ear-piercing shriek.

"You're supposed to be dead," she screamed, pointing a finger at Doris. "I saw you fall over the cliff. You're supposed to be dead!"

"The constable isn't here," an astounded Baxter protested, springing to his feet as Cecily burst unceremoniously into his office demanding to talk to P.C. Northcott.

"Well, where is he, then?" She fought for breath as Baxter continued to stare at her with growing apprehension in his face.

"Samuel couldn't find him, madam. He's most likely out on the Downs with his men, waiting for the kidnapper."

"I saw Samuel a little while ago," Cecily said, fighting her frustration.

"He returned to the hotel in order to meet the train, madam. He left word for the constable to come to the hotel immediately upon his return."

"Then we shall just have to go without him." Cecily headed for the door, then looked back at him. "For heaven's sake, Baxter, don't stand there looking at me. We have to get up to the Downs right away. I only hope and pray we are not too late."

"Madam, if you are planning to catch the murderer single-handedly, I strongly suggest—"

"You can strongly suggest all you like, Baxter, but do it on the way, please. I will explain everything on our way there."

To her intense relief, he followed her to the door. Quickly she recounted the events of the morning and her suspicions. Baxter uttered not one word while he listened.

Samuel had already left with a footman to pick up the visitors arriving for the weekend. Cecily waited anxiously as Baxter harnessed the remaining horse and trap, and then scrambled in before he had a chance to assist her.

For once he did not argue when she insisted on leaving the canopy down. As they set off at a fast clip, she tied her scarf under her chin to anchor her hat and buttoned her coat.

"Perhaps we shall meet the constables on the Downs," Baxter said over his shoulder as the bay trotted smartly down the Esplanade.

"I certainly hope so—" Cecily broke off, staring down the street ahead of them in disbelief.

"Baxter, do you see that man and woman riding toward us on the black horse?"

"Yes, madam. It isn't often one sees a couple riding together nowadays."

"That's Lord Withersgill," Cecily said, her excitement growing. "And I do believe . . . Baxter! That's Daisy riding with him."

"Upon my word, so it is, madam." Baxter tugged on the reins, bringing the snorting animal to a halt as the rider and his passenger passed by without apparently noticing them.

Lord Withersgill, Cecily noticed, looked as immaculate and elegant as he had appeared in Dr. Prestwick's office. Daisy, on the other hand, seated in front of him, was covered in mud, her hair matted with the stuff, and she wore a bemused, almost dazed expression on her face.

"Turn the trap around, Baxter," Cecily said sharply. "We must get back to the hotel immediately."

The horse was already turning as she spoke.

Although they raced back to the Pennyfoot at a speed too

fast to be prudent, the debonair horseman had disappeared when they arrived. Hurrying into the lobby while Baxter returned the horse and trap, Cecily encountered Mrs. Chubb, her face wreathed in smiles.

"Oh, madam, I'm so glad you're back," she said as Cecily rushed over to her. "You'll never guess what happened. Daisy just wandered in here as right as rain."

"She is unharmed?" Cecily exclaimed in relief.

"She is indeed, mum. Very dirty she is and hasn't quite got hold of her wits as yet, but she says she's all right. Just a bit bewildered, that's all."

"Has she told you what happened to her?"

Mrs. Chubb shook her head. "No, mum. I didn't think it was a good time for questions. I sent her to her room to have a good wash. I was on my way to find Doris to tell her the good news."

"Very well, Mrs. Chubb. I'll wait for Daisy to clean herself up. Then I'd like to talk to her."

The housekeeper nodded. "I'll send her to the library, shall I, mum?"

"If you will, Mrs. Chubb. Thank you."

After the excitement of the past hour or two and the relief of knowing that Daisy was safe, Cecily was beginning to feel quite light-headed herself.

Heading for the library, Cecily sent up a silent prayer of thanks for Daisy's deliverance. She couldn't wait to find out how Lord Withersgill came to be involved.

Baxter joined her in the library a little while later. She barely had time to exchange a word or two with him before a light tap on the door announced Daisy's arrival.

She looked a different girl now that she had washed the mud from her face and hair. She appeared to have recovered from her trance and even managed a slight smile as Cecily led her to a chair at the long table.

"Do you feel like telling us what happened?" Cecily asked as Baxter took up his usual stance by the fireplace.

"Yes, mum," Daisy said, folding her hands in front of her.

"I feel a lot better now, thank you. For a while there I didn't think I was ever going to see the Pennyfoot again."

Her lower lip trembled for a moment. Then she appeared to recover herself.

"Take your time, Daisy," Cecily said, seating herself at the head of the table. "Just tell us in your own time exactly what happened from the moment you left the kitchen last night."

Daisy nodded, staring into space for a moment or two before beginning to speak in a low voice. "I went out to empty the ashes," she said, looking down at her hands. "It was getting dark, but my head felt like cotton wool, it was that fuzzy; so I was going to go for a walk along the seafront."

She shivered, and Cecily leaned forward in concern. "Are you cold?"

Daisy shook her head. "I was last night, though, and that's a fact."

"Go on," Cecily said gently. "What happened after you emptied the ashes?"

"Well, I was on me way across the yard when I saw someone trying to climb in the hotel through the pantry window. I thought it was a gypsy, and I was in two minds whether to rush back into the kitchen and tell someone or wait for the thief to come out." Daisy heaved a long sigh. "I should have gone back to the kitchen. Then none of this would have happened, but I was afraid the gypsy would get away. Mrs. Chubb was so cross with us already because food was missing, I thought she might not believe me if I said it was a gypsy what took the grub."

"So you waited for the gypsy to come back out of the window?"

"Yes, mum, I did. And I caught her and all. Only it wasn't a gypsy at all. It was Cynthia Chalmsford."

"I see," Cecily murmured.

"Well, mum, you could have knocked me down with a

feather when I saw who it was. There she was, all dirty and messy, with a sack in her arms stuffed with food."

"Did she say where she had been?" Cecily asked, exchanging a glance with Baxter.

"Yes, mum, she did." Daisy paused and cleared her throat. "She told me as how a bad man had taken her up to the Downs and hid her inside a cave at the bottom of the cliffs. She said as how he had made her come back to the hotel for food and that he said he would kill her if she didn't do what she was told, just like he killed Freddie."

Daisy shuddered at the memory. "She said she didn't know what he looked like or what his name was. She kept saying he had something on his head, like what knights wear. I don't understand that bit."

"So what did you do then?" Cecily prompted, as Daisy paused.

"Well, I told her we should tell someone at once. I said as how the police would capture the man and then he couldn't hurt no one no more. Not even her."

Cecily nodded her approval. "What did she say to that?"

"She said that the man told her that if she wasn't back by nine o'clock, he was going to move to another hiding place so no one could find him. Then he was going to wait until he had a chance to come after her and kill her. She said as how there wasn't no time to tell no one, because she had to be back by nine o'clock or he'd be gone, and the police wouldn't find him before he came to kill her."

She paused for breath, and Baxter muttered, "Ingenious."

"Indeed," Cecily murmured, giving him a warning look. "So you agreed not to tell anyone?"

"Yes, mum. I couldn't think what else to do since there wasn't a lot of time left. So I made up this plan. I told Miss Cynthia that I'd go back to the Downs with her. She could show me the hiding place, then go back there with the food while I came back here for help."

"What did Cynthia say to that?"

"Well, she wasn't too sure about it at first. But when I told her as how I couldn't let her go back there without knowing where she was going, she said it was all right. I knew she was frightened because she kept crying, but I didn't know what else to do. I didn't have no time to think proper. That was the trouble."

"It's all right," Cecily said soothingly as the girl's voice rose. "You did the right thing. Now, what happened when you went back with Cynthia?"

"Well, mum, it was right creepy, I can tell you," Daisy said with a shudder. "There we was, out on the Downs in the dark—it were that foggy I could hardly see me hand in front of me face. I was scared silly, so I knew Miss Cynthia had to be scared. She had to go back to that man. At least I didn't have to do that."

She paused as her yawn interrupted her words. "Oh, sorry, mum," she muttered, "I didn't get any sleep last night."

"I don't suppose you did," Cecily said, glancing at Baxter. "Anyway, tell us what happened next."

"Well, there we was, creeping across the Downs toward the cliffs with the sea crashing about on the sands. I asked Miss Cynthia how we was going to get to the cave, and she said as how there was a path what went down the side of the cliffs to the beach." Daisy stopped talking and stared into space, her hands clenching as if she were facing the horror all over again.

"Take your time, Daisy," Cecily said, reaching out to pat the girl's arm.

Daisy started, then focused on Cecily's face. Her voice was hushed when she spoke again. "Cynthia pointed down the cliffs and said as that was where the path was. I leaned over to take a look and the next thing I knew . . ." Daisy swallowed twice. "Someone gave me a hard shove in the back, and over I went."

A tense silence followed her words. Baxter's face registered shock, pity, and disgust in rapid succession as Cecily watched him.

"I could've easily been killed," Daisy said, her voice shaking.

"But you weren't." Cecily covered the housemaid's cold hands with one of hers. "How did you manage to save yourself?"

Daisy shrugged. "I don't know. I was just lucky, I s'pose. One minute I was falling, and the next I landed on a ledge so hard it knocked all the wind out of me. I sort of grabbed a hold of some grass what was growing out of the cliff and hung onto it. All night I was there, afraid to move or go to sleep in case I fell off the ledge." She drew in a long breath. "I prayed a lot," she said, looking at Cecily with wide eyes. "I reckon He heard me."

"I believe He must have done." Cecily smiled and patted the small hands. "How did you manage to climb back up the cliffs?"

"I didn't." Daisy's expression changed, growing softer. "I watched the sun come up," she said, her voice tinged with awe. "It were a beautiful sight, I can tell you. I kept thinking all night I weren't never going to see the sun again. Then I got scared again, thinking maybe no one would ever see me, and I'd die up there on that ledge or fall off into the sea."

"It must have been dreadful for you," Cecily murmured.

"It were, mum, I can tell you. Until I heard the horse coming. I could hear the hoofbeats long before it got close to me. By then I was screaming at the top of me lungs."

"Ah," Cecily said, nodding. "You were rescued by the young man."

Daisy looked surprised. "How did you know?"

"We passed you on the Esplanade when he brought you home."

"You did? I never saw you." Daisy clasped her hands together and stared dreamily into space. "I never saw much at all, tell the truth. It were so wonderful, sitting up there on his horse. He was so brave, climbing down like that to rescue me. Used his horse, he did, to pull me back up."

She came back to earth, her face heating as she met

Cecily's gaze. "Never had much time for men," she said awkwardly, "but he was a proper gentleman, that he was. Nobody's ever treated me like that. He was so nice and so gentle . . ." Her voice died on a sigh.

"He obviously made a good impression on you," Cecily said, smiling. "Our new lord of the manor has at least one enthusiastic advocate."

Daisy's eyes grew wide again. "Lord of the manor?" she repeated faintly.

"Yes, Daisy. Your rescuer was none other than the new Lord Withersgill." Cecily almost laughed at the girl's thunderstruck expression.

"Strewth," Daisy whispered. "Wait 'til I tell Doris. She'll have a pink fit, she will."

"I dare say she will," Cecily agreed.

Daisy shook her head, as if trying to clear her thoughts. "It must have been the murderer what shoved me," she said, traces of her earlier fear returning to her eyes. "I never saw him come up behind me in the dark. What do you think he'll do to Cynthia, now that he knows she told on him?"

"It was the killer who pushed you," Cecily said gently. "You did, however, see who it was. The person who killed Freddie and who pushed you over the cliff was the same person who led you up onto the Downs. I'm afraid, Doris, that our killer is Cynthia Chalmsford."

CHAPTER

❖ 18 ❖

"You'll never believe who pushed me over that cliff," Daisy said a little later as she joined Doris in the dining room to help her lay the tables for lunch.

Doris paused with a bundle of forks in her hand. "No, who was it, then?" she asked, staring at her sister. She still couldn't believe how close she had come to losing Daisy. Her stomach felt squiggly inside every time she thought about it.

"It were that Miss Cynthia Chalmsford all the time. She waited until I was leaning over the cliff, and then she shoved me over."

Doris gasped in horror. "That little kid? What'd she go and do that for?"

"I don't really know yet," Daisy admitted. "Madam said

as how she was going to talk to her, and she'd tell me everything later." She looked over her shoulder to see if anyone was around. "You'll never guess what," she whispered. "If I tell you, you've got to swear you'll keep your mouth shut. Madam said I wasn't to tell no one until she'd talked to the constable."

"I swear," Doris said fearfully, wondering what was coming next.

"All right." Daisy looked around at the empty tables again and then whispered, "Madam says that Cynthia killed Freddie, too."

"Oo, 'eck," Doris whispered. Her tummy felt really cold inside. "How could a little kid like her kill someone?"

Daisy shrugged. "Don't know. All I know is what madam told me. I reckon we'll find out soon enough, after she's talked to the constable."

"I still can't believe it," Doris said, shaking her head. "Fancy a little kid like her. She almost killed you as well."

"Yeah, I know," Daisy said, carefully placing knives at the side of the placemat. "She didn't, though, did she."

Doris looked at her sister with curiosity. "You never did tell me about the man what rescued you."

Daisy's face lit up. "No, I didn't, did I. That were another shock, let me tell you."

"What, that somebody rescued you?"

"No, silly." A closed expression crept over Daisy's face, as if she were hugging a special secret.

Doris stared at her suspiciously. "Well, what, then?"

"I meant it were a shock to know who he was."

"You said you didn't know who it was." Doris raised her eyes to the ceiling and clasped her hands to her bosom. Mimicking Daisy's voice, she said breathlessly, "He were such a handsome man and such a gentleman. To think I shall never know his name . . ." She looked back at her sister. "That's what you said when Mrs. Chubb asked you about him."

Daisy nodded, smiling in a way Doris had never seen her

smile before. "I know who he is now, though," she said in the same dreamy way she'd talked to Mrs. Chubb. " Madam told me. She saw him bring me home on his horse."

Doris slapped a fork down on the table. "So who is he, then?"

"He's the new lord of the manor, Lord Withersgill. That's who."

Doris jerked her chin up to stare at her sister. "Go on! I don't believe you. You're having me on."

"I am not. You ask madam if you don't believe me." Daisy poked her nose in the air. "I was riding on a horse in front of Lord Withersgill, and he had his arms clasped around me waist. It were real romantic, I can tell you."

Doris felt a strong urge to throw the forks at her. "It's not fair," she muttered, turning her back on Daisy. "Why couldn't it have been me what met him? You don't care nothing about men, and you go and meet a toff. All I ever seem to met is stupid, poor, common buggers like Roland Young."

"What about that American man what follows you about?" Daisy asked slyly. "He looks nice."

"He's nothing, is he," Doris muttered. "He's a foreigner. Besides, he's a lot older than me."

"That don't make no difference." Daisy gathered up the rest of the knives and danced across to the next table. "Just wait 'til you get on the stage. You'll have all sorts of men hanging around the stage door. Old and young ones, fat and thin . . ."

"And rich, I hope." Doris sighed. "But I've got to get on the stage first."

"Well, you've got a start tomorrow night, don't you? You never know who'll be there."

"Yeah," Doris said, beginning to feel more cheerful. "Per'aps Lord Withersgill will be out there. He'll hear me sing and immediately whisk me off to Piccadilly."

Daisy dropped her knives with a clatter. "Blimey! Do you think he will be here tomorrow night?"

Doris studied her sister's flushed face and felt yet another sharp pang of envy. "Who knows?" she said, shrugging. "All I know is, I got to sing me song. I just hope they don't throw Lydia off the stage before she has a chance to play for me."

"I hope so, too," Daisy said, giving her sister a rare smile. "You're good, you are, and everyone will love your singing, you'll see."

Doris felt her resentment slipping away. "I'm really glad you got rescued," she said. "I don't know what I would have done if you'd been killed."

Daisy looked embarrassed. "I'm glad I did, too. I was really scared, I don't mind telling you."

"So was I." Doris put her arm about her sister's shoulders and gave her an affectionate squeeze. "I'm really glad that Lord Withersgill came along when he did and saved you." She meant it, too. Only she just wished it could have been her instead.

"I'm so sorry to disturb you again," Cecily said when Lord Chalmsford opened the door of his suite. "I wonder if I might have another word with Cynthia?"

"I really don't see—" Lord Chalmsford began, but his wife's voice interrupted him.

"Is that Mrs. Sinclair? Do ask her in, dear."

Taking advantage of the man's hesitation, Cecily marched into the room, closely followed by Baxter. She saw Cynthia at once, huddled on the window seat with a book on her lap. She was scribbling in it with a red crayon.

Lady Chalmsford came toward Cecily with a smile. "Have you had any news about my necklace, Mrs. Sinclair? I am most anxious now to retrieve it."

"Not as yet, I'm afraid," Cecily said, glancing at Baxter. "I do feel quite sure, however, that the pendant will be returned to you in the very near future."

She looked across the room at the child. "Hello, Cynthia."

The little girl went on scribbling as if she hadn't heard her.

"Cynthia," Lady Chalmsford said sharply. "Please have the manners to answer when someone speaks to you."

Cynthia looked up, her face tight and drawn. "Hello, Mrs. Sinclair," she said politely.

"Do you feel like talking to me now?" Cecily asked, moving slowly toward her.

The little girl shook her head and drew back in her seat as if afraid someone would attack her.

"Really," Lord Chalmsford said, sounding a trifle testy, "I think the child has been through enough. She must have told you everything she knows."

"Not quite everything, I'm afraid, Lord Chalmsford," Cecily murmured, keeping her gaze fixed on Cynthia. "Have you, Cynthia?"

The child backed even further into the corner, her face frozen in fear.

Feeling desperately sorry for the child, Cecily drew closer. "No one is going to hurt you, Cynthia, I promise, just as long as you tell us the truth."

"Mrs. Sinclair—" Lord Chalmsford began, but again his wife interrupted him.

"Hush, darling. I am quite sure Mrs. Sinclair would not insist unless it was something very important."

Cecily flashed her a grateful smile. "Thank you, milady." She looked back at Cynthia. "I want you to tell me, Cynthia, where you were when you saw Freddie come into the stables."

For a long time the little girl stared at Cecily with terrified eyes. The only sounds in the room were the ticking of the clock on the mantelpiece and Lord Chalmsford's harsh breathing.

Finally he said in a voice curt with impatience, "You've already told us once, Cynthia. Tell Mrs. Sinclair again."

The child's eyes flickered at her father before she whispered, "In the loft."

Aware that she must proceed with extreme care, Cecily said quietly, "You were playing with the equipment for the tournament, weren't you, Cynthia?"

The little girl nodded.

"And then you saw Freddie come in."

Again the child nodded, her lower lip beginning to tremble.

"He didn't have anyone with him, did he, Cynthia? You didn't really see a man with a knight's helmet on, did you?"

Cynthia shook her head and began digging the crayon into the book, tearing the page.

"Are you telling me you lied, child?" Lord Chalmsford said, taking a step forward.

Again fear flashed in the little girl's eyes.

"Lord Chalmsford," Cecily said, keeping between father and daughter, "perhaps it would be better if I handle this for now."

"Oh, do sit down, Geoffrey," Lady Chalmsford said irritably. "Allow Mrs. Sinclair to finish, if you please."

The irate man looked as if he was about to argue. Behind her, Cecily heard Baxter clear his throat. Turning her head, she saw him take two steps forward. She gave him an almost imperceptible shake of her head in warning.

To her relief, Lord Chalmsford muttered something under his breath and sat down heavily on the elegant tapestry ottoman.

"Now, Cynthia," Cecily said after silence once more settled over the room, "Freddie came into the stables. Did he see you playing in the loft?"

Cynthia nodded.

"Did he speak to you?"

Again the child nodded.

Cecily felt exceedingly thankful for all the years she'd spent dragging information out of Baxter. The practice would serve her well now. "What did Freddie say to you, Cynthia?"

"He was cross," Cynthia said, darting a wary look at her

father. "He told me to come down at once or he would come up there to get me. He frightened me."

"What did you do? Did you try to run away?"

Cynthia nodded, tears welling up in her eyes. "I jumped up, and my foot banged into the spears. One of them fell off and . . . and . . . it hit Freddie." She burst into noisy tears, and Lady Chalmsford rushed to her side, while Lord Chalmsford swore and rose to his feet.

Turning a white, shocked face toward Cecily, Lady Chalmsford said, almost pleadingly, "I'm sure she didn't do it on purpose, Mrs. Sinclair."

Cecily nodded. "I'm quite sure she didn't." Speaking once more to Cynthia, she added, "Don't cry, Cynthia, nobody is going to blame you for hurting Freddie. Just tell us what you did next."

The child gulped, then mumbled, "I climbed down, and he was lying on the ground with the spear sticking out of him, and he was bleeding so I knew he was hurt and I . . ." She paused with a loud sniff, and Lady Chalmsford produced a handkerchief for her daughter.

"Go on, precious," she said, patting the child's trembling hand. "Tell Mrs. Sinclair all of it."

"I didn't know if he was dead yet, so I tucked him up like I do my dollies to make him comfy, and then I found the magic dust in my pocket that Miss Pengrath gave me, so I sprinkled some on Freddie to make him all better."

Lord Chalmsford groaned while Cynthia's mother hugged the little girl. "It's all right, precious," she said. "We'll take care of you."

"Why did you run away, Cynthia?" Cecily asked, feeling immensely sorry for the stricken parents. They had been through so much in the last few days. This latest revelation had to be devastating for them.

"I was afraid what everyone would do to me if Freddie didn't get better," Cynthia said, casting another terrified look at her father. "I just ran and ran, and I saw the trap all hooked up to the horse, and I climbed inside and made him go fast. He went all the way up to the Downs before he stopped."

"How did you find the cave?" Cecily asked, amazed that the child had managed to take the trap that far.

"Daddy showed it to me when we were here last summer." Cynthia uttered a shuddering sigh. "I climbed down the cliffs to get to it. I almost fell lots of times."

"Oh, my dear Lord," Lady Chalmsford whispered, holding her daughter close.

"So it was that cave," Lord Chalmsford muttered. "I'd forgotten all about it."

"So you hid in the cave," Cecily prompted as the child looked anxiously at her father.

Cynthia nodded. "Then I got really, really hungry. I didn't eat all night or all day and my tummy hurt, so I came all the way back to the hotel to get some food."

"And no one saw you?" Cecily asked, wondering what the child would say if she knew she'd been hiding at the end of the passageway that ran beneath the hotel.

"I didn't see anyone, but I heard them talking. I climbed in the pantry window, and I heard Mrs. Chubb and Gertie talking about a bad man who had taken me away and was going to keep me until Mummy and Daddy gave him some money."

"So that's where you got the idea," Cecily said softly.

Lady Chalmsford stared at her in amazement. "Cynthia, did you write that ransom note yourself?"

The child nodded. "I found a big picture of the tournament on the wall, and I tore it down and wrote the words with my crayon." She held the crayon up for her mother to see. "I didn't know how much money to ask for, so I put the necklace down as well, because I really liked it."

"Oh, my," Lady Chalmsford murmured, her hand straying to her throat.

"I said to put the money in the tree, and then I put the note in the stables. I was going to wait for the money and take it and then pretend the bad man let me go. Only I couldn't get it because the policemen were there and they would've seen me, so I had to wait until they went home to sleep."

"And you got hungry again," Cecily said, beginning to see the rest of the story taking shape.

Cynthia nodded. "I couldn't say the bad man had let me go until I took the money, so I came back here for more food, but then Daisy was waiting outside the window when I climbed out. She really made me jump."

Lord Chalmsford made an angry sound in his throat. "Why didn't you just come and tell your mother and father what had happened? Do you have any idea the trouble you caused, the dreadful fright you gave us running away like that?"

Cynthia began to sob again, while Lady Chalmsford gave her husband a long, hard look. "She was frightened to tell us," she said coldly. "And with very good reason."

Lord Chalmsford snapped his mouth shut and sat down again, his face dark with anger.

"You told Daisy that there was a bad man who would kill you if you didn't go back with the food," Cecily reminded the child.

Cynthia nodded. "She wanted to know what I was doing with the food, and I couldn't tell her, so I told her about the bad man and she wanted to come with me to see where he was. I didn't want her to come, but she wouldn't let me go back on my own."

Cecily sighed, knowing that this part of the confession was bound to upset the parents further. It had to be brought out, however, and it was unlikely anyone would believe what the child had done unless she admitted it herself.

"Daisy went with you up onto the Downs," Cecily said, wishing that this interrogation wasn't necessary. It was hard on the little girl, and she had the distinct impression that Lord Chalmsford could be quite ruthless when meting out punishment to his small daughter. She could only hope that Lady Chalmsford would step in and protect Cynthia against his wrath.

"Yes," Cynthia said in a small voice. "Daisy wanted to see the cave, and then she was going to tell everyone about it. I knew if she told that everyone would know there wasn't really a bad man."

She started to cry again, babbling through her sobs so that it was difficult to understand what she was saying. "I didn't want to hurt Daisy. I really, really didn't."

Lady Chalmsford's face looked drained of color. "Oh, my God," she whispered, staring at her child in shocked dismay. "Whatever did you do to that poor girl?"

Cecily glanced at Lord Chalmsford, who sat with his hands pressed between his knees as if afraid he might do something terrible with them if he released them.

Cynthia cried even harder. "I thought the constable would put me in prison for hurting Freddie if he found out, so I told Daisy to look down on the sand to see the cave, and when she went to look down . . . I . . . pushed her."

Lady Chalmsford uttered a cry of horror, while her husband stared at his daughter as if he'd never seen her before.

"It's all right, Lady Chalmsford," Cecily said quickly. "Daisy is quite unharmed. She fell onto a ledge and was rescued this morning by Lord Withersgill, who happened to be passing by. I'm so sorry to put you through all that, but I needed to hear Cynthia tell us what she had done."

"What will happen to her now?" Lord Chalmsford mumbled in a voice numb with disbelief.

"I shall have to report the events to the constable, of course," Cecily said, moving with Baxter to the door. "Since Freddie's death was obviously an accident, I doubt if P. C. Northcott will pursue it further. As for what happened after that, Cynthia simply panicked, trying to resolve one problem by creating another."

She reached the door and looked back at the unhappy family. "Daisy has survived the fall with little more than a few bumps and bruises, and she has no wish to make trouble for the child. Under the circumstances, I will do my best to persuade the constable that Cynthia is not a bad child, but a victim of unfortunate circumstances."

Lady Chalmsford rose and came toward Cecily with tears brimming in her eyes. "We will all be exceedingly grateful if you would do that, Mrs. Sinclair," she said unsteadily. "I assure you, Cynthia will be made to understand what a dreadful thing she has done."

Cecily waited for Baxter to open the door before answering her. "Cynthia will most likely need some special care for a while," she said quietly. "I can recommend a good doctor in the field. His office is in Harley Street. I will see that you get his card. In the meantime, your daughter will need a lot of attention and reassurance from you both." She gave Lord Chalmsford a direct look and was satisfied to see him glance sheepishly at his wife.

Once in the hallway, she let out a heartfelt sigh of relief. "I am so glad that is over," she murmured.

"May I congratulate you, madam," Baxter said, looking down at her with respect glowing in his eyes. "You handled the situation with the utmost tact and just the right amount of consideration. I was most impressed."

"Why, thank you, Baxter," Cecily said, smiling in delight. "Your approval means a great deal to me. Now all that is left is to pray that the St. George's Day ball and the tournament proceed without too many mishaps."

"I am quite sure you have nothing to worry about there, madam," Baxter assured her as he followed her down the stairs. "Compared to the unfortunate events of the past few days, anything that might happen now would surely be trivial."

"One would hope so," Cecily murmured. "Wherever Phoebe is concerned, however, one never knows. Let us just hope that this time her presentation goes off without the usual chaos."

CHAPTER

❖ 19 ❖

Doris could feel her heart banging so hard that she thought it would put a hole in her chest. Here she was, standing in the wings, about to set foot on her very first stage as a real live singer.

She smoothed her hands down the folds of the print cotton frock. Mrs. Chubb had sewn it for her, without her ever knowing a thing about it. The housekeeper must have worked all night to make it.

Doris looked down at her feet peeking out from under the hem of the lace-trimmed skirt. Madam herself had lent her a pair of pink satin shoes to go with the dress. They were a bit tight on her, but they looked so pretty that she wasn't about to breathe a word about it to no one. Besides, she was too nervous even to notice if her feet pinched.

They had all promised to come and hear her sing. Daisy and Mrs. Chubb, even Michel said he would poke his head in the door. Gertie promised that if she could get the twins asleep by the time Doris sang, she'd be there, too.

Doris twisted her hankie into a tight knot. The string quartet were halfway through their third piece. They seemed to be inspired by the audience and actually sounded quite good to Doris's critical ear. She was on next. Lydia had arrived at the back door of the kitchen a little while ago and was now tucked away behind the back curtain where no one would see her until she walked on stage.

Doris peeked anxiously at the folds of the curtain. They hung smooth and straight, with just the slightest of bulges where Lydia stood.

Doris had written down all the words to the song on a sheet of paper for Lydia, and the pianist had promised her that she would learn the song by tonight. All Doris could do now was hope that Mrs. Carter-Holmes wouldn't stop the show and order the accompanist off the stage.

A voice behind her spoke her name, and Doris jumped. Swinging around, she saw the American gentleman smiling politely at her. "I don't have time to talk now," she said, her nerves making her voice sharp. "I have to go on in a minute."

"I just wanted to wish you well." He glanced at the quartet on the stage, who were all sawing away furiously. "I would like a word with you after the performance. I'll wait for you in the ballroom."

This, Doris thought, with a little rush of excitement, was her first stage-door beau. Not that she wanted anything to do with him, of course. She was going to wait for a real toff. This was, however, her first chance at handling unwanted admirers, so she might as well practice on him.

Straightening her shoulders, she looked directly into his glasses. "Mr. Keen—" she began, but he interrupted her.

"Kern," he said with a little bow. "Jerome Kern."

She had to start all over again. "Mr. Kern. It's very nice

of you to want to speak to me, I'm sure, but I have to tell you that I am not interested in making your acquaintance. I must ask you to please leave me alone and stop bothering me like this."

She wondered if she should add that she would have someone forcibly remove him from the premises, but she wasn't sure who would do that. Besides, this was the Pennyfoot Hotel, and madam might not like it if she threatened one of the guests.

To her relief, the warning appeared unnecessary. Once more, the gentleman gave her a slight bow of his head, then said in a resigned voice, "Very well, Miss Hoggins, I'll respect your wishes. Please forgive me if I've caused you any distress. I only regret that I could not interest you in my proposition. I believe you have a great deal of potential. I wish you luck, and if you ever come to America, please feel free to look me up."

He left her, and she stared after him, amazed at his cheek. If she ever got to America, she thought indignantly, he'd be the one who would have to try to see her.

The round of applause took her by surprise, and she clutched her stomach as the ladies on stage took a bow. Now it was her turn. "Keep your fingers crossed, Lydia," she muttered under her breath. Then, fixing a stiff smile on her face, she marched onto the stage.

Standing on the floor at the side of the stage, Phoebe looked on with pride as Doris made her appearance. The quartet had surpassed themselves, sounding better than she had ever hoped. Apparently the rehearsals here in the ballroom had served their purpose well.

Esme had assured her that Doris had learned the aria well enough, though her pronunciation was somewhat inept. Phoebe was hopeful, however, that the audience would enjoy the singing and disregard the girl's lack of expertise with the Italian language.

Esme finished her announcement of the aria and introduced Doris. A smattering of polite applause greeted her words, but then, to Phoebe's astonishment, Doris raised a hand.

In her firm, clear voice, she announced, "Ladies and gentlemen, I would like to introduce my accompanist for my presentation. Miss Lydia Willoughby."

Phoebe stared in outraged shock as the scrawny, bespectacled woman fumbled her way from behind the back curtain and came forward, clutching a sheet of paper in her hand.

Whatever was the child thinking of, Phoebe thought, inwardly fuming. How could she possibly expect Lydia Willoughby, of all people, to play an Italian aria? Keeping a determined smile on her face, Phoebe glared at the woman as she paused in the center of the stage beside Doris.

Catching Phoebe's eye, Lydia visibly started. The sheet of paper fluttered from her hand, and there was a moment or two of confusion while the pianist clumsily chased it down.

Phoebe tried in vain to attract Doris's attention in the hope of quietly ordering her to get rid of the girl and sing with the quartet as arranged. Doris directed her gaze steadfastly ahead, however, and Phoebe had to stand seething while Lydia chased all over the stage after the paper.

Finally the woman seated herself at the piano, which had been pushed to the back of the stage in order to accommodate the quartet. The slight murmuring that had arisen subsided, and Lydia lifted her hands.

Phoebe momentarily closed her eyes, bracing for the opening notes of the aria. She snapped them open again a second later. Her entire body bounced with the shock waves from the raucous chords resounding from the piano.

The awful pounding seemed to vibrate throughout the entire room. Sending a frantic glance at the ladies in the quartet, Phoebe could see her own amazement reflected on their stunned faces.

Snapping her face back at Doris again, she frowned furiously at the girl, who studiously avoided her gaze. In fact, to Phoebe's horror, the housemaid was now gyrating her hips to the rhythm in the most appallingly debauched display Phoebe had ever seen in her entire life.

The thought of this performance actually going on in front of the entire audience made her want to swoon dead away. She might have done, if Doris hadn't at that moment opened her mouth to sing.

What came out of that innocent child's mouth was enough to raise the devil himself. Phoebe didn't understand all the words. She caught the gist of them, though.

"Give me a shilling and I'll be oh, so willing," Doris sang, turning sideways to stick out the lower part of her anatomy. "Give me a wink and I'll be tickled pink . . ." This was accompanied by a promiscuous leer that proved just too much for Phoebe. Clutching a hand to her heart, she slowly sank to the floor.

Standing on the balcony above the ballroom, Cecily held her breath as she surveyed the scene. Baxter stood silently by her side, and she didn't have to look at him to know his expression. She had once dragged him to the Hippodrome for a Variety performance, from which it had taken him days to recover.

Mrs. Chubb had appeared from nowhere and was busily fanning Phoebe's face while Doris gamely bellowed out the song, doing her best to overpower the awful noise coming from the piano. Lydia seemed oblivious of everything as she slammed the keys with red-faced enthusiasm.

"Heaven preserve us," Baxter murmured when at last the song mercifully came to an end.

Doris dropped down in a respectful curtsey, which seemed incongruous after her risqué performance, while Lydia stood by the piano, her face flushed with triumph. Silence settled over the audience, each person seemingly frozen in shock.

Then, from the back of the ballroom, Gertie's voice rang out. "Encore!" she yelled, clapping furiously. "Bloody well done, Doris!"

Across the room in the corner, Daisy stepped into view, clapping just as hard.

Baxter groaned, but just as Cecily was about to nudge him to join in the applause, someone in the audience began to clap politely. Someone else joined in, then another, the noise gathering momentum as one by one, the majority of the gentlemen and even a few ladies stood up, wildly applauding.

Cheers rang out and shouts of "Bravo!" echoed around the ballroom, as Doris, looking near to tears, took her bows again and again. Esme Parsons was the first of the quartet to recover. Stepping forward, she grasped Doris's arm and forcibly dragged her off the stage while the applause continued, then slowly faded away.

Looking thoroughly sick at having to follow such a tumultuous performance, the ladies once more began sawing at their instruments. It was some time, however, before the audience settled down enough to listen to them.

Somewhat shaken by the event, Cecily waited long enough to see Phoebe being escorted from the scene by Mrs. Chubb and a grinning Samuel and then made her way from the balcony with Baxter following behind.

Descending the stairs at the back of the ballroom, she saw the American gentleman standing by the doors.

He greeted her as she approached him, saying, "What a marvelous evening, Mrs. Sinclair. A wonderful dinner and such delightful entertainment—I'll have some great memories to take back home with me."

"I'm so glad you enjoyed it, Mr. Kern," Cecily said, trying to sound as if the entire performance had been planned. "I hope the tournament tomorrow will prove just as fascinating."

The gentleman shook his head with a look of regret. "I'm afraid I shan't be able to stay for the tournament. My ship sails from Southhampton tomorrow evening."

"Such a pity," Cecily murmured. "I'm sure you would have enjoyed the jousting."

"No doubt." Jerome Kern glanced back at the stage. "It's too bad the little lady isn't interested in talking to me. She has a lot of talent. I could have done something with her."

He looked back at Cecily and inclined his head. "Nice to have met you, Mrs. Sinclair. You too, Mr. Baxter. You have a fine hotel here. I shall look forward to visiting you again some time."

"Please do," Cecily said as he turned to leave.

She waited until the doors had closed behind him, then looked up at Baxter. "Could have done something with her? Whatever did he mean by that?"

Baxter shrugged. "I have not the slightest idea, madam. I must say, however, that it's not surprising the man was so familiar in his attitude toward Doris, after the lascivious way she behaved."

"Oh, come now, Baxter," Cecily said, laughing. "You know very well that that kind of song is perfectly acceptable on the stage nowadays. Why, even some members of royalty enjoy the performances. I do believe that Marie Lloyd and Vesta Tilley are among the king's favorite artistes, both of whom are Variety performers. Doris could do a lot worse than to emulate them."

Baxter stretched his neck above his collar. "All I can say is that I would not wish to see a lady I cared about cavorting around in public in that disgusting manner."

Cecily shook her head, knowing it was futile to argue the point with him. Baxter would not change his attitude, no matter what she said. It was better to allow him his opinions and live in the hope that one day something would happen to enlighten him as to what was happening in the world around him.

"I must find Phoebe and make sure she has recovered sufficiently to return home," she said as they left the ballroom together.

"Very well, madam. Though I would like to discuss the matter of Freddie's murder with you later if you can spare the time. I must confess to being curious as to how you arrived at the conclusion that Cynthia Chalmsford was responsible."

Cecily smiled. "I'll be happy to tell you. Give me a few minutes with Phoebe, and I'll join you in your office for a cigar."

Baxter rolled his eyes to the ceiling. "When you told me this morning that you'd heard from your son, I was rather hoping you would not be in need of such a detrimental form of relaxation."

"I admit I do feel a great deal better now that I know he and Simani have safely reached their destination," Cecily admitted. "I have never been more happy to receive a letter from him than I was this morning. There are other pressures that still plague me, however. Surely you would not begrudged me my one source of consolation?"

"You are in dire straits, indeed, madam, if that is your only source," he said, shaking his head in a mournful way that made her want to laugh. "Since my formidable warnings about ruining your health, not to mention your reputation, appear to have no effect whatsoever, I shall just have to resign myself to your addiction, I suppose." With an exaggerated sigh, he strode off down the passageway.

Poor Baxter, Cecily thought, looking after him with a rush of affection. All these social changes going on, and he was unable to do anything about it.

Baxter was a man who needed to be in control, of himself and of the situation at all times. It must be disturbing for him to see so many of the ideals and morals he held so dear being obliterated by progress and the rebellious unrest of an enlightened society.

She found Phoebe a few minutes later resting in a comfortable armchair in the drawing room. She was sipping a glass of sherry which, she informed Cecily, had been kindly brought to her by Mrs. Chubb.

"Such a treasure, your housekeeper," Phoebe said as she sank back against the cushions with a little sigh. "I really don't know what I would have done without her. That dreadful girl. How could she have disgraced me in that disgusting manner?"

"As a matter of fact, Phoebe," Cecily said, seating herself by her side, "I heard several comments from the audience as I left the ballroom. By and large, I would say that this was our most successful presentation so far. Everyone seemed to have enjoyed the performance tremendously, and some even congratulated me on our efforts in keeping up with the modern times by presenting the revue."

"Well!" Obviously at a loss for words, Phoebe fanned herself with a small embroidered fan.

"I think that as long as the audience was satisfied, we should be grateful that everything turned out well." Cecily peered closer at her friend. "I trust you have recovered from your little upset?"

"Upset?" Lowering her fan, Phoebe sat up. "My dear Cecily, you have no idea. As if it wasn't bad enough that I was subjected to that scandalous display, I was met with yet another shocking revelation when I went to discuss the matter with the musicians afterward."

"Why, what happened?" Cecily exclaimed, wondering what could possibly surpass Doris's little surprise.

"My dear, you will never guess. I was so agitated by Doris's performance that I wasn't paying enough attention to where I was going. Quite by mistake I opened the door of the gentleman's dressing room instead of the ladies'."

Cecily frowned as Phoebe fanned herself harder. "But there were no gentlemen in the dressing room. The member of the ladies' string quartet were the sole performers tonight, apart from Doris."

"Quite," Phoebe said dryly. "Which was why I was so shocked to find a gentleman in the room. Imagine my confusion when I saw who it was. Beryl Barrett, the bass player. Can you believe? She was actually a man all the time."

"A man?" Cecily suppressed a strong desire to burst out laughing.

"Yes, my dear. A man. Apparently the original fourth member of the quartet retired from the entertainment business. Hilda's brother was the only bass player the ladies could find to replace her. They were afraid that they might not procure any more bookings if a man were to play in a ladies' string quartet, so Beryl . . . er . . . Bernard, I do believe his name is, dressed up as a woman. Can you imagine the lengths some people will go to in order to make a living?"

"I must admit," Cecily said evenly, "that is rather an unusual solution to the problem. Were the ladies upset at your discovery?"

"I don't believe so." Phoebe took another large sip of her sherry, draining the glass. "I think the subterfuge was becoming very difficult for Beryl . . . er . . . Bernard. It also made things very awkward for the other ladies."

"Yes," Cecily murmured. "I'm sure it did."

"Then, to top it off," Phoebe said, putting down her empty glass, "that old fool of a colonel came barging up to Esme and demanded to know where the bass player was hiding. Little did he know that she was standing right in front of him, dressed as a man."

"Oh, dear," Cecily said, no longer able to keep a straight face. "What happened?"

Phoebe folded her fan and tucked it inside the bodice of her dress. "Well, Bernard told him in his deep voice that he was the bass player. I thought the colonel was going to faint dead away. He went stumbling off, muttering something about giving up drinking. As if he could."

"It might slow him down a little," Cecily said, smiling broadly.

"Well, I'm glad you find it all so amusing. I, for one, am thankful this night is over." Phoebe rose, shaking out the folds of her blue satin tea gown. "I must get back to the vicarage. Poor Algie will be wondering where I am."

"Samuel will take you home," Cecily said, getting to her feet. "He's waiting for you at the door. Thank you so much for all your efforts, Phoebe. The entertainment was an unqualified success, as always."

"Yes," Phoebe murmured, sounding mollified, "I suppose it was. I'm quite looking forward to the next event now. It will be quite a challenge to outdo this one."

Having apparently forgotten that she had deemed the performance a disaster a few short minutes earlier, Phoebe went off well pleased with herself, leaving Cecily to wonder what her friend might possibly conjure up for next time.

When Cecily reached Baxter's office later, she found his door standing open. Thinking he might be resting, she peered cautiously around the corner.

Baxter sat at his desk, his chin buried in his hands. His expression was so bleak that all her previous anxieties about him forcibly returned.

Loath to let him know she had seen such dejection on his face, she withdrew, then made a great deal of noise approaching the door again.

This time, he sat looking expectantly at the door as she walked in. Rising at once to his feet, he said with forced enthusiasm, "I trust Mrs. Carter-Holmes has recovered from her trauma, madam?"

Cecily smiled as she seated herself. "Quite. I managed to persuade her that the performance was a success and that everyone was delighted with the entire proceedings."

"I have to admit," Baxter said, making a great display of tidying his desk, "I was astonished at the reception the girl received. Unfortunately it will only serve to encourage her to pursue her unfortunate ambitions. Why she should want to sacrifice her reputation by appearing on the stage I can't imagine."

"I really can't understand why a stage career is still considered a sin for women—one more instance of intolerance toward women and their choices."

He gave her a steely look. "You sound a little peevish tonight, madam. I do hope you are not feeling ill."

"I am perfectly well," Cecily said firmly.

"I am happy to hear it. Then perhaps you will tell me how you discovered that Cynthia Chalmsford was responsible for Freddie's unfortunate death?"

"After you offer me one of your wonderful little cigars," Cecily said, giving him a cheerful smile.

A moment passed before Baxter pulled the package from his pocket and offered her one. She waited for him to light it for her, then settled back to enjoy the fragrance.

"I had all the clues, you know," she said after a moment or two. "I simply failed to add them all up at the time. Taking into consideration the bad spelling of the ransom note, the fact that it was written in crayon—as was the picture Cynthia had drawn for her mother—the way Freddie had been carefully tucked up in bed, and the fragrance around him that reminded me of Madeline's potpourri which she had given to Cynthia, I should have concluded the child was involved."

"What was it, then, that made you finally realize she was the culprit?"

She smiled. "It was when you told me about the branch killing Roland Young's father. Up until then, I had thought of the murderer as a tall person. I even suspected Beryl Barrett, or Bernard, which I believe is his real name. He certainly had the height and the build to have thrust the lance into Freddie's chest."

Baxter looked thoroughly confused. "I beg your pardon?"

Cecil dismissed his question with a wave of her hand. "I'll tell you about it later. As I was saying, once I had eliminated Roland Young and the American gentleman, both of whom had alibis, I felt it had to be one of the quartet. I thought they might have kidnapped Cynthia for the money, considering their somewhat impoverished condition."

"The thought had crossed my mind also," Baxter admitted.

It was Cecily's turn to be surprised. "Really? Why didn't you mention it?"

"I wouldn't be so presumptuous, madam."

She chose to ignore that, sensing the sarcasm behind his words. "Once I realized that the lance had actually fallen from the loft," she continued, "the rest all fell easily into place. I have to tell you, Baxter, I feel a distinct chill when I think I was almost too late. If it hadn't been for that ledge on the cliffs, or the fortuitous appearance of Lord Withersgill, poor Daisy might have . . ."

She let her voice trail off, silenced by the dreadful thought of what could have happened.

"You cannot blame yourself for what happened, madam. You did your utmost to discover the culprit and, as always, accomplished a remarkable achievement."

She smiled wearily at him through a cloud of smoke. "Thank you, Baxter. It's very kind of you to say so. I feel terribly sorry for the child, of course. So many children of wealthy parents would seem to have everything yet are desperately lonely and unhappy. It would seem that the adage is right. Money can't buy happiness after all."

"It would certainly help in some situations," Baxter muttered so quietly she barely caught the words.

She gave him a sharp look. "Is that what you have been worrying about lately? You have a financial problem?"

"In a manner of speaking," Baxter admitted.

She watched him run a finger around the inside of his collar. He cleared his throat, and she braced herself, knowing instinctively that he had something important to tell her. Now that he was apparently about to explain what had been troubling him so much lately, she wasn't at all sure she wanted to hear it.

"I would say this is as good a time as any, madam," Baxter said in a voice fraught with tension, "to inform you that I have been offered a position elsewhere. I am considering accepting the offer."

If he had raised his hand and slapped her, she could not have been more shattered. Tears threatened as she worked to rid herself of the hard lump in her throat. "I am sorry you are so unhappy working at the Pennyfoot," she said when she felt able to speak with at least some semblance of composure.

Baxter's look of despair was painful to see. "I am not unhappy at all, madam. Quite the contrary. I have spent some of the happiest moments of my life here at the Pennyfoot, but sometimes desperate situations call for desperate measures, so to speak."

She sat up, trying hard to understand what her mind insisted couldn't possibly be happening. "Is it money, Baxter? If so, I'm quite sure the business can afford a raise in your salary. Please tell me what you need—" She broke off, knowing by his expression that she had offended him deeply.

His voice sounded placid enough, however, when he said. "It is not the money, madam, but I thank you."

Inwardly pleading with him to make her understand, she demanded, "Then what is it, Baxter? I feel I have a right to know why you are deserting my hotel."

He looked at her for a long moment, while she struggled to withhold the tears. Finally he said softly, "Cecily, this decision does not mean the end of our relationship. That I can promise you. I wish I could explain, but I'm afraid this is not the time. I can only tell you that I sincerely hope it will not be too long an interval before I can make everything quite clear to you. In the meantime, I must ask you to trust, and respect, my decision."

It was a long speech for Baxter, and a painful one, judging by the wounded look in his eyes. Quickly she stubbed out the cigar and rose. She had to leave at once, before she made a complete fool of herself in front of him.

"Of course, Baxter," she said, forcing a lightness to her tone. "I shall miss you a great deal, but I will not stand in your way. You have my blessing and my very best wishes in whatever venture you wish to follow."

He lifted his hand in a helpless gesture that just about broke her heart and then he took her hand, apparently too moved to say more.

"Goodnight, Baxter," she said softly and left the room, closing the door behind her. The soft click of the latch sounded like a death blow. As she walked down the hallway, the glow of the gas lamps seemed misted through the veil of her tears.

What on this good earth was she going to do without him? The departure of Michael faded into significance compared to this catastrophe. The prospect of life without Baxter didn't bear thinking about.

Yet somehow she couldn't help feeling that a promise lay behind his words. A promise of what, she couldn't imagine. Or maybe she preferred not to dwell on it, for fear she should jump to the wrong conclusions.

Yes, she would sorely miss her manager. Yet she, of all people, knew that great happiness often came from drastic changes. She would just have to be patient and wait for whatever this change might bring.

"I ask only one thing, Baxter," she whispered as she climbed the stairs to her suite. "Please don't make me wait too long."